An Excerpt from *Three*

Aidan looked into the c
the shower was sexy. His biceps flexed as he bent to soap himself. His groin was flat, with a mound of bushy brown hair at the root of his thick, semihard dick. He scrubbed himself with no self-consciousness, enjoying the soap and the clean water. When the man turned his back, Aidan salivated over a perfect bubble butt with a narrow trail of dark hair running between the cheeks.

He closed his eyes and imagined the man's big hands roving over his own naked body, the feel of fingers wrapped around his dick, a tongue lapping at his puckered asshole. Bee-stung lips on his, kissing him in a way he hadn't been kissed in years. The scent of another man filling his nostrils. The taste of a man as his tongue roved from collarbone to belly button. And how much more wonderful all that would be if he were in love.

Then he remembered he was in a Muslim country. They stoned gay people here, didn't they? He turned away from the window, afraid someone would see him staring, and realized that his erection had given him away, tenting his shorts. He adjusted himself, but one of the men at the table had already noticed.

As the man approached, Aidan marked his bushy eyebrows, gold front tooth, black hair slicked back from his forehead. He was older than he'd appeared at first; lines creased his dark skin. Muscles bulged from his upper arms. Aidan's pulse raced again. Would the man accuse him? Hit him?

Loose Id ®

ISBN 13: 978-1-60737-626-2
THREE WRONG TURNS IN THE DESERT
Copyright © September 2010 by Neil Plakcy
Originally released in e-book format in September 2009

Cover Art by Croco Designs
Cover Layout and Design by April Martinez

DISCLAIMER: Many of the acts described in our BDSM/fetish titles can be dangerous. Please do not try any new sexual practice, whether it be fire, rope, or whip play, without the guidance of an experienced practitioner. Neither Loose Id nor its authors will be responsible for any loss, harm, injury or death resulting from use of the information contained in any of its titles.

This book is an original publication of Loose Id. Each individual story herein was previously published in e-book format only by Loose Id and is a work of fiction. Any similarity to actual persons, events or existing locations is entirely coincidental.

Printed in the U.S.A. by
Lightning Source, Inc.
1246 Heil Quaker Blvd
La Vergne TN 37086
www.lightningsource.com

THREE WRONG TURNS
IN THE DESERT

Neil Plakcy

Dedication

To Marc. Everybody's got a hungry heart—thanks for satisfying mine.

Acknowledgement

Christine Kling and Mike Jastrzebski provided valuable critiques in the early stages of the book, helping me clarify the characters and the story. Laura Baumbach encouraged me to enter the world of M/M romance, and my editor, Maryam Salim, helped me pull this manuscript together.

Thanks to all the fans, bloggers, and reviewers who have supported my writing, both in mystery and in romance. Thanks, too, to the professional groups that have helped me learn to writer better, to make contacts in the world of writing, and to promote my work: Mystery Writers of America, Romance Writers of America, and Sisters in Crime.

I'm grateful to Broward College, where I teach, for the sabbatical term off that allowed me to get so much writing done, as well as to the many wonderful writers and teachers I work with.

The Bar Mamounia

If Aidan Greene had stuck to the main streets, he probably would have been fine. But he was restless, walking all day, killing the three days between his arrival in Tunisia and the start of his teaching job. Though he loved the contrast between the stark white buildings and the bright blue, often cloudless sky, the plazas strung with tiny red flags, and the narrow cobblestoned streets of the medina, he didn't want to think of himself as merely a tourist; he was going to be living in Tunis, working there, starting a new life.

He passed the broken remnants of the Roman aqueduct, confusing signs in Arabic that might have been warnings or simply directions, pavements stained with centuries of sewage, rows of low whitewashed buildings with exposed wires leading to decaying poles.

Men approached him asking for cigarettes, children for baksheesh. He ignored them all and wasn't even nervous, until the dark-skinned boy in the torn T-shirt approached him as he walked down a narrow alley. The two- and three-story buildings leaned in toward him, blocking the sky, making him feel like a caged animal. "American?" the boy asked. "You give me dollars?" He was eight or nine, wearing sandals and a pair of ragged shorts.

Aidan shook his head, said, "No," in a firm voice, and kept walking. Behind him, he heard a second voice, speaking what he assumed was Arabic. When he glanced back, he saw a second boy in his early teens.

He remembered the way he'd felt sometimes walking through the gay neighborhood of Philadelphia, afraid of being bashed by random toughs. But in other parts of the city, he'd felt safe—he was often mistaken for Italian or Greek because of his olive skin, and his deep-set eyes and dark eyebrows made people think he was more dangerous than he really was.

At the end of the alley, two more boys were waiting, both in their early teens. "American," one of them said. "Dollars."

Aidan's heart accelerated. The street ahead was wider than the alley but nearly deserted. It was late in the afternoon, the sun broiling above, and most sensible people were inside somewhere waiting for the night to cool things down. Somewhere in the distance he heard the heavy backbeat of Arabic music. A man's voice, high and almost whiny, twisted through the rhythm of the strings. It reminded him that he was in a foreign place, one with lurking dangers.

He had no idea where he was. His usual strategy was to keep walking, and eventually he'd run across a landmark, refer to his guidebook, and orient himself.

Looking ahead, he saw one of the older boys holding something that glinted in the bright sun—probably a knife. Another alley branched to the right, toward a broad plaza, so he took off at a run.

Back in Philadelphia, Aidan had walked everywhere—to his job, teaching English as a second language to recent immigrants at a private college in Center City, to the grocery, the dry cleaner, the gay bookstore where he went to readings now and then. But he hadn't run much, and he knew he couldn't hold out for long, especially not in the heat, when he was dehydrated from a day on the pavement.

What a stupid idea it had been, he thought as he sped toward the plaza, the boys behind him. Giving up everything he had known back home to run away to a strange country, just to distract his broken heart. He had thought he could put aside the waste of eleven years on Blake Chennault, a man who had probably never loved him.

Years before, right after graduating with his master's degree in English as a second language, he had traveled through Europe teaching, jumping from job to job and country to country as the mood took him. Then he had gone back to the States to visit his family, met Blake, and settled into a succession of tedious part-time jobs and a dull life that had never satisfied his desire for adventure. Once Blake had kicked him to the curb, he'd thought he could resume that itinerant life. But had he gotten too settled, too sedate, to survive on his own again?

The boys shouted and chased him, and it was sheer panic that kept him moving. He rounded a corner onto the plaza and saw that it was nearly empty too.

His heart was pumping, and sweat was pooling under his arms, dripping across his forehead, streaming down his back. Where could he go? He didn't know a soul in the city—he hadn't even met his boss-to-be, Madame Habiba Abboud, having communicated with her through e-mail.

Aidan kept running, his heart thudding, his feet slamming against the rough concrete pavement. He rounded another corner and saw a blessed sight—a neon beer bottle glowing beside a curtained doorway.

One of the teenagers was gaining on him. Aidan could almost feel the boy's breath on his back as he reached the beadwork curtain that led into the bar, and pushed through. His guidebook had indicated that the few bars outside hotels were often seedy and not recommended for tourists. But it was too late to be squeamish.

The walls of the dim, high-ceilinged room were whitewashed stucco, the floor an indecipherable mosaic tile pattern. Three slim-hipped Tunisian men in jeans and cotton shirts sat at rickety metal chairs around a small square table painted bright blue and inlaid with chipped tile patterns.

He had a sudden memory of high school, the way he'd often run into the library to escape bullies. He felt the same sense of sanctuary. The men looked up as he burst into the room, panting and sweating. He rushed to the bar, where a dark-skinned bald man in a clean white T-shirt was working behind an elaborate brass coffee urn. Aidan slid onto one of the three bar stools and pointed at a bottle of lemon soda.

He looked behind him. None of the boys had dared follow him inside, which was good. He worried that they might be waiting outside, though. It would be dark in a few hours, and he had no idea where he was or how he could get back to the little apartment he'd rented.

Stupid, he thought to himself as he took a long drink of lemon soda and waited for his racing heart to calm. How could he have been so stupid? Not just to get himself lost and in trouble in Tunis—but to have ended up here in the first place? He didn't speak the language, didn't know more about the country than he'd read in his Lonely Planet *Tunisia Travel Guide*. It had all been a knee-jerk reaction to being dumped.

When his heart rate had returned to a manageable level, he paid for his soda, then walked over to an opening in the back wall—you could have called it a window, if there had been a frame around it, a piece of glass. But it wasn't that kind of bar. He looked out at a small dirt courtyard—and a naked man standing under an open showerhead.

The sight was startling enough that for a moment Aidan forgot the boys who had been chasing him. His dick surprised him with an erection as he watched the water cascade over muscles and gleaming skin. The man had close-cropped brown hair, high cheekbones, and a few days' growth of beard. One small gold ring pierced each fat brown nipple, which sat on a pair of almost square pecs. From there, his body formed a V down to a narrow waist. He was tanned a deep brown, all over, almost as dark as the Tunisian men in the bar.

Aidan lounged against the wall, enjoying the sight of the naked body, daydreaming a bit about touching and being touched. The roughness of another man's cheek against his, the taste of another man's lips. That initial intoxication with someone new, learning the ins and outs of his body, what turned him on, and the things he would do that would surprise Aidan with his own responses.

But that led him to the pain of breaking up. Was it worth it? To have your heart torn open when a man you thought loved you enough to last forever walked in one day and said it was time for you to move out?

Aidan looked into the courtyard again. Damn, the guy in the shower was sexy. His biceps flexed as he bent to soap himself. His groin was flat, with a mound of bushy brown hair at the root of his thick, semihard dick. He scrubbed himself with no self-consciousness, enjoying the soap and the clean water. When the man turned his back, Aidan salivated over a perfect bubble butt with a narrow trail of dark hair running between the cheeks.

He closed his eyes and imagined the man's big hands roving over his own naked body, the feel of fingers wrapped around his dick, a tongue lapping at his puckered asshole. Bee-stung lips on his, kissing him in a way he hadn't been kissed in years. The scent of another man filling his nostrils. The taste of a man as his tongue roved from collarbone to belly button. And how much more wonderful all that would be if he were in love.

Then he remembered he was in a Muslim country. They stoned gay people here, didn't they? He turned away from the window, afraid someone would see him staring, and realized that his erection had given him away, tenting his shorts. He adjusted himself, but one of the men at the table had already noticed.

As the man approached, Aidan marked his bushy eyebrows, gold front tooth, black hair slicked back from his forehead. He was older than he'd appeared at first; lines creased his dark skin. Muscles bulged from his upper arms. Aidan's pulse raced again. Would the man accuse him? Hit him?

Instead, the man smiled broadly and placed his hand on Aidan's groin. He said something in a language that had its roots in French. Though the words were unknown, the meaning was clear.

Equally clear was Aidan's reaction to the man's touch. His dick deflated faster than an escaping hot-air balloon. The man looked puzzled, and Aidan dropped the soda bottle on a nearby table and hurried out of the bar, forgetting the danger that lurked outside.

Two Glasses of Vieux Magon

Fortunately, by the time Aidan left the bar, the boys who had chased him had given up and disappeared, and after walking a few blocks, he found a sign leading to the Avenue Bourguiba, a broad boulevard with thick stands of trees along one side. The presence of tall buildings and taxicabs was reassuring, and he walked the remaining blocks back to his apartment without incident.

The next morning, he awoke with an erection and realized he'd been dreaming of the naked man showering behind the bar. He'd seen handsome men in Philadelphia, of course, and sometimes been physically attracted to them, particularly when it had been a while since he and Blake had made love.

But those men had never invaded his dreams, never engendered the sense of longing Aidan felt when he remembered that naked body under the cascade of water. As he went into the bathroom to relieve himself, he thought it was probably just a knee-jerk reaction to losing Blake. It was silly, but he needed to feel he could be attractive again.

Then why had his dick deflated the minute the Tunisian man had touched him? Was he only interested in the unavailable? The naked man had looked as straight as any

Aidan had ever seen—from his short, military-style haircut to his muscled body. None of the gay men he knew back in Philadelphia had physiques like that, even the ones who spent every available minute at the gym.

He sighed. He thought he'd got over longing for straight guys when he found Blake, who was tough and demanding, a football fan who disdained opera and ballet. In a way, Blake was a gay man's fantasy—a straight-appearing guy who was willing to have sex with another man.

But the naked man behind the bar was another story. He was a show-off; why else shower in a quasi-public place? But there had been a "look, don't touch" message from his body language.

Maybe that was what he found attractive, Aidan thought as he fixed himself breakfast. A man who could satisfy his fantasies without any danger of emotional involvement. Sex without all the messiness of love. No more heartbreak. Just a little fun in an exotic location. Would his fantasy man, when dressed, wear one of the hooded white robes Aidan had seen on men in the medina? Did men wear anything under those robes?

He kept thinking of the naked man all morning, and at least to shut up his subconscious, he retraced his steps to the place he discovered was called the Bar Mamounia. A pair of Tunisian men sat in one corner of the bar as he pushed through the beadwork curtain once again; he couldn't tell if they were the same men who'd been there the day before. The same bald bartender was behind the bar, this time working on what looked like accounting, rows of numbers interspersed with sprawling Arabic script. He looked up at Aidan and said, "*Salaam aleykum.*"

Aidan knew that meant hello, and that the proper response was "*Aleykum salaam.*" But just so the bartender didn't get the wrong idea, he said the only other Arabic phrase he knew, "*Mish bakalum arabee,*" which meant, "I don't speak Arabic."

The bartender just looked at him. Aidan pointed at a bottle of Sidi Rais, which the guidebook had said was a dry white wine, and asked for a glass in his schoolboy French.

The bartender seemed to understand. Aidan asked, continuing in French, about the man he'd seen the day before.

"Monsieur Liam," the bartender said, pronouncing it *Lee-ahm.* In French, he said, "Yes, he stays across the yard." He pointed out the window to a small stucco one-story house, hemmed in on both sides by taller buildings. A faded off-white, it had rough walls and windows that were merely slits. Closer examination showed a cistern on the roof, with a hose that ran to the shower.

Aidan drank his wine while thinking how stupid he was to have come back this way. He had a picture of the sexy, naked man imprinted in his brain, and that would have to be enough for a while. He sipped from his glass, and then a voice behind him said, "The white wine in this place tastes like horse piss. You've got to drink the red."

He turned around and saw Liam there. He was even better looking up close than he had been across the yard, sexier somehow in clothing than he had been naked. His sheer physicality was awesome—his height, his brawn.

Aidan's dick sprang to attention. "Have you tried it?" he asked. "Horse piss?"

Liam laughed. "You bet. Camel piss too. Horse is saltier." He beckoned to the bartender and said something in Arabic. Aidan caught the words *Vieux Magon*, which he assumed was the name of the wine.

Then Liam turned to Aidan. "Don't get many Americans down this way. I'm always pleased to meet another." He extended his hand. "Liam McCullough."

Aidan was too astonished to even tell the man his name. The fact that his fantasy had come to life, and was talking to him, was so surprising, so erotic, that all he could do was nod along. The bartender brought two balloon glasses of rich, ruby-colored wine, and Liam said, "Let's take a table."

He led Aidan across the room to the far corner and sat down, straddling the metal-backed wooden chair. He wore a vest of supple leather, which hung open, exposing his muscular chest, though Aidan noted that the two nipple rings were gone. Liam's dun-colored cotton drawstring shorts reached just below his knees. On his feet, he wore a pair of brown leather sandals.

Up close, he smelled like lavender. Aidan could see that Liam's hair was longer than he'd thought the day before, and a fuzz of light brown hair covered his chin, like a scruffy Hollywood movie star. Aidan took a sip of his wine. It tasted as rich as it looked, with notes of cherry and lemon. He'd taken a wine-appreciation course back in Philadelphia, but he didn't remember tasting anything like that.

"We're going to be spending a lot of time together," Liam said. He smiled, and Aidan's heart did a quick flip-flop. "So let me spell out some ground rules. I have to know where you are all the time, and if I say you can't go somewhere, you can't go. You don't know Tunisia like I do."

He took a drink of wine. Aidan just stared at him. Who the hell did he think he was? And he'd thought Blake was controlling. Maybe he'd been wrong the day before. Suppose this handsome god of a man was gay, and he'd noticed Aidan staring at him. Or not—Blake had always said Aidan's mannerisms gave him away as gay. The guy could have come into the bar and pegged Aidan for a quick fuck.

He had goose bumps up and down his arms at the thought of this man touching him, holding him, entering him, and he couldn't help smiling back. It was gaydar, he thought. A straight man wouldn't look you in the eyes, wouldn't return a glance of interest.

Aidan's dick, which had stiffened as soon as he laid eyes on Liam, was still jammed against the fabric of his shorts. He longed for some physical contact to confirm his feelings— perhaps just pressing his leg against the other man's in passing, the casual touch of Liam's fingers on Aidan's shoulder.

They talked for a few minutes—what Aidan thought of Tunis, the sirocco wind, the taste of the wine. It had been a long time since a man flirted with him, and Aidan felt like one of the Roman ruins the guidebook said had been covered by centuries of sand, finally exposed by the desert wind. His heart beat faster, and his dick pulsed in his shorts. The wine was going to his head, and he enjoyed the sense that he had no idea what was going to happen next.

Then Liam drank the last few ounces of his wine in a single gulp. "Let's go," he said. "I want to see your place."

He stood up. Aidan couldn't help it; he thought the guy was incredibly sexy. He'd always been attracted to take-charge men, though Liam was coming on stronger than any guy he'd ever met. But hey, he'd been out of the dating pool for eleven years, so maybe the rules had changed. He tossed down the rest of his wine and stood himself, unsteady on his feet.

The bartender called Liam over, and Aidan stepped out into the intense sunshine ahead of him, his eyes wincing at the brightness. It was earlier than when he'd visited the bar the day before, and there was a lot of activity on the street: young kids playing noisily, two women in head scarves and floral print dresses arguing, a motorcycle gunning just ahead.

Coming toward him, Aidan saw a man, obviously American, about his height, age, and build. Looking at his face, Aidan felt a shock of recognition. It was almost like looking in a mirror, distorted a bit by age and coloring.

The man wore a dark suit, a white shirt, and a navy blue tie, and sweat dripped down his forehead. Tunis was hot, hotter than any place Aidan had ever been. He was sweating himself, and he was wearing a lightweight cotton T-shirt and shorts.

The man's eyes darted left and right as if he was scanning the street for danger, and Aidan wondered if that's the way he looked roaming around the streets of Tunis with only half an idea of what was going on. The traffic of the street eddied and swirled around the American, but there was an invisible barrier around him that no one wanted to cross.

The motorcycle Aidan had heard gunning came up close behind the American, and with horror Aidan watched as the cyclist raised a hand holding a gun. Three short bursts of noise blasted across the street, and the American fell to the street as the motorcycle sped away.

Out of the Dating Pool

Liam stepped out of the beaded curtain from the Bar Mamounia to the street. "What's going on?" he asked Aidan.

"That man…" Aidan pointed to the body on the street.

All around the man, women were screaming and running, men were cursing in Arabic and shaking their fists. But no one moved to cross that invisible barrier around him.

"Come on," Liam said, grabbing Aidan's arm. "We're not running, but we're walking fast."

"What?" Aidan said. "That man was just shot. We have to try and help him."

"Not our business."

Looking back at the man lying motionless in the street, Aidan felt helpless, carried away by the moment and the gorgeous guy tugging his arm. Liam was a few inches taller than Aidan, with longer legs, so Aidan had to hustle to keep up. They hurried through a maze of narrow alleys as police sirens rose and fell in the distance. Finally they came out by the open plaza of the Jardin Habib Thameur, where mothers pushed babies in strollers along the broad avenues and young couples sprawled in the shade of the tall palms. Liam said, "Which way to your place?"

The guy was single-minded, Aidan had to give him that. Some poor man had just been gunned down in the street, and Liam still wanted sex. There was a real urgency in his voice too. Fortunately the building where Aidan had found an apartment was just a few blocks farther away.

"Not bad," Liam said as Aidan unlocked the front door to the six-story building. "Though I expected you to be staying in a hotel." It was about fifty years old and wouldn't have been out of place on a Paris side street. It hadn't been painted in years, so the bright sun had faded the color to a dirty off-white. The walls were thick and the blue-framed windows small, and the hallways smelled of cumin.

The tiny, metal-grilled elevator had been out of service since Aidan had moved in three days before, so they climbed the two flights to his apartment. Aidan's pulse was racing, all thoughts of the dead man in the street gone. He imagined how quickly he and Liam would strip their clothes off, how good it would feel to be in the big man's arms, how much he wanted to kiss those full, dry lips. The hell with Blake. He was about to embark on a new romance, and it felt amazing.

The skinny brown dog was lying in front of Aidan's door, as she had been every time he'd come home for the last couple of days. He wondered if she had lived with whomever had the apartment before him, or if she'd adopted him as a soft touch.

"Your dog?" Liam asked as Aidan bent down to scratch behind her ears and she rolled over.

"I guess. I feed her, and she sleeps with me, but she's on her own during the day."

"Dogs are good," Liam said. "She bark?"

"Don't know," Aidan said, opening the door.

Liam's cell phone rang as they walked inside, and he stepped over to the French doors that led out to a narrow balcony to take the call. While he did so, Aidan pulled bottles of cold water from the half-size refrigerator. He poured some water into a bowl for the dog, and she lapped it up eagerly.

His dick strained against his shorts, and he felt trapped by his T-shirt. He was ready to strip naked and offer himself up to Liam as soon as the big man got off the phone.

As Aidan returned to the living room, Liam snapped his phone shut and looked at him. "Who the fuck are you?" he asked.

Aidan's romantic fantasies evaporated in an instant. They had been too foolish to come true anyway.

What kind of mental case was this guy? First the take-charge attitude, now this about-face to anger. And Aidan had done the stupidest thing imaginable. He'd brought this stranger back to his apartment. This was what being out of the dating pool did; it dulled your senses, let you get caught up in a moment too easily. You wasted your time on fantasy when you should have been alert.

And wasn't that the problem with Blake too? Aidan hadn't been paying attention to possible problems with Blake, just as he'd ignored all those warning signs with Liam—running away from the dying man, the desperate urgency to get to Aidan's apartment.

Aidan remembered a personal-safety training course he'd taken at one of the colleges where he'd taught. If a student became angry or violent, you had to talk to him calmly, try to defuse the tension.

"I'm sorry. I guess I never told you my name. Aidan Greene. I'm from Philadelphia, and I just got to Tunis three days ago. I start teaching ESL at the École Internationale on Monday."

"Fuck me," Liam said, but from the tone of his voice, Aidan could tell it was an expletive rather than an invitation. "No chance you're also a courier from New York planning to head out into the desert? Go by the alias Charles Carlucci?"

"I think you should go," Aidan said, trying to keep the tremors out of his voice. He walked over to the door and put his hand on the knob. "I won't say anything or do anything. I promise. Just don't hurt me."

Liam looked disgusted. "I'm not going to hurt you. I'm a bodyguard, and I thought you were my client." He stood framed in the bright glare from the French doors, the same stance he'd used in the shower.

Only this time it was light cascading off his perfect body instead of water, though Aidan could see that square chest under the loose vest. He even thought he could make out the shadow of a semierect dick beneath the loose cotton of Liam's shorts. His own hardened as he remembered seeing Liam naked, even as it was clear their connection was about to end.

So much for falling in love—or even lust. He'd just run halfway around the world to escape the pain of a breakup; how had he even considered starting up with someone else so quickly? It was stupid, just plain stupid, despite how wonderful he had felt for those few minutes in the bar and on the desperate rush back to the apartment.

Aidan stepped toward Liam. The light in the living room was beautiful, dazzling and slightly yellow. Behind Liam, through the French doors, Aidan could see the sunlight glinting off the dome of the Zitouna mosque. In the distance, he heard a muezzin calling the faithful to prayer.

"You always meet your clients in bars?"

"This one was twitchy. He wanted to meet me on my turf. Didn't trust anybody." He grimaced. "Turns out he was right. That must have been him who got shot in front of the bar."

Aidan was confused. "Then you're not gay?"

Liam snorted. "What the hell does that have to do with the situation?" He looked at Aidan and then burst into laughter. "You thought I…" He laughed again.

Aidan thought he would fall through the floor with embarrassment. What a fool he'd been to consider that this god of a man was gay—and interested in him. Not only had Blake betrayed him—now he knew for a fact that he couldn't even trust his own body, his own instincts. Look at how he'd narrowly escaped danger the day before, running from those boys.

He needed to lock himself up in his apartment, play with the dog, and teach his students and shut down everything else. "Thank you very much for that charming opinion of my sexual attractiveness," he said. "And now, like I said before, I think you should leave."

Before Aidan realized Liam was moving, the big bodyguard was right next to him, his arms wrapped around Aidan, his lips on Aidan's lips.

Aidan hadn't kissed anyone but Blake in years, and it had been a long time since Blake had really kissed him. Liam's lips were chapped and his beard was rough, but there was such passion in the kiss that Aidan's head spun. With his big hands, Liam pulled Aidan close, their bodies meshed together, and Aidan felt the smooth leather of Liam's vest, the heat rising from his bare chest.

Aidan understood the meaning of the word *swoon*. He felt light on his feet, his heart racing, all sensation gathered at those points where his body met Liam's. Those lips! Pressed against his own, at first confused, now yielding, his mouth opening a little against the assault. Inhaling Liam's scent, Liam's arms wrapped around him, pulling their bodies close.

How was it possible he'd never felt something like this before? He'd been no virgin when he met Blake—and he'd thought what he felt with Blake was so much deeper than it had been with any man before.

That had been love, he thought. Despite all Blake's flaws, Aidan had loved him—and that made any contact between them, however brief, feel deeper and richer. And yet with this stranger, he felt more than he had ever felt before—the sense that he could fall into this handsome man's arms and stay there forever.

Liam broke the kiss first. "That should answer any questions you might have," he said, backing away. "And now, I've got to figure out who killed my client. See you around."

The Hotel Africa

After Liam left, Aidan walked around the small apartment in a daze. He believed in monogamy, so he had remained faithful to Blake even as the intervals between their sexual encounters grew longer and longer. He thought his own libido had all but disappeared until the moment he saw Liam showering behind the Bar Mamounia.

He opened the French doors and stepped onto the narrow balcony. Below him, Liam exited the building, then stopped and opened his cell phone. At the fruit vendor's stall across the street, women in faded floral-print dresses, with kerchiefs tied around their heads, shook melons and argued with the owner. Old men in white robes with the round red *chechias* on their heads sat in the shadows of doorways. Birds screeched in the trees, and somewhere Aidan heard a donkey braying. In the open lot across the road, young boys in T-shirts and brightly colored athletic shorts congregated to kick around a soccer ball.

Below him, Liam spoke for a moment, then looked up. He spoke again, then closed the phone. "I need to come back up," he called.

"I don't know how to work the door from up here," Aidan said.

"Then come down."

Aidan hesitated. Liam had behaved so strangely, at the bar and then again just a few minutes before. Did he want to get involved with this guy, no matter how his body reacted to Liam's touch?

"Please," Liam called up.

Aidan had always been a sucker for manners. And then there was that kiss. He went downstairs and opened the door.

"I need a favor. You have any nicer clothes?"

Aidan was wearing a Tiffany window T-shirt he'd bought at the Philadelphia Museum of Art, cargo shorts, and sandals. "Nothing I have will fit you," he said as he led the bodyguard back upstairs. "You're bigger than I am."

"I'm sure. But it's not for me; it's for you. I need you to be Charles Carlucci."

Here we go again. Was this guy ever going to speak a language he could understand?

"The man I was supposed to protect," Liam said as they reached the apartment door. The dog, which Aidan had yet to name, was sitting in the doorway waiting for his return. "He was supposed to be carrying something. My contact says that it wasn't on his body—which means it may be in his hotel room."

"What does that have to do with me?"

"I need you to go up to the desk at the Hotel Africa and tell the clerk you were mugged and your ID and room key were stolen. He'll make you a new key card."

Aidan had passed the Hotel Africa as he walked. It was big and modern; its flat facade would have fit in any big city. It wasn't the kind of place Aidan would ever stay—too impersonal, too corporate—too Blake. "Can't you just pick the lock?"

"Not as easy as it looks," Liam said. "And those electronic locks keep a record of every entry. There may be an alarm that goes off if someone gets in without a card. I don't have time to waste finding out if that's the case."

"Why would the desk clerk believe me?" Aidan asked. Then he remembered that shock of recognition when he had seen Carlucci on the street. They did look enough alike to pass for each other among strangers.

"Trust me, it happens all the time in Tunis. Plus they have Carlucci's passport in the safe."

Aidan wondered if he owed Carlucci something, because they had looked alike, and because Aidan had witnessed his death. He felt a strange connection to the dead man—as if looking at him was like looking at himself in a fun-house mirror. Perhaps this was a service he could perform to honor Carlucci's memory or appease his spirit.

He had one lightweight suit with him, navy, and a single white dress shirt. He stepped into the bedroom to get ready while Liam spoke on the phone again in the living room. A few minutes later, Aidan was fully dressed.

"You'll do," Liam said appraisingly. "Come on, we've got to move."

"What about you? Do people parade through the Hotel Africa dressed like you are?"

"You'd be surprised. Remember, I'm not the businessman from New York. I'm a bodyguard. I'm supposed to stand out."

As they walked downstairs, Aidan asked, "Why?"

"I want anybody who's considering harming my client to know that I'm there. Your ordinary street criminal, the pickpocket, the guy with a rusty knife, he'll back down right away."

"You think you could have protected this Carlucci guy?"

Liam shrugged. "If he'd agreed to meet me at the hotel, he wouldn't have been out on the street like that, vulnerable. Somebody must have either known he was coming to meet me or been following him. I might have been able to ditch the tail or protect him from the gunshots." He frowned. "But I couldn't."

Outside, he hailed a cab and gave the driver the address of the hotel. "He's in room 1801," Liam said. "As you pointed out, I'm pretty visible. If I'm with you, the clerk is going to wonder how come I didn't protect you from the mugger. So I'm going to head to the elevator. I'll meet you on the eighteenth floor."

"You make it sound so easy," Aidan grumbled, but when the cab pulled up in front of the hotel and the bellman opened the door, he stepped out and walked directly toward the desk, hoping to channel Charles Carlucci even though he'd only gotten a brief glimpse of him outside the bar.

But Aidan had lived with Blake Chennault for eleven years, and on occasion, when he'd had to argue on Blake's behalf, he'd been able to be him—to assume the air of privilege that surrounded him, the idea that he was better than anyone else and that the world was there to accommodate him.

Aidan had to wait while an overweight, sunburned British couple got restaurant suggestions, and out of the corner of his eye he saw Liam glide across the lobby to the elevator bank. A shiver ran through him as he remembered that amazing kiss in his apartment, the feel of Liam's body against his. Would there be any more?

The young blond clerk behind the counter was German; his name badge read *Heinrich.* Treating him the way he knew Blake would, Aidan explained that he'd been mugged and his key card stolen, and that he'd need a new one, please. "Carlucci. Eighteen-zero-one." He said it with a tone of exasperation, that somehow, by living here in this lousy country, Heinrich was responsible for his problems, and he expected the clerk to make things right as soon as possible.

"May I see some identification, please?" Heinrich asked.

"Weren't you listening?" Aidan asked. "The bastard got everything."

He frowned. Then, as if remembering, he said, "But you've got my passport in your safe. I warn you, though, it's a terrible picture. Those shots always are."

"Just one moment, please," Heinrich said, and he disappeared into the back office. As Aidan stood there, he had the feeling he was being watched. He scanned the lobby, keeping his lip curled in the attitude of disdain Blake demonstrated in even the most luxurious of settings.

A tracery of Arabic curlicues ran just below the high ceiling, and each of the doorways into other parts of the hotel was surmounted by a pointed arch. The floor was marble, the overstuffed sofas upholstered in dark brown leather. Bright red flowers like oversize poppies, with yellow centers and fringed petals, clustered in vases on the tables.

In one corner, an African man in a bright yellow and orange dashiki sat hunched over a laptop. Two Japanese men in business suits stood near the front door. The superior complained, in guttural tones, and the lesser man bowed frequently and said, "*Hai!*"

A Tunisian in a beige djellaba spoke on a cell phone near him, but Aidan couldn't understand a word he said. The other clerk, an Indian woman in a bright blue sari, continued to check in new customers. No one seemed to be staring at him, but Aidan couldn't escape the feeling of being watched.

By the time Heinrich returned, five minutes later, Aidan was sure that he'd summoned the cops, who were going to arrest him for Carlucci's murder. Or that one of the men in the lobby was going to come over and demand whatever it was Carlucci was supposed to have, or strong-arm Aidan out of the hotel. With Liam gone, Aidan would be on his own. Sweat was pooling under the arms of his suit and across his forehead. He struggled to keep channeling Blake Chennault.

Heinrich held the passport up, looked at Aidan, looked down again, then up again. "Thank you for waiting, Mr. Carlucci," he said. He took a plastic key card from a stack, typed a few keys into his keyboard, and then swiped the card through a slot. "Here you go, sir."

The Indian woman was checking in the Tunisian who'd been on his cell phone. She was apparently having a problem with his reservation and said, "Heinrich, can you help me here?"

While Heinrich's head was turned away, Aidan slid the passport across the counter and pocketed it. He took the elevator to the eighteenth floor, where the doors opened on a hallway that reminded him of luxury hotels where he'd stayed with Blake. The carpet was plush, patterned like an Oriental rug, and light came from a cove just beneath the ceiling. At the far end of the hall was a housekeeping cart, but otherwise the hallway was empty.

He didn't see Liam, so he walked over to room 1801 and pulled the key card from his pocket. Without a sound, Liam was beside him. "That's creepy," Aidan said. "The way you move around so quietly."

"Put these on," Liam said, handing him a pair of thin rubber gloves, the type nurses use. Aidan wondered if Liam had lifted them from the maid's cart.

"You're always prepared. Were you a Boy Scout?"

"That, and Navy SEAL," Liam said. He took the card and slid it into the door. He put his finger to his lips and very slowly pushed the door open.

It looked like Carlucci had left in a hurry. The mahogany-framed, king-size bed was unmade, a pair of Brooks Brothers pajamas strewn over the covers. The top of the credenza was covered in a messy pile of newspaper sections, the *New York Times* and the *International Herald Tribune.*

Ornate Arabic scrollwork decorated the bed, the bureau, and the nightstand. On one wall hung a portrait of a Tuareg man in the traditional blue robes, silhouetted against golden sand dunes.

"Start packing Carlucci's suitcase," Liam whispered, pointing to the open roll-on bag on a small luggage stand by the closet. "Everything goes in the bag. Leave nothing behind." He began a systematic search of the room, taking apart the phone and the bedside lamp, checking under the surfaces of tables and drawers.

Aidan wiggled his hands into the plastic gloves and got started. He didn't ask what Liam was looking for; he just did what he was told. Blake had traveled a lot for work, and they'd taken a fair number of pleasure trips as well, so Aidan was a fast and experienced packer, despite the fact that his heart was racing at about double its normal pace.

Out of the corner of his eye, he saw Liam bend to the floor, the leather vest slipping aside to show a tantalizing glimpse of flat, tanned skin, and it was like an electric shock to Aidan's groin. He nearly moaned out loud with longing. Just to touch that skin again. To be held in those arms.

Aidan folded Carlucci's slacks carefully, maintaining the creases, though the man would never wear them again. He saw Liam bent over the bedside telephone, his shorts stretched taught against his round ass. Aidan licked his lips and tried to concentrate on packing.

"Thought so," Liam said, holding up the phone's entrails. "Bugged. Somebody knew Carlucci was meeting me at the bar."

"Which means they know who you are."

"And they know we're here, if they're paying attention. Which means we need to get out of here as fast as possible."

Liam put the phone back together, replacing the bug. They passed each other often, never touching, as Aidan folded Carlucci's clothes, slid the shoes into their cloth bags, wrapped up the complimentary toiletries from the bathroom. It took him under ten minutes, but the time felt like it was going so slowly—and he worried that hotel security would burst through the door any minute.

Aidan admired Liam's economy of movement. Everything he did was deliberate and careful. He seemed hyperaware of the space around him, and despite his size and musculature, his moves were precise. He didn't drop anything, bump into the furniture, or second-guess himself. Aidan felt butterflies in his stomach. Was it the tension of the situation or the memory of the handsome man's hands on him? He didn't know.

In addition to the roll-aboard bag, Carlucci had a leather portfolio filled with papers and maps. Aidan slid the newspapers into the portfolio and zipped it. He picked both pieces up as Liam gave the room one more pass and then carefully opened the door.

Liam held a small mirror out through a crack, manipulating it left, right, up, and down. Aidan hovered behind him, wanting nothing more than to be in his arms again. Heat rose from Liam's body, and Aidan wondered if they would ever embrace or kiss again.

Once assured, Liam opened the door wider and did one more visual check before giving Aidan an all-clear sign and stepping into the hallway.

Liam slipped the door to Carlucci's room closed. He peeled off his rubber gloves, and Aidan did the same. "Now we get out of here," Liam said. "Casually. Not attracting attention."

They were heading for the elevator when they heard the chime that indicated it was coming to a stop on eighteen. "Change of plans," Liam said, and he grabbed Aidan's arm and moved him down the hall to the exit stairs. With his hip, he eased the door open.

"Eighteen floors?" Aidan said as they entered the stairwell.

Behind them, Aidan heard excited conversation in Arabic, and a quick glance over his shoulder revealed Heinrich, the desk clerk, and two uniformed police.

Silver Knife

Liam bodychecked the door to keep it from slamming behind them. They waited there for a moment, until Liam was sure they hadn't attracted any notice; then he took the suitcase from Aidan, leaving him the portfolio, and started down the stairs fluidly, moving almost without effort.

After about ten flights, Aidan found himself toiling. "Can you move faster?" Liam asked from below. "I want to get away from this hotel."

"Working on it." Aidan panted.

Finally, they reached the ground level. "Give me your jacket and tie," Liam demanded as they stood just inside the door to the ground floor. Despite the circumstances, as he peeled off his jacket and undid his tie, Aidan wished he could strip even further down, get naked with Liam right there in the cinderblock stairwell.

As Liam folded the jacket and tie and stuffed them into the top of Carlucci's roll-on bag, he said, "Open your collar and roll up your sleeves." Aidan did as he was told as Liam repeated his mirror trick with the fire door.

Liam handed Aidan his sunglasses and said, "Put these on top of your head. Then walk next to me."

He opened the door, and Aidan followed him out. Each step on the marble floor sounded as loud as a rifle shot, and Aidan couldn't believe they wouldn't attract attention. They were at the far end of the lobby, and he could see another pair of uniformed policemen at the front desk, talking to the Indian woman who had been working with Heinrich.

"Slowly," Liam said. "We're just two guests having a conversation. Keep your face turned toward me."

He put his arm around Aidan's shoulder and laughed. Aidan felt the heat of Liam's skin radiating through his body, felt his dick stiffening once again in his navy suit pants. He said something mindless, and they walked across the lobby to the front doors. One of the policemen looked at them, then turned back to the Indian woman. The bellman called over a cab and held the door open.

Liam ushered Aidan in and then followed. He gave the cabdriver Aidan's address. "I'm going to drop you at your place, and then I'll get out of your hair," he said. "Don't tell anyone you know me, or say anything about what we did today."

"Are you going back to that little house behind the bar?"

"Don't come looking for me. It's not safe for you."

"Liam. If someone knew Carlucci was going to meet you, isn't it likely he knows who you are and where you live?"

"Fuck."

"Come to my apartment. You can figure out what to do from there."

"All right." He leaned forward and spoke in Arabic to the driver. When he came back to Aidan, he said, "I'm going to need some stuff from my place, and we've got to move fast. I want to know if somebody's watching me already."

The ride was bumpy, the driver taking curves so rapidly that Aidan was tossed against Liam, and he reveled in the brief moments their bodies touched. If this was all he was going to get, he was going to enjoy it. The heat of Liam's bare leg against Aidan's suit pants, Aidan's hand brushing the leather vest, the tip of his index finger grazing Liam's smooth, tanned chest. He wanted to close his eyes and savor every bit of contact, inhaling Liam's lavender scent, now overlaid with a musk of sweat. He stole a glance at Liam's dick, which lay semihard under the thin fabric of his cotton shorts.

A few minutes later, the driver pulled the cab over in front of a shop selling elaborate metalwork. "Wait here," Liam said. "If I'm not back in ten minutes, go directly to the American embassy and give Carlucci's luggage to a guy named Louis Fleck. Got that?"

Aidan nodded. Liam spoke to the driver in Arabic again and then got out of the cab. Aidan tried to watch where Liam was going, but his whole body language changed as he walked, and despite his height, he melded into the crowd.

Aidan stared into the window of the shop. Elaborate silver trays and swords lined the front, along with an array of knives. He said to the driver, "You speak English?"

"*Non, Monsieur. Arabe ou français.*"

"*Attendez-moi, s'il vous plait,*" Aidan said, asking him to wait, and the driver nodded.

Aidan looked around before he got out of the cab. No snipers appeared perched on any of the low rooftops, so he scurried into the shop. The proprietor was a fat old man wearing an embroidered cap. "A knife," Aidan said, pointing to the display in the window. "Small." He motioned with his hands to simulate the opening of a switchblade.

The old man got up and shuffled to the display. Aidan kept looking out to the window, expecting to see Liam rushing to the cab in a rain of bullets. His raised adrenaline level made him twitchy; he couldn't stop shuffling from foot to foot. The old man pulled a selection of knives from the window, and one caught Aidan's eye. It was a simple silver case, with a delicate scrollwork of Arabic lettering on the hilt. It popped open easily, exposing a wickedly sharp blade.

Aidan took a quick glance to the street. No menacing characters had appeared near the cab.

The knife held six blades in total, a kind of Arabic version of a Swiss Army knife. Aidan had had one of those for years, so he knew how they worked. "I'll take it," he said. "How much?"

While the man figured the price, Aidan took one more look outside. Still clear.

Aidan splayed out some paper money, and the old man took a few bills. Aidan thanked him, pocketed the knife, and stepped to the door.

Trying to calm his heart, he did what he thought Liam would do. He looked left, right, up, and down. All seemed clear, so he ducked back into the cab.

He looked at his watch. It had been nearly ten minutes, and Liam still had not returned. He scanned the passing crowd for the big bodyguard and couldn't see anyone his size, anyone who was so conspicuously American. He kept switching his glance between the street and his watch, waiting for the seconds to count down, until he saw two soldiers approach, carrying rifles.

Liam's House

Through years of practice, Liam McCullough had trained himself to blend into his surroundings. After he climbed out of the cab, he pulled a red chechia, the round felt cap Tunisian men wore, from his pocket. He put it on his head and donned his dark sunglasses, and his whole body language changed.

With his tanned skin, his Tunisian-made cargo shorts and leather vest, he no longer looked quite as American, though his height, unusual among Tunisians, still made him stand out a bit. But with his posture relaxed, he appeared at least a few inches shorter than he was.

He moved slowly down the street, keeping pace just behind a pair of men wearing long white cloaks. His gaze swiveled from right to left and back again as he surveyed the area around him. It was possible that whoever shot Charles Carlucci only knew his destination, not Liam's name or address, and he'd be able to get into his house easily and without surveillance.

But things were rarely that simple in North Africa. Since the first time he'd come to Tunisia, nearly ten years before, as part of a SEAL operation, Liam had come to accept that

Murphy's Law applied to all dealings with the Arab world. If something could go wrong, it would.

He couldn't forgive himself for mistaking Aidan for Carlucci. If he'd been more alert, he might have seen the sniper ready for Carlucci, might have protected him. That was his job, after all. Protection.

A block from his house, he caught sight of the first policeman. The man lounged against a wall, his rifle hanging from his shoulder. He might just be taking a cigarette break, or he might be watching for Liam.

There was another on the opposite corner. Unlikely that two policemen would take a break across from each other. And even more unlikely that two more would have chosen to take a break at the next cross street.

Liam focused on his pulse rate, willing it to slow. He turned the corner, not attracting any notice from the police. They were watching his doorway, not watching for him. Big mistake on their part.

Their second mistake was not watching the Bar Mamounia. The police disdained the bar for its reputation among a certain kind of men—the kind who occasionally found their way across the courtyard and into Liam's bed.

Liam's experience as a SEAL had taught him to keep his emotions closed. When he was in the military, he hadn't been able to be open about his sexuality, so he'd learned only to approach men who wanted what he did—a quick release. If a man expressed interest in more, Liam disappeared.

There was no one watching the entrance to the Bar Mamounia, so Liam crossed the street, willing himself not to rush, and entered the cool darkness, the beads hardly rustling as he passed through them. The bartender looked up, nodded, and went back to his crossword puzzle. The usual drunks were occupying the shady corners of the bar, skinny older men who didn't care about the bar's reputation as long as they could get alcohol there. Liam walked past them nonchalantly. He was nearly to the courtyard when he heard his name called, and the corners of his mouth turned down.

"Liam! Liam! Why you not love me anymore?" the young man said in Arabic.

Abdullah was a skinny, dark-skinned Tunisian in his early twenties who painted kohl around his eyes and wore American-style tank tops, often with misspellings. Today's read *University of Princeton.* "Not now, Abdullah."

"Why not? You found someone you like better?"

In a quick move, Liam had his hand over Abdullah's mouth. Why had he ever agreed to take the idiot to bed? It had been one night, but Abdullah had not let it go. "I'm busy now, Abdullah. I don't have time to talk to you or to mess around with you. Do you understand?"

Abdullah's eyes gleamed as he nodded. Liam removed his hand, and the Tunisian began to speak—until he saw the look in Liam's eyes, and he stopped midword. "Tomorrow I will buy you a drink," Liam said. "You understand? Tomorrow?"

"Yes, tomorrow," Abdullah said. He tagged along behind Liam as the American moved toward the courtyard.

"Stay here, Abdullah," Liam said.

"I come to your house," Abdullah said. "I make you feel good."

Liam looked at the bartender, who called out to the Tunisian. With a pout, Abdullah turned and stomped over to the bar. Liam paused at the two French doors that led to the courtyard. From there he could see no one on the roof of his house, no one in the corners of the yard. He stepped outside and, keeping to the sides of the building, made his way through a narrow alley to the front.

From his vantage point, back against the stucco wall, he could see the officers watching the front door. The bright sun had already begun to sink from its zenith, so he was fully in shadow, the rough wall digging into the part of his back unshielded by the leather vest.

The policemen hadn't moved, and the sand in front of the door, which Liam always groomed after leaving, was undisturbed, which meant no one had gotten into the house.

He returned to the rear of the building, where a door led out to the courtyard and his makeshift shower. He always kept this door locked too. Holding his breath, he slid the key into the lock and pushed the door open.

He waited at the side of the door for a long moment, getting a sense of the house, but there was no one in the living room, and he stepped inside. After a quick survey of the other rooms, he grabbed a duffel bag and began to pack.

He moved quickly, not knowing how much time he had, thinking as he worked. Why were the police watching for him? Did they think he was a suspect—or were they working with whoever had Carlucci killed? Who was responsible for the shooting? Why? And who was trying to implicate him? What had Carlucci been carrying—and why was it so important, so deadly?

Then there was the teacher from Philadelphia. Liam hated to rope in civilians, but he hadn't had any choice; things were moving too quickly and in unexpected directions. He'd get back to the teacher's apartment, make some calls, and figure out his next move.

He froze, listening, as loud voices shouted in Arabic outside his front door. Someone in authority had shown up and was demanding to know if this was Liam's house.

Damn. Had to get out fast. He grabbed his duffel bag and hurried out of the bedroom as he heard the sound of his front door splintering.

Hidden Numbers

Aidan was just about to tell the driver to go when the cab door popped open and Liam jumped inside carrying a canvas duffel. He said something in rapid Arabic to the driver, and they were off. Twisting around to look out the rear window, Aidan saw the soldiers talking and gesturing to each other, one of them pulling out a radio.

The cab turned the corner, and the soldiers disappeared from view. No siren-blaring police cars pulled behind them as they navigated the narrow, crowded streets to Aidan's apartment. That was good news. "There were police watching my place," Liam said quietly. "I managed to sneak out the back just as they broke down my front door."

"So they know who you are."

Liam shifted the duffel bag between them but said nothing, his mouth set in a grim line. At Aidan's apartment, Liam made Aidan wait in the cab until he had checked that the way was clear, and then they hurried through the elaborate grillwork door to the lobby.

Liam carried the suitcase, with his duffel slung over his shoulder, and climbed the stairs effortlessly. Aidan followed, stopping to pet the dog outside his door as he fumbled for his keys.

Once inside, Liam took his cell phone over to the window, and Aidan poured fresh cold water into the dog's bowl. While she lapped noisily, Aidan hoisted Carlucci's roll-aboard to the table and started lifting things out. Liam appeared next to him a moment later and began to survey each item, opening the lining on Carlucci's suit jacket and feeling inside.

"What are we looking for?" Aidan asked.

"Don't know," Liam said. "Anything that doesn't belong where it is."

Aidan inspected the toiletries. There were no diamonds stuck at the bottom of the shampoo bottle, no false bottoms or secret compartments in anything. They worked for an hour and came up empty-handed.

Liam's cell phone rang again, and he stepped away to take the call. Aidan thought it was a good thing there was nothing romantic between them, or he'd start to get very jealous of all these secret calls.

When Liam returned, he said, "We're looking for an account number and a password."

"How do you know?"

"We're going to have to read through everything. Look for patterns—the number may be camouflaged in something else, a letter or a memo."

Aidan was cranky over the secrecy, but he had to remind himself that he wasn't a spy or a bodyguard or a former Navy SEAL or whatever it was that Liam was. He was just an ESL teacher who'd been dumped by his boyfriend and set off for an adventure on the other side of the world.

As time passed, Liam got increasingly frustrated. He even bumped into Aidan once, which was quite unlike him; he usually moved with such catlike grace that he had passed by before Aidan even knew he was near. He cut open the lining of each of Carlucci's garments and analyzed the labels with a magnifying glass. When Aidan saw him holding up a pair of Carlucci's boxers to the light, he couldn't help laughing. They were patterned with red-and-white-striped candy canes—probably someone's Christmas gift to him.

Then he remembered Blake, who had bought Aidan a pair of white cotton boxers patterned with cupids for their first Valentine's Day. He'd worn them a lot those first few years together, but as intimate moments between them had become fewer and fewer, the boxers had faded and been torn up for cleaning rags. Regret twisted at his heart, though he wasn't sure if it was for Carlucci or for what he'd lost with Blake.

Four hours later Aidan's stomach was grumbling and they hadn't found anything. Whoever had hidden the account number and the password had done a damn good job of it. "You want something to eat?" Aidan asked, standing up and stretching. His back ached from hunching over the table. Through the French doors, he saw that the sun was setting, the last golden rays reflecting from the dome of the Zitouna mosque in the distance.

"What have you got?"

"Rice and vegetables," Aidan said. "I make a mean stir-fry."

"Sounds good. Got any beer?"

"In the fridge."

While Aidan sautéed the vegetables and boiled the water for the rice, Liam kept on reading. Aidan could see he was the type who wouldn't give up so easily.

They sat to eat, and suddenly Aidan felt Liam staring closely at his bottle of beer. Water had condensed on the side of the bottle, and you could clearly see his fingerprints there.

"Have you ever had your prints taken?" Liam asked quietly.

"At one of the colleges where I worked," Aidan said. "Post 9/11 rules. Why?"

His mouth was a thin line, and his lips hardly moved when he spoke. "Did you handle Carlucci's passport at the front desk?"

"Sure."

"So they may be able to get a print from it and match it to you." He jumped up and began to pace. "We've got to get out of here."

"Hold on. I forgot. I took Carlucci's passport from the clerk when he wasn't looking." He got up to retrieve it from his jacket pocket, and Liam was by his side a moment later. Before Liam accepted the passport, he took Aidan's face in both his hands and kissed him. It took Aidan by surprise, those rough, full lips against his, the feeling of Liam's body so close. It was over way too quickly; Aidan wanted to linger with Liam's hands on his face, their mouths tasting each other. But Liam backed away.

"Wow. What was that for?" Aidan asked as he handed Liam the passport.

"For surprising me."

Liam smiled as he opened Carlucci's passport and started leafing through the pages. "Our man got around," he said, pointing to the visa stamps from various North African countries, Morocco, Libya, and Sudan among them.

"Can you even go to those places?" Aidan asked.

"He could." Liam flipped to the back of the passport, where there was a row of tiny letters printed across the bottom of the back page. "What the hell?"

He held the book up close to his face. "Damn, this is tiny." He opened his duffel bag and rummaged around inside for a moment. He pulled out a pair of cheap reading glasses and squinted at the writing on the inside of Carlucci's passport. "Numbers," he said. "And a word."

"The account number and password?" Aidan asked.

"I think it must be. Carlucci was a courier. He was supposed to meet me at the bar, and I was going to escort him to a Tuareg camp at an oasis in the south of the country, where he would hand over this account number."

"What do you do now? Take the account information yourself?"

He shrugged. "Got to make a call." He stepped over to the French doors once again, which now led only to darkness.

While he did, Aidan went into the bathroom and tried to wash the tension from his face. He took a bunch of deep breaths. It had been an interesting day, to say the least. Trying to recover the adventurer he'd been before he settled down with Blake, he'd taken action—he'd chased down a guy he found attractive. And look where it had led.

When Aidan came out of the bathroom, Liam was sprawled on the couch. "You can stay here if you want," Aidan said. "If you can't go back to your place for a while. As you can see, the couch is pretty comfortable."

A faint smile played at the corners of Liam's mouth. "Only the couch? I can't do anything until I hear from my contact, which leaves me at loose ends."

He slipped off his vest, exposing all that gorgeous, muscular chest. Their eyes met, and Aidan remembered the brief passion of that kiss. So did his dick, which sprang to attention. Once again, he thought about the adventure he'd come to Tunisia to find. "Getting pretty hot in here," Aidan said. He began unbuttoning his shirt too.

Liam stood and came over to him, and they embraced, both of them shirtless. Liam's chest was sun-browned, with a couple of small scars, and it was warm against Aidan's. They kissed, and the electricity of their previous contact was there again, a burning that began in the pit of Aidan's stomach and rose throughout his body. Liam's lips were rough against his, but the pressure of them against his mouth was enough to make Aidan's pulse race and his dick stiffen.

Aidan opened his mouth a little, and Liam's tongue darted in. *Damn, this guy knows how to kiss.* His brawny arms wrapped around Aidan's back, and he pulled Aidan close to him, his hands exploring the waistband of Aidan's shorts and snaking down to the crack of his ass. Aidan put his hands on Liam's back, his fingers resting on Liam's prominent shoulder blades.

Their tongues dueled, tasting each other, the lingering flavors of dinner and the local Tunisian beer, called Stella.

Aidan closed his eyes and savored every sensation, from the rhythm of Liam's heartbeat to the feel of Liam's rough cheek against his own.

Liam's lips slid over Aidan's chin, then slid down and began nibbling on his neck as Aidan arched his back in pure pleasure.

Then Liam's phone rang.

Aidan knew the drill from eleven years with Blake. If he and Blake were talking, or on that rare occasion, enjoying a moment of intimacy, and Blake's phone rang, his BlackBerry vibrated, or his laptop beeped to indicate a new e-mail, his attention immediately shifted.

If Aidan had been paying attention, he supposed he might have foreseen the breakup of their relationship as soon as Blake started caring more about unknown callers or e-mailers than he did for the man who was supposed to be his life partner. At least with Liam, Aidan knew where he stood from the first moment.

Liam stepped over toward the French doors. Aidan didn't know if he got better reception over there, or if he just didn't want to be overheard. Aidan told himself that he didn't care. Liam was a momentary distraction, someone who'd be out of his life as soon as something happened to draw the bodyguard away. He knew he had to keep his distance, because he couldn't afford to be hurt again so soon after Blake. He didn't know if he could recover from another disappointment so soon.

For fun, Aidan faced Liam as he listened to his caller. Aidan touched his index finger to his own right nipple, drawing gentle circles around it and teasing it into stiffness.

Liam looked up and noticed what he was doing, grinned, but refocused on his phone call.

Aidan moved to the left nipple, playing with it for a moment. Closing his eyes, he imagined it was Liam's hand on him, Liam's finger exciting the nipple to a hard nub. Then both hands, one on each nipple. He could feel his dick leaking precum. He felt loose and adventurous, the way he'd felt when he was younger, traveling Europe and tasting her men. When he opened his eyes, Liam waved a hand at him. "Got a pen?" he asked.

Aidan gave up. He handed Liam the pen and then sat down on the couch like a sulky adolescent. It was silly to think he could tempt a six-feet-four porn star with a body to die for, ripped abs, killer biceps, a tight, round ass, and a dick of death. He was a scrawny English teacher on the brink of middle age who hadn't been properly kissed, or made love to, in years. He wasn't that sexy young thing he'd been right after college, full of energy, excitement, and lust. He had nothing to offer Liam except a way to waste time while the bodyguard waited for his next move.

Which appeared to be coming.

Liam hung up the phone and asked, "Have you been to the medina yet? You really shouldn't miss it. *Medina* is Arabic for city, and it's one of the most interesting things to see here. Really the heart of Tunis."

Aidan looked at Liam like he'd lost his mind. The ex-SEAL soldier of fortune had turned into a tour guide? "I've been to the medina. It's a tourist trap. All those narrow streets, the little stalls selling trinkets. I think I'll pass. But you can head out anytime you like."

"I'd really like to show it to you," Liam said, coming over to him. "I can show you things you wouldn't see as a tourist." His right index finger grazed against Aidan's right nipple.

It was such a transparent effort to bend him to Liam's will that Aidan slid backward on the couch. He was through being taken advantage of, even if it meant forfeiting the chance to fool around some more with such a gorgeous guy. Maybe he had learned something since the last time he'd been on his own.

Aidan picked up his shirt. "I don't know what you're playing at, Liam, but I'm tired. It's been a stressful day. I don't normally impersonate dead men and sneak into hotel rooms."

Aidan was tired, and the adrenaline hits he'd felt throughout the day had drained him. All he wanted to do was collapse in bed—alone.

Behind him, out the French doors, the city was dark, just a few lights shining here and there. Liam looked at his watch. "You're right. I didn't realize how late it had gotten. The souk closes at sunset. We'll have to go there first thing tomorrow."

"You're not listening to me." Man, how many times had Aidan said that to Blake? "I'm not going to the medina with you, today or tomorrow. Pack up all of Carlucci's crap, and your little mercenary duffel bag, and hit the road."

Something that looked a bit like hurt flashed across Liam's handsome face, but then it was gone, back to the impassive mask of the soldier of fortune. "I'm not a mercenary," he said quietly. "I'm a bodyguard. And the client

I was most recently supposed to protect is dead. I appreciate your help, and I'll get out of your hair."

He began to pack up Carlucci's bag, and after a minute or two Aidan said, "Where will you go? You can't go back home."

"I've got friends," Liam said, moving efficiently to pack up Carlucci's stuff. "I'll find a place."

Aidan had never been able to stay mad for long, no matter how much he'd been hurt. He tended to store up his anger, sometimes letting it out in inappropriate ways. He'd yell at women whose grocery cart blocked his, at parents with cranky babies. And then he'd feel miserable for getting mad at them.

"Wait. I'm sorry. Why don't you stay here tonight?" Liam's eyebrows rose, and Aidan said, "On the couch. And then we'll see what happens in the morning."

Aidan had a feeling that if he made a pass at Liam, the big, sexy guy would accept. But Aidan knew he'd feel like a fool in the morning—and he was tired of that feeling. It was time for him to take some more control of his life.

"Thanks," Liam said. "I appreciate it. I know you've been through a lot today, and I apologize for dragging you along."

Aidan shrugged. "I came to Tunisia for an adventure," he said. "Monday morning I start teaching, and there's not much adventure in that. So I'm good."

"Well, I'm going to look through the paperwork Carlucci had with him one more time." Liam sat on the sofa with the paper around him, donning his reading glasses once again. For just a moment Aidan envisioned a future with the bodyguard, evenings spent like this. But he brushed the thought away as soon as it appeared.

Aidan went into his bedroom, stripped down, and got into bed. Through the open window, he heard birds chirping, the sound of a far-off motorcycle. He lay there for a long time, wondering if Liam might appear in the doorway, tempting him. Would he have the strength to go on saying no?

But sleep claimed him instead.

A Trip to the Medina

Aidan woke to the rays of the rising sun streaming in through his bedroom window and the slightly bitter scent of coffee coming from the kitchen. He made a pit stop in the bathroom, then pulled a pair of cargo shorts over his boxers and walked out to the living room.

Liam was sitting on the couch, reading an Arabic newspaper, a mug of fresh coffee next to him. On the low table sat a tray of flaky pastries topped with drizzled honey. "There's coffee in the pot," Liam said. "Morning."

"Good morning." Aidan impulsively leaned down and kissed the bodyguard's cheek as he passed.

He'd done that so many times to Blake, and so often Blake had flinched as if Aidan's lips were poisonous. Liam didn't flinch; in fact, he smiled.

Aidan poured a mug of coffee and then sat in the easy chair across from Liam. He picked up a pastry, flaky layers of dough, honey, and nuts, and took a bite. It tasted a lot like baklava. "Mmm. These are fabulous."

"Best bakery in Tunis." Liam folded the paper and put it down next to him.

"Anything about Carlucci in there?"

Liam shook his head. "The police don't like to release bad news about foreigners. Bad for the tourist trade."

"And someone may be hiding what happened to him."

"Maybe."

Aidan finished the pastry and licked his fingers. "So, the medina. You think there's something you can show me I haven't already seen?"

A smile crept across Liam's face. "I'm sure there are things I can show you that you haven't seen." Then he paused, for effect. "In the medina."

Flirting felt good. Aidan hadn't done it for so long, and he'd thought he'd forgotten how. He guessed he could probably still ride a bicycle too.

He fed the dog breakfast, and she followed them outside, then went off to do her business. As they walked, Liam said, "In the medina, the souks run by the clean trades are closest to the Zitouna mosque, while the dirtier ones, like metalsmiths and fabric dyeing, are farther away. They still weave silk by hand at the Souk de la Laine, and there's some beautiful jewelry in the Souk des Orfevres, the goldsmith's market. That's where we're going."

It was a brilliant, sunny day, hardly a cloud in the sky, and Aidan was sure as the clock ticked toward noon the temperature would keep rising.

They passed the empty field across from Aidan's building, where sheep grazed and a couple of local kids kicked a ball around and feral cats slunk under the palm trees. The streets smelled of jasmine bushes, coffee, and automobile exhaust, and over the noise of car and bicycle horns and spoken Arabic, they heard Elvis Presley singing "Hound Dog."

At the Bab el Bahr, the arched gateway to the medina, men and teenage boys sheltered under the overhangs of white stucco buildings, clutching fistfuls of sunglasses, baseball caps, and round, red felt chechias. They were interspersed with shoeshine boys, vendors standing over flaming grills, and other small merchants. Though he knew they were staying close to the buildings for shade from the bright sun, Aidan still felt there was something shadowy about their failure to step forward.

They passed a poster Aidan thought was advertising a movie, but because he couldn't read the Arabic script, it could have been pushing mouthwash. High, wailing music blared around them, and the crowds got heavier, men with gold teeth bumping into Aidan and moving on without apologizing. He began to feel how alien he and Liam were in this world.

Even though Liam lived in Tunis and spoke Arabic and French, his size, his complexion, and his light brown hair marked him as an outsider. With Aidan's dark hair and Mediterranean looks, courtesy of centuries of desert-dwelling Jews, he fit in better. But he was sure his clothes and bearing still screamed *American.*

"This area dates back to the end of the seventh century," Liam said, and through his easy, conversational tone, Aidan could tell that the bodyguard was aware of everything that went on around them. His eyes never stopped moving, and he walked close to Aidan as if he could shelter him with his body. "Until the French arrived in the late 1800s, everyone lived, shopped, and worked in this part of the city. These narrow, winding alleys haven't changed in centuries, though most people live outside in the modern city now."

As they took the main route into the medina, the narrow cobblestoned street filled with people moving through or stopping to survey what the tiny souks had to offer. Occasionally a man with a handcart tried to squeeze past them. Fat women in bright-colored dresses swished by, including one in a burka, completely masked except for a narrow strip where her dark eyes shone through.

"Most women in Tunisia don't wear the burka," Liam whispered as they passed her. "It's very progressive for an Arab country. Most women wear Western clothes, and it's illegal to wear the burka in places like government offices and schools. There have been stories that women in burkas have been arrested, even raped, by the police."

"Nice," Aidan said. "Bet that doesn't make it into the tourist guides."

Liam continued to scan the area around them, moving his head slowly from left to right. So close to him, Aidan could tell that the bodyguard's whole body was on alert, as if the slightest touch could send him into attack mode. It was hard to see far ahead, and it would be easy for a man with a knife or a gun to squeeze right up next to them.

Seeing Liam's heightened reactions, Aidan became more agitated himself. What were they doing there? This wasn't a casual sightseeing outing. Not with police outside Liam's house, with a dead American and a Swiss bank account number.

"What's up, Liam? Why are we here?"

"We need to pick something up," he said. "Actually, you need to pick something up from one of the vendors."

"Me? Why me?"

"Because you look like Carlucci."

Aidan sighed. "Not again."

"This is the last time, I promise. It's just that the vendor has been given a picture of Carlucci and told to hand over what he has only to him."

"And what is that?"

Liam shrugged. "We'll see when he hands it to you."

Aidan blew a big breath out through his lips. Of course. That's why Liam was still being nice. He still needed Aidan's help. It was Philadelphia all over again. Blake had needed him and used him. Why should Liam be any different? And what about that sexual tension of the night before—had that all been manufactured?

Liam wore the same vest as the day before, though it had been cinched across his chest with leather straps. The pockets of his cargo shorts were full of sharp-edged things that banged against Aidan's legs when they touched. With his new realization, Aidan couldn't stand to be next to the bodyguard. It was as if he'd developed an allergy to the man's lemon scent, to his smooth, tanned skin. He stepped away.

"Hey, come back here," Liam said, grabbing his arm.

"Let me go," Aidan said. "I'll go with you until you get your little package. But then I'm out of here."

"Don't get pissy. I've got enough to watch out for without any tantrums from you."

"I'm not a child, Liam. As you'd have figured out if you hadn't wimped out last night and stayed in the living room."

Where had that come from? Aidan wondered. It had been his choice not to have sex, hadn't it?

"You made it clear what you wanted from me last night. And that was to be left alone." Liam shook his head. "You're crazy, you know that? Men like you are why I prefer my sex without strings. I don't have the patience for stupid games."

Aidan didn't respond, having lost track of why he was angry in the first place. The sounds in the medina were overwhelming, from the calls of the merchants in harsh Arabic to the methodical pounding of the repoussé artisans and the Arabic pop music blasting from speakers.

They passed souks full of carpets, elaborate birdcages with pointed arches, brass teapots, and cotton blouses in a rainbow of colors, embroidered with intricate designs. He saw a souk stocked with the long, hooded cloaks called djellabas and thought he might buy one to wear at night while relaxing and grading papers.

Sweet aromas wafted out of the spice vendors' souks; the leathermakers' stalls were pungent. They even passed the perfumers' souks, where the flowery scent combined with the delicate colorful bottles to assault the senses.

At the fez-maker's souk, an old man was proudly demonstrating the traditional process. Finally they came to the goldsmiths' street, what Liam had called the Souk des Orfevres.

"Is there a password I should know?" Aidan asked Liam. "Some secret word or signal? Or do I just go in and say that I'm Charles Carlucci?"

"I assume someone will recognize you from the photo."

Liam paused in front of a souk lined with glass display cases. Rows of gold bracelets and necklaces and trays of charms glinted in the slanting sunlight that penetrated through the medina. He nudged Aidan, who took the hint and walked in, while Liam remained at the street.

Aidan smiled at the elderly man at the counter. "Monsieur?" the man asked.

In halting French, Aidan asked if the old man spoke English. When he shook his head, Aidan muddled on, asking if the man had anything for him. "*Mais oui*," the man said. He pulled out trays of rings and pendants. Yet he made no move to offer Aidan any one in particular, and Aidan was baffled. Was this the right shop? Aidan asked if the old man was alone in the shop, thinking perhaps another clerk might recognize him, and the old man looked at him suspiciously, as if Aidan were planning to rob him.

Finally in desperation Aidan showed him Carlucci's passport. Recognition dawned in the old man's eyes. "*Un moment*," he said, and he disappeared behind a beaded curtain.

What was going on? Suppose the police had been alerted that Carlucci, or someone using his passport, would appear here? What if, when the old man returned, he was carrying a gun or accompanied by police?

Aidan looked out at Liam, but the bodyguard's back was to the wall, his head swiveling as he surveyed all approaches to the shop. Behind the curtain, Aidan heard the sounds of an argument in Arabic. A deeper voice, probably the old man, and a higher female one.

A young woman emerged from the beaded curtain. She wore a T-shirt with Tupac Shakur's name and face on it, only the name was spelled "Shaker."

"You are Carlucci?" she asked in English.

"Yes."

"My husband thought you were dead."

Aidan didn't know what to say. Carlucci was dead, after all. The woman stared at him.

"Your husband was right," Aidan said after a long pause. "I am not Carlucci. He is dead. But I have what he was to deliver to the Tuareg, and I need to know how to find them."

She eyed him suspiciously. "How can I trust you? You could be from the police."

He laughed. "Do the Tunisian police hire Americans?"

He took her hand. He remembered seeing Carlucci shot down in the street, and the power of that moment energized him. "I saw Carlucci just before he died. He gave me the account information and asked me to carry out his mission. You must believe me. You must help me."

She looked at him and nodded. "My husband is not here now. The police, they come and ask many questions. So he left to go to El Jem. Maybe he will be safe there. I hope so. He has a friend, another from the same school, who runs the pharmacy next to the amphitheater. You must look for my husband there, and he can tell you how to reach the people of the veil."

She reached up behind her head and unlocked the chain from around her neck. "Give him this, to prove that you have been to see me and that I trusted you." She showed him an eyeball on a thin gold chain.

At least it looked like an eyeball. Aidan recognized it as one of the eye charms you saw all over the Muslim world, though this was particularly beautiful and encased in an elaborate gold filigree case. She motioned him to lean forward, and he did. She undid the catch of the chain and slipped it around his neck, then hooked it closed. "Do not remove this until you reach my husband," she said. "It will protect you and guide you."

"Thank you," Aidan said, lifting his head. "But where do I go? You said your husband is in El Jem? Is that another city, or a neighborhood in Tunis?"

The old man leaned out from behind the curtain and began to argue with the woman again. She waved her hand at him and said a few curt words. He ducked behind the curtain, leaving the beads rustling.

"There is a train to El Jem, in the south," the woman said to Aidan. "Now you must go. There are eyes all over the medina. You may already have been seen."

Aidan bowed and said, "Salaam aleykum."

"Aleykum salaam," she said. "May Allah protect you and our country."

As Aidan stepped out into the chaos of the souks, Liam took his arm and steered him back the way they had come. "You got whatever it was you were supposed to?"

"No. The goldsmith was questioned by the police, and he left for a friend's place in some other city. I convinced his wife that we were trying to help, and she gave me an eye charm on a chain around my neck. I'm supposed to take it to her husband in this other city, and then he will tell us how to find this tribe. She called them 'the people of the veil.'"

"We'll figure it all out at your apartment. Let's focus on getting out of the medina for now," Liam said grimly.

"The woman, I think she must have been the merchant's daughter or daughter-in-law, she said there are eyes everywhere, that we may already have been spotted. Spotted by whom?"

"I don't know," Liam said. The smell of the food around them was intoxicating, and Aidan's stomach grumbled despite the coffee and pastry they'd had for breakfast. They passed chechia-wearing men sitting on wire chairs, sipping mint tea and smoking *chicha* pipes.

As they reached the Bab el Bahr, ready to move back into the modern city, Liam grabbed Aidan's arm. "There are police up ahead," he said. "See, on the right and the left. They haven't spotted us yet, but they'll get us as soon as we walk through that arch."

"Not if we're in disguise," Aidan said. "Follow me."

"Aidan," Liam said, but Aidan was already on his way back into the medina, heading to the souk he'd noticed that sold the Moroccan-style djellabas. When they reached it, recognition dawned in the bodyguard's eyes. "Good idea," he said. In rapid Arabic, he negotiated with the vendor for two djellabas. Aidan's was off-white with vertical black stripes. Liam pulled the hood over his head and nodded his approval.

The only djellaba in the souk large enough for Liam was decorated in an elaborate scrollwork motif. He didn't look happy with it and negotiated an extra minute with the vendor, clearly asking if it was the only one. The merchant just shrugged. Liam pulled some dinars out of his pocket, paid the man, and shrugged into his djellaba.

Disguised, they hurried back to the Bab el Bahr. Focused on the police ahead, neither of them noticed the three men approaching from the rear.

Looking for Liam

Two of the men went for Liam. The squat, bulky man took one arm, and the oldest one, a middle-aged man with a grizzled chin and a shirt studded with epaulets, took the other. The man who grabbed Aidan was small and wiry, with a gold front tooth that glinted in the sunlight. The crowd made a space around them, and out of the corner of Aidan's eye he saw two police officers rushing toward them.

Liam kicked the younger of the men holding him in the chest, which knocked his left arm free, and then he used that arm to punch the older one, who ducked and twisted, maintaining his vise grip.

Aidan leaned in close to Gold Tooth and kissed him, hard on the lips. The man reacted as Aidan expected, backing away with an expression of disgust on his face. Then, with his free right hand, Aidan reached for the Arab's groin. He found the man's dick, grabbed hold, and squeezed. Gold Tooth shouted a curse in Arabic and relaxed his iron grip on Aidan's left arm for a moment.

That was all Aidan needed. He twisted free and ran, picking up the bottom of the djellaba. As soon as he'd turned into a crowded street, he stepped close to a building and pulled the djellaba off over his head. It wasn't as good a disguise as he'd expected.

Across from him, a souk sold tourist crap—T-shirts, ball caps, postcards, and other souvenirs from a happy trip to Tunisia. He darted in there and bought an oversize T-shirt with *Bienvenue à Tunis* scrolled across it, a cap with a deep brim, and a pair of big, cheap sunglasses.

He dumped the djellaba into a plastic bag, pulled the T-shirt over his own, and slapped on the cap and the glasses. Checking his reflection, he looked like a different person. He hoped whoever was chasing him would agree.

As he walked back into the medina, Aidan heard the rise of angry voices behind him, but he spotted a group of American and European tourists, mostly middle-aged, overweight, wearing T-shirts and sun visors, and slid his way into their midst. For several blocks he kept his head down, surrounded by what he figured out was a tour group from a cruise ship. He half listened to the French-accented guide's descriptions of the various souks and the history of the area, keeping his eye out for Liam or for anyone who might be chasing him.

After about fifteen minutes, Aidan ditched the tour group and exited the medina. Liam was nowhere in sight when he approached his building, and there were no cops or unsavory characters lurking around. He acted as he thought Liam would, looking around, trying to identify places where someone might hide, evaluating the purposes of all those around.

Inside, the dog was sprawled in front of his apartment door. He paused and rubbed her behind the ears. If Liam had already been here, he'd have let the dog in, wouldn't he? Even so, Aidan hesitated before putting his key in the lock. He took a deep breath, slotted the key, and turned the handle. The door squeaked as he opened it, and the dog pushed ahead and went to the kitchen. Aidan sighed, walked inside, and locked the door behind him. He gave the dog some fresh water and drank a full bottle of orange soda.

By the time evening fell, with no sign of Liam, Aidan was sure the bodyguard had been arrested. He had a feeling that Liam would hold up under questioning, at least for a while. But Aidan kept worrying. Should he leave the apartment? Where could he go? What if Liam were killed? What should Aidan do with the eye charm? What if the police showed up at his door?

There were two voices in Aidan's head. One voice said that he was lucky to be rid of Liam, and that Aidan would be a fool to put himself in harm's way to find out what happened to the ex-SEAL. The other voice remembered Liam's kiss, the feel of his body. That voice reminded him of Carlucci's murder outside the bar. If Liam was in danger, Aidan owed it to him, and to Carlucci's memory, to do something.

Aidan decided to go back to the Bar Mamounia to see if Liam had returned to his little house or if the police were still there. He dressed in his most touristy clothes, with the ball cap he'd bought at the medina clamped on his head.

Tunis was a different place once the sun had set. There weren't many streetlights, and every door slam, shout, or car horn seemed more ominous. He hurried toward the bright lights of the Avenue Bourguiba, and once there felt less conspicuous.

He walked past the Bar Mamounia twice before daring to venture in. It reminded him of his first desperate attempts to visit a gay bar in Philadelphia so many years before. Then, too, he'd been eager yet nervous, his body racing with adrenaline.

The inside of the Bar Mamounia was a big disappointment—just as those first few gay bars had been. Five or six men stood around drinking, fast Arabic music playing too loud, with a backbeat that reverberated against Aidan's spine. A few men swiveled eyes toward him as he entered, but then went back to their conversations.

He ordered a glass of the Vieux Magon, the red wine Liam had ordered for him. The man behind the bar wasn't the one who was there during the day, and Aidan hesitated to ask about Liam. What if he'd been alerted by the police that Liam was wanted? Aidan could be putting himself in grave danger.

He looked around the bar, which seemed even darker and more disreputable than it had during the day. Liam wasn't there, and though he'd had no reason to expect he would be, Aidan was disappointed. But was he in his house, across the courtyard? Aidan took his glass and strolled over to the opening in the wall through which he'd first witnessed Liam showering.

The courtyard was dark, a single square of light falling on the dirt floor through the window. The shadowy bulk of Liam's building loomed across from him.

He felt a hand on his back. "Bonsoir, Monsieur," said a man in heavily accented French. Aidan turned. He didn't recognize the man—but did the man recognize him?

"Bonsoir," Aidan said.

The man rattled off something fast that Aidan couldn't follow with his schoolboy French. He stepped in close and whispered in Aidan's ear. He was Tunisian, with sun-baked skin and close-cropped dark hair. He wore a plain gray T-shirt and a pair of black pants with Nike sneakers. "Liam?" Aidan whispered back to him. "*L'américain?*"

"*Ah, vous êtes Américain,*" the man said. "*J'aime les Américains.*"

The man leaned forward and stuck his tongue in Aidan's ear.

Well, that was easy to understand. The man didn't know Liam. He didn't have anything to do with Charles Carlucci, eye charms, or Tuaregs in the desert. He simply wanted to have sex.

Aidan was so relieved, he laughed. Gently he put his hand against the man's chest and pushed. "*Non, merci.*"

The man said something else in French, something low and urgent, and for a moment Aidan worried that he'd mistaken the message. But the man's hand on Aidan's crotch was an unmistakable gesture.

"Non," Aidan said more firmly. He finished his wine and stepped away from the Tunisian to leave the empty glass on the bar. Then he walked outside.

Ever hopeful, the Tunisian man followed him to the door. Aidan looked back at the man and shook his head. The man accepted the decision and stepped back inside.

Aidan walked around the block, passing the front of Liam's house. The front door was in splinters, as if someone had broken in. Did that mean that Liam had returned home and the police or the military had apprehended him there? Or had they merely broken in to search for him?

A policeman stood at the corner, and Aidan nodded to him the way any tourist might. The officer ignored him, lighting a cigarette.

So the police were still watching Liam's house, which meant that they didn't have him in custody—or that they were hoping his accomplice might show up. If they were waiting for Aidan, they were doing a lousy job of it.

It was late by then, and Aidan was worn-out. On the way back to his apartment, a couple of drunken Arabs turned onto the street in front of him, laughing and shouting and banging into each other.

Aidan crossed the street to avoid passing them, tripped on a stone, and fell against a building. The men seemed to think he was drunk as well and shouted something across to him. He ignored them and walked faster.

By the time he got home, Aidan had gone over the situation with Liam a dozen times. There was nothing else he could do, though, but go to bed. He had to meet Madame Habiba Abboud the next morning at the École Internationale and begin teaching. But even after he stripped down and got into bed, sleep eluded him.

A Game of Shkouba

Liam battled the men who had set on him and Aidan in the medina, angry that he'd been taken by surprise. He brought his right leg up and kneed the assailant who gripped his right arm, and the man spiraled away in agony.

That left the one in the military shirt. Liam bent his head and then brought it up hard under the other man's chin. He heard the snap of bone against bone, felt the man fly backward. Liam twisted away and slid into the crowd surrounding the fight just as two policemen ran into the far end of the street.

He had lost track of Aidan in the scuffle and had no idea where the teacher from Philadelphia had gone. But there was no time to look for him; the soldiers raised their rifles and pushed through the cluster of spectators. A young woman stepped aside, making an escape valve for him, and he slipped through.

His blood was racing, and he focused on calming himself, resisting the urge to rush through the crowd like a loose bull. That would only draw attention to his path. Instead he pulled his red chechia from his pocket and slapped it on his head, relaxing his posture and resuming his self-confident swagger. The crowd closed around him, and he strolled out of the street of the goldsmiths, surrounded by tourists and Tunisians.

It was always easier for him to blend into a mixed crowd; he stood a head taller than most Tunisians, who hadn't had the benefit of the nutrition available in New Jersey when he was a child or fathers who stood over six feet themselves. Among Americans and Europeans, he didn't stand out so much.

He maintained a dark tan year-round and kept his light brown hair cut short as well. But fitting into his surroundings was about attitude and posture more than height or hair color. Americans walked quickly, without much concern for their surroundings. On the streets of Tunis, you could always pick them out—they moved in a combination of confusion and implied superiority.

Perhaps that was why he had mistaken Aidan for Carlucci back at the bar. He had a picture of Carlucci but hadn't paid much attention to it, assuming his client would be the only American in the bar.

And look where that single mistake had led. He walked from street to street, struggling between the urge to flee and the knowledge that flight would make him more visible. He turned into the street of metalsmiths and saw two police officers just in front of him. He looked the younger one in the face and smiled, nodding.

The man returned the greeting; then his colleague elbowed him, and he turned away. Liam took a deep breath. His mind raced through his knowledge of the medina. He was sure that there would be police stationed at the exits, and just because he'd fooled a young recruit didn't mean he could pass a police gauntlet.

Where could he stay out of sight for a while? As he neared the street of silk weavers, he knew he had his answer.

The year before, he had been hired to retrieve a woman and her two children who had been kidnapped. He had tracked the kidnappers to a ramshackle building in the center of the medina, near the silk weavers' souks, and he'd established an observation post across from the building, a tiny space above a bar.

Before entering the bar, though, he strolled past, looking all around. A policeman stood at the far end of the street, questioning a young boy. Across from him, a pair of German tourists negotiated for bolts of dark red silk striped with gold. The sun was directly overhead so that the whole street was lit, the only shadows cast by the mix of Americans and Tunisians, the old man pushing a wheelbarrow loaded with bolts of cloth.

From across the street, he watched the bartender through the open door. The man was polishing the counter, looking up periodically as if expecting customers. The few customers were clustered around a table in the back.

He waited, lurking in a niche where two buildings met. The policeman cuffed the boy alongside the head and let him go, and Liam saw him scurry off. The officer started walking toward Liam, looking in at each souk. Across from him, one of the men at the table called to the bartender, who busied himself preparing a drink. Liam took that moment to dart across the street, inside the bar, and through a gap in the wall to an abandoned staircase that led to the second floor of the building.

The ceiling up there had collapsed, so no one used the space. Liam had made himself a lookout post with a view of the street through a crack in the wall. He was pleased to see that the space was undisturbed.

Light striped the floor in the pattern of the ruined ceiling, though there was enough protection from the heat of the sun, and rain, when it came. The room smelled musty, overlaid with the aroma of spicy *harissa* from whatever the family next door was cooking. He remembered that certain boards creaked when you walked on them, but could not recall which ones.

He stood there at the top of the stairs, calming his breathing, listening for any indication that the bartender below, or one of the drinkers, had noticed him enter. All he heard was some raucous laughter, someone calling out insults in street Arabic.

He crossed the room to the gap in the wall he'd used to survey the street. Looking outside, he saw the oldest of the attackers. The man had a cell phone to his ear, and he walked slowly down the street, checking alleys, looking into every door. Liam focused on steadying his pulse as he watched the man proceed.

The man moved out of sight as he ducked into the bar below. Liam didn't move, worried that any sound might give away his position, nearly holding his breath until he saw the man step back out of the bar and continue down the narrow street.

Liam let his breath out and relaxed. He knew he had to stay hidden for a while, until he was certain that the man and his accomplices had given up their search. He wondered what had happened to Aidan. His last sight of the teacher from Philadelphia had been as he ran from the men who had attacked them.

On the street below, a young man approached carrying an old-fashioned boom box. The sound of American rap music blasted, and he could see older women wearing long dresses, with their heads covered, whose body language showed they disapproved. However, they were often accompanied by teenage daughters wearing very tight jeans and exposed-midriff T-shirts, who seemed to like the music, and the young man, much more.

Liam relaxed and took a short catnap, knowing he couldn't leave the crawl space for at least an hour or more. He woke to the sound of a group of soldiers approaching the bar, laughing and knocking each other around. With a sinking sensation, he realized that they were heading for the bar downstairs. There was no way he could slip out with a gaggle of soldiers below, even if they were all drunk.

Quickly his small space filled with the noise of the bar below. Listening carefully, he caught bits and pieces of dialogue. It appeared that the soldiers had just come off a long shift, and they planned a night of music, cards, and alcohol. They were playing *shkouba*, the most popular card game in the country, and one that could go on for hours.

Leaning against the wall, he considered his situation. He felt an obligation to see Carlucci's mission through. He should have been more assertive with Carlucci, insisting on a meeting at the Hotel Africa. He shouldn't have mistaken Aidan Greene for the courier. Those mistakes had cost a man his life. Years in the military had drummed a sense of responsibility into Liam; discharge papers, however honorable, couldn't change that.

With an effort of will, he calmed his impatience and slowed his breathing. It was going to be a long night.

Mme. Habiba Abboud, BA

When Aidan arrived at the address Madame Abboud had given him, a few blocks from the Zitouna mosque, he was confused. Where was the school? The building in front of him was run-down, with stucco that hadn't been painted since the French retreated forty years before. The blue paint on the ornamental grillwork had faded, and the stone stoop was cracked in half. The ground floor was occupied by a hair salon, and a narrow staircase at the far end led up to the second floor.

A small sign directed him up to the second floor, where ÉCOLE INTERNATIONALE had been painted on a wooden door in a flowing, Arabic-style script. He knocked, and a woman's voice called out, "*Entrez!*"

He opened the door to a single drab room brightened by posters of American sights: the Grand Canyon, the Statue of Liberty, and the Golden Gate Bridge.

Madame Abboud was a small, dumpy lady in an American-style business suit that looked like black silk. She sat behind a dented metal desk piled haphazardly with papers. "Ah, you must be Monsieur Greene," she said to him in English. "I am Madame Habiba Abboud, BA. Welcome to my office."

They shook hands, and he sat across from her in a spindly metal chair. "Your country is very beautiful," he said.

"Yes, it is. How long have you lived here?"

"I arrived five days ago. I left the US right after our e-mail correspondence."

She looked disturbed. "You came here to teach?"

"Yes. I was looking for a job somewhere outside the US, and when you offered, I decided Tunisia was a good place."

"So you did not receive my further e-mails?"

He shook his head.

"I am afraid I have some bad news. As soon as I heard from you, I applied for the proper permits so that you could work in Tunisia. My request was denied."

Aidan was surprised. "What does that mean?"

"Every time the United States commits some act against the Arab world, the Tunisian government retaliates against those, like myself, who hire Americans." Her accent was somewhat British, overlaid with hints of French and Arabic. "Last week your government censured the Saudis for something foolish. That resulted in a taboo on hiring foreign teachers, for the present." She shrugged but smiled. "These things, they come and go. It all depends on who is in charge."

"But what can I do?" Aidan asked.

She straightened a pile of papers on her desk. "I can try again in one month. Unfortunately, not before."

Aidan's pulse raced. "But I gave up my home and flew all the way here."

"This is the way of the Arab world. May I suggest that you do some sightseeing while you wait? The island of Djerba is lovely this time of year."

"I don't have the luxury of vacationing. I need a job. Can I work without those permits? Just until you are able to receive them?" Back when Aidan had taught in Europe, there had always been ways around the rules. Surely the same had to be true in Tunisia.

"Alas, no," Madame Abboud said. "I have a license, you see, and to employ someone without the proper papers— well, if it were discovered, that would be the end of the École Internationale."

She stood up. "I am so sorry for your predicament, Mr. Greene. But you know, I did e-mail you several times to let you know about this problem."

Aidan felt powerless to argue. He had no way of knowing whether she had e-mailed him; his account was under Blake's name, and Blake had probably already shut off his access. He thanked Madame Abboud and promised to be back in touch within a month.

He trudged down the stairs to the dark vestibule, then stepped back into the glaring sunshine. He winced at the brightness, squinting his eyes shut, then stood there on the broken sidewalk, letting the world swirl around him. What could he do? Where could he go? Could he afford to wait around Tunis for a month or more until a job materialized at the école?

Standing there, he felt the weight of the chain around his neck that held the eye charm that the goldsmith's wife had given him the day before. Well, that was something he could do. He'd go back to the souk and return the charm.

The sense of a mission, even a short-term one, gave him energy. He consulted his map of the city and began walking toward the Bab El Bahr. Within a few blocks, he was sweating heavily, so he shucked his suit jacket, loosened his tie, and unbuttoned the first few buttons of his shirt.

Even so, he was drenched by the time he reached the Souk des Orfevres, the goldsmith's market. The souk bustled with tourists, with shopkeepers calling bargains out into the street. He ignored their entreaties and searched for the shop where he'd been given the amulet. It was shuttered, though all the others around it were open and busy. He went into the one next door and asked, in fractured French, for the elderly shop owner or his daughter-in-law. "*Ils avaient parti*," the old man behind the counter said. "*Hier soir.*"

They had left the night before. But for where? Were they fleeing the police as well? What had he gotten himself into?

He noticed the shopkeeper picking up his cell phone and decided to get out of the medina as quickly as possible. He must have bumped into a dozen men and women as he rushed back toward the Bab el Bahr, and when he couldn't find it right away, his fear began to take over. Finally he saw the arched gate, set in a stone wall, ahead of him. There were no police loitering there, so he strode forward, back into the modern city. He needed a shower, a bottle of cold water. And a plan.

As he walked back to his apartment, he realized how bad his situation was. He had used the thousand dollars Blake had given him, as well as his savings, for the flight to Tunisia and the rent on the apartment. He had a single credit card in his name, which he'd almost never used because Blake had paid for everything. So he had a ridiculously low limit on the card, barely enough to buy himself a plane ticket back to Philadelphia.

And what would he do when he got back there? It was early August, and no schools started until September. He wouldn't have a paycheck until the end of the month. How could he find a place to live and support himself until then? He'd have to find someone to stay with, then get online and look for a few private ESL clients, students who needed a review before starting college in the fall, immigrants preparing for a citizenship exam.

Going back to Philly would be difficult. But staying in Tunis was no easier. He didn't know a soul in Tunis beyond Liam McCullough, and the bodyguard had disappeared, perhaps into police custody. Aidan thought he should get on the first flight back to the States. But what if the police knew his name and had alerted the immigration authorities to be on the lookout for him?

Making a decision required energy and determination, and he had none. It was all he could do to keep putting one foot in front of the other and make his way back to his apartment—where the rent was paid only through the end of the week. Without a job, he'd be homeless in Tunisia.

As he walked, the tears he'd hardly shed over Blake finally came, blurring his vision so that he didn't see the hands that grabbed him as he neared his building.

Making Lemonade

"You really ought to be more aware of your surroundings," Liam said.

Aidan didn't realize how much he'd been worried about the bodyguard until he appeared there. That realization only loosed his tear ducts further. Liam put his arms around Aidan and hugged him. "It's okay," he said. "Everything's going to be all right."

Aidan sniffled and wiped his nose with his sleeve. He was embarrassed that this macho man had seen him so vulnerable. "Can we go inside?"

Aidan nodded. They didn't speak again until they'd climbed the stairs to Aidan's apartment. "You got away all right?" he asked Liam.

The bodyguard shrugged. "It took me a while. You?"

"Yup." Aidan gave the dog her water and then reached around and unhooked the gold chain that held the eye amulet. "Here. This is what the woman at the souk gave me."

Liam took it and examined it, then looked at Aidan. "Tell me what she said."

Aidan repeated as best he could while Liam paced around the apartment. He wore the same clothes he'd worn to the medina the day before—his leather vest, cinched tight across his chest, khaki cargo shorts that ended midthigh, leather sandals. "She trusted you," Liam said. "She trusted you with that charm. So her husband will be expecting you in El Jem."

Liam turned back to Aidan, who could feel the dried tears on his cheeks. But he was too tired even to wash his face. He slumped into a chair at the kitchen table.

"Are you all right?" Liam asked.

Aidan blew his nose and said, "I'm fine."

"Aidan. You're not. Tell me what's the matter." Liam pulled the other chair out and swung it around, as he'd done at the bar, so he was straddling it, his leather vest once again hanging open and exposing that muscular chest.

"Turns out I don't have a job after all. The government denied me a work permit. The woman I went to see said she had e-mailed me to notify me, but I had already left Philadelphia by that point." He looked away, embarrassed. "I was an idiot. I shouldn't have rushed over here without working everything through."

"So what do you do now?" Liam asked. He pulled a tissue from his pocket and wet the end of it with the tip of his tongue. And then, very carefully, he wiped the dried tears from Aidan's cheeks.

It was such a tender gesture, so unexpected from a big, tough guy like Liam, that it almost made Aidan cry again. But the time for crying had passed. He had to figure out how to get out of the mess he'd made.

He tried to smile. "You know the saying, 'When life hands you lemons, make lemonade'?" Liam nodded. "Well, I just happen to have a bunch of lemons in my refrigerator. You want a glass?"

Liam smiled back. "That would be great. I'm going to make a call."

He stepped over to the French doors, and Aidan went into the kitchen. He draped his suit jacket over one of the chairs and hung his tie over it. Then he looked in his wallet. He had about fifty bucks in American dollars and Tunisian dinars. He was pretty sure he had enough available credit to buy a plane ticket back to the States, but that would wipe him out.

He refused to ask Blake for a penny—not that he'd hand over anything. He ran through his list of friends—most of them as poor as he was, scraping by on part-time jobs. One was an actor who worked as a waiter, another a writer who did temp work. Most of his friends lived in studio apartments or shared with roommates. He realized he didn't know anyone he could impose on who had a spare room for guests.

He pulled the lemons from the refrigerator. In turn, he rolled each one on the counter, loosening up the juice. He busied himself with bottled water, lemons, and sugar until Liam came back from the French doors and said, "I need to tell you about how I get work."

"Okay." Aidan handed him a glass of the lemonade and then followed him back into the living room. He sat down on the couch, and Liam sat across from him.

"I know a guy who used to be high up in the Tunisian police," Liam began. "Now he works on his own, handling problems on a freelance basis. Occasionally he uses outside contractors, like me. If a visiting diplomat needs a bodyguard, for example. Sometimes I retrieve stolen property. Last year I rescued a woman and her two children who were being held captive."

Aidan clasped the glass of cold lemonade in his hands, feeling the chill rise through them.

"My guy knows a lot of people who know a lot of people," Liam continued. "Someone put him in touch with Carlucci, who worked for a private foundation in the US. Carlucci was coming to Tunisia to deliver some money to a Tuareg tribe, and he wanted a bodyguard."

"But he wouldn't let you come to his hotel. His fatal mistake."

"He didn't think there would be any threat until he got out into the desert."

"But if Carlucci was your guy's client, and Carlucci's dead, then there's no client anymore, is there?"

"Carlucci worked for the Counterterrorist Foundation. It's a think tank on terrorism, funded by a billionaire whose son died in the attacks of September Eleventh. A bunch of scholars who write papers and research counterterrorism activities."

"Why are they interested in funding this tribe?" Aidan asked.

Liam shrugged. "I don't know. I've heard a little about them—their agents infiltrated a terrorist cell and destroyed it, and they pass information on to the CIA and the FBI." He sipped his lemonade. "They say they're also trying to shut down terrorists by making life better for the people who might be recruited. My contact has been in touch with them, and they want to hire me to deliver the money. It's to help this tribe transition from nomadic to settled. Build them houses, a school. But I don't know where to go, and it's a big desert. I have to convince the goldsmith, the one who went to El Jem, to give me the directions, and I need you for that because you were able to get his wife to trust you."

Aidan pushed his chair back from the table and crossed his arms. "No, Liam. I went back to that souk this morning. The shopkeeper and his daughter-in-law are gone. They ran off last night."

"All the more reason you should come with me to El Jem. They may be in trouble. And you're a teacher, right? Don't you want to see the kids from this tribe get an education? They need schools and computers to survive in the modern world. You can help them get what they need."

Aidan hated when people made emotional appeals like that. They always made him think of those sappy TV commercials that made him cry. But he was determined not to let his emotions control him. "The shopkeeper next door said something about the police."

"I admit, I still don't understand how the police are involved," Liam said. "There were officers stationed outside my house when I went there on Saturday. But the safest way to stay off their radar is to head out into the desert for a while, until the heat is off."

"You have an answer for everything, don't you?" Aidan asked.

Liam leaned forward, causing Aidan to back away farther. "The police are in this somehow—maybe just investigating Carlucci's death. But they wouldn't have known anything about the goldsmith." He shook his head. "There's something more going on here. Those men who attacked us in the souk weren't cops."

"I don't want to know. I'm getting on a plane back to the US. I don't have a job here—I can't even afford to stay in this apartment after Wednesday. I don't have time to waste going out into the desert with you."

"What are you going to do when you get back to the States?"

"Look for a job."

"In August? There's no school in session."

"That's true. But it will start in September."

"You can be back by then. It'll only take us a couple of days to get out into the desert, pass on that bank account and the password, and get back to Tunis."

Liam reached over and took Aidan's hand. "Please, Aidan. I need your help. And it's not just that you look like Carlucci. You know how to handle yourself in a crunch—I saw that back at the souk. And you're a good sounding board for me." He smiled, the corners of his mouth making tiny dimples. "I've been a lone wolf for so long, I forgot how great it feels to have someone else on my team."

"I don't have any money," Aidan said. "Travel, hotels, food. I can't afford to spend a penny. I need to save everything I have to get back home and get my life going again."

"Not to worry. Carlucci's foundation advanced me some cash when I agreed to be his bodyguard, and they've agreed to cover all expenses for delivering the information to the

Tuareg tribe, as well as give me a hefty bonus, which I'll split with you fifty-fifty."

Liam named a figure that made Aidan's mouth drop open. Who knew there was so much money in the bodyguard business? His half would be enough to get him a flight back to the States, give him the first and last months' rent on a new place, even leave him some cash left over to carry him through until he got his first paycheck. It didn't seem like he had much choice.

"How would we get to El Jem?"

"The train," Liam said. He released Aidan's hand and sat back. "There's a Roman coliseum there, and lots of tourists go to visit. We'd have good cover."

"What can I do with my stuff?" Aidan asked, looking around the apartment. "We'll need to travel light."

"I can make a call," Liam said, smiling.

Spicy

Something changed in the air between Liam and Aidan after Aidan agreed to go to El Jem. For the first time, Aidan felt like he was a part of whatever it was Liam was doing. It wasn't just that he looked like Carlucci and was a convenient tool for Liam to use. He had convinced the goldsmith's wife to trust him, and he had impressed Liam with his quick thinking at the souk and with his ability to work under pressure.

As Liam stepped over to the open French doors to make his call, Aidan felt like he was getting back to the person he'd been before he met Blake and settled down. Once more, he could think on his own, adjust to uncertainty. Even the thought that thugs had chased him through the medina didn't bother him that much. He'd been clever enough to get away from the guy who held him, and then by slipping in with that group of American tourists, he'd eluded his pursuers. It felt good to be that guy again, the one who'd been willing to experience the world firsthand.

Liam snapped his phone closed and came over to him. "I have a great restaurant I'd like to show you."

"You think it's safe to go out? What if someone's watching?"

"I don't think anyone has identified you yet, so there's no reason for anyone to be watching your building. And even though they know who I am, as long as I stay away from my usual hangouts, we should be okay."

"I should change," Aidan said. He was still wearing his dress shirt and suit pants, though it seemed like days had passed since that morning, when he'd dressed to impress Madame Abboud.

"I think you look fine just like that," Liam said. He was dressed much more appropriately for the climate in his leather vest and khaki shorts.

"Nice of you to say," Aidan said, smiling. "But I still want to switch to shorts and a lighter shirt." While he did, he said, "I haven't had a chance to eat much Tunisian food yet. I didn't want to eat in a restaurant by myself, so I've been cooking here."

"In my line of work, you spend a lot of time on your own," Liam said as he put his hand on Aidan's back and they began to walk toward the door. "So you get accustomed to eating restaurant meals by yourself." He laughed. "Especially if you're as lousy a cook as I am. It'll be a nice change to have a handsome face across the table from me."

Aidan felt a warm glow rise up from the pit of his stomach and was embarrassed. Liam thought he was handsome! In all the years he and Blake had been together, Blake had hardly complimented him—he told Aidan once he'd get too big an ego if Blake was always saying nice things.

Liam slipped off his leather vest, and Aidan's heart skipped a beat at that beautiful torso, a work of art

Michelangelo would have been proud of. Liam was darker than the David, which Aidan had ogled during his Italian travels, but so much warmer. It was a terrible shame when Liam pulled a lightweight white cotton shirt from his duffel bag and put it on.

"Tell me about your line of work," Aidan said as they walked down the staircase. "How did you get into it?"

At the building's front door, Liam paused, out of habit, Aidan guessed, and surveyed the street before they stepped outside. The day's heat had begun to burn off, and a light breeze swept down the nearly empty street. Liam said, "I think I told you I was a Navy SEAL. I ran up against a little rule called 'don't ask, don't tell.'"

"I've heard of it. Did someone ask?"

"I told. I came off a mission in Iraq, where I did a pretty stupid thing—I ran in front of a bank of enemy artillery to rescue a buddy who'd been shot. I realized I had been totally fearless because I didn't care if I lived or died, and I knew there wasn't anybody back in the States who cared either."

"I doubt that. You just told me this guy was your buddy. I'm sure there were lots of guys in your platoon who'd care what happened to you." Aidan didn't touch the question of who Liam had back in the States, if anyone. That was something to save for a more intimate discussion.

A husband and wife hurried past them, the wife cradling a child against her chest, and Liam waited until they'd passed to continue speaking. "Yes, I had friends. Guys who'd do for me what I did for that buddy. But I couldn't help feeling that they might not have if they'd really known me."

That was deep, and Aidan didn't know how to respond. He'd been out of the closet since he was in his early twenties, and the academic environment had always been welcoming to him. He'd never had to worry about losing a job because he was gay or getting kicked out of an apartment. He'd been frightened, once in a while, about walking down dark streets near gay bars, fearing that almost mythical pickup truck full of redneck gay bashers with baseball bats, but that was about it.

They arrived at the restaurant. "Not my favorite," Liam said, opening the door, "but the food's good, and it's close to your place."

The restaurant was dim, lit only by candles in glass globes, and the dark-skinned young waitress led them to a table in the corner. Liam sat facing the door.

The first thing he ordered was a bottle of the red wine they had shared on their first meeting. "Tunisian cooking is a blend of European, Asian, and desert cuisine," Liam said. "I have to warn you, it's very spicy." He smiled. "There's an old wives' tale that says a husband can judge his wife's affections by the amount of hot peppers she uses when preparing his food. If the food becomes bland, then his wife no longer loves him."

Aidan liked heat on his tongue, and he was relishing the chance to spice things up a bit. "Blake—my ex—liked his food bland, and when I was mad at him, I'd sneak a couple of grinds of pepper into dinner. Usually gave him indigestion."

Liam laughed. "You're always surprising me."

"So what do you recommend? I've been dying to eat some couscous. I took a cooking class back home and learned how to use this special kind of double boiler."

Liam looked interested, so Aidan continued. "You start with semolina in the top half. You boil your meat and vegetables in the lower half. The top half has holes in the bottom, and the steam rises to cook the grain."

Liam laughed. "I've lived in this country three years, and you know more about the food than I do."

Aidan blushed. "Blake liked to watch TV and sleep when he wasn't at work, so I had a lot of time on my hands. You should have seen our kitchen—stacked with every kind of appliance imaginable."

"And you left it all behind?"

Aidan nodded. "Blake paid for it all. And I needed to travel light. I didn't know where I was going to end up."

The waitress brought the bottle of red wine and two glasses and poured for them. Liam lifted his in a toast. "To ending up here," he said, smiling. "Together."

Aidan felt an electric current rise up from his groin and run through his body as he clinked his glass against Liam's. "So, we still have to pick what to eat."

Liam spoke rapidly in Arabic to the waitress, and she nodded several times. When she walked away, he said, "We're starting with *chorba*. A peppery soup. We'll see if you really like your food hot."

"I may surprise you." Aidan shifted in his seat, and his leg brushed up against Liam's. The touch of his bare skin against Liam's sent another heat wave through his body. It felt so good to have a man's skin against his own.

In the candlelight, he could see Liam smile back, and the bodyguard maintained the pressure of his leg against Aidan's. He remembered their embrace on Saturday night, the feeling of Liam's body against his. The longing for that touch again nearly knocked him back against his chair.

"After the soup, a veal and olive tagine," Liam said, smiling. "You probably had one of those in your kitchen in Philadelphia, didn't you?"

Aidan knew that a tagine was the name for both a conical-lidded pot and the stew that was cooked in it. "Yes, I did."

"After that, a couscous with beef and lamb." Liam increased the pressure of his leg against Aidan's, more waves of heat rising from the friction of skin against skin. Liam moved his leg up and down against Aidan's, and he felt the pressure of his dick stiffening against his shorts. He worried there'd be a wet spot on the cloth by the time dinner was over.

Liam pulled his leg away, and Aidan wanted to cry out to have it back. "After we've eaten, we'll discuss dessert," Liam said. He leaned back in his chair, and Aidan felt the big man's bare foot exploring his calf, then his thigh. His mouth dropped open, and he caught his breath. Liam's toes grazed Aidan's crotch, and he reached under the table and grasped Liam's ankle. Liam raised his eyebrows and smiled.

It had been so long since Aidan had flirted with another man, since he'd been out on a date with a good-looking man who found him attractive too. The wine only contributed to the heady nature of the evening.

When the waitress brought the soup, Liam pulled back his foot and sat up. As promised, it was spicy. It made Aidan's eyes water, but he loved it. "You were telling me about what caused you to leave the navy," he said as they ate.

"I didn't think you'd let that slide." Liam sighed. "Looking back on it now, I see I was immature and foolish. Depressed too, and probably suffering from shell shock. But I had this idea that until I faced the truth about myself, I was going to keep undervaluing my life and putting myself in danger."

"Sounds pretty mature to me."

"I went to see my buddy in sick bay," Liam said. "The one I rescued. We were sitting around chewing the fat, and he mentioned his girlfriend back home. I said something like, 'Yeah, I wish I had somebody back home. A nice guy waiting for me.' I waited to see if he'd say anything, but he didn't."

He finished the last of his soup and pushed the bowl away from him. "The next day, another one of the guys in my unit asked me if I was gay." He laughed. "You know, I wasn't scared at all running in front of that artillery, but I was scared as shit right then. I said that I was and asked if it was a problem for him."

Aidan finished his soup, and he reached over and squeezed Liam's hand. Liam's knuckles were rough, his fingers strong and thick. Aidan wondered if the bodyguard's dick would be as beefy as his hands. "What did he say?"

"He said no. But within a couple of days every guy in the platoon knew, and it was only a matter of time before my CO called me in." He pursed his lips together and shrugged. "He asked me if it was true, and I said yes."

"I thought he wasn't allowed to ask?"

"He said it was disrupting the platoon, some guys minding, some guys not."

The waitress brought the tagine and laid the plates out before them. Liam inhaled deeply. "Smells good, huh?"

"Yes. But finish the story, Liam."

"Not much more to it. The CO thought it would be best for me to muster out, and I did. He made sure I got an honorable discharge, and I washed up here. End of story."

Aidan was sure there was more to it than that, but he let it go. His leg stretched out, pressing against Liam's, and they both smiled at each other. They ate the delicious tagine, the spiciness bringing more tears to his eyes.

"You think Blake is home missing you right now?" Liam asked.

"Don't know. He may be missing the things I did for him—the food, the laundry, and so on. But right now he's probably just happy to have the house to himself."

"Are you going back to him when we're finished?"

"Nope. Not a chance."

"You seem pretty sure about that."

"I am. Sometimes it takes something traumatic to make you wake up and look around." Aidan smiled. "Fortunately nobody took a machine gun to me. But Blake kicking me out of the house made me realize I'd been wasting my time there. I deserve the chance to be loved, and I wasn't getting what I needed from Blake. At the same time, I don't think I'd ever have had the courage to pick up and walk out on my own. So he did me a favor."

"I think you'd be surprised at what you have the courage to do," Liam said.

They ate their way through the tagine and then the couscous. Their feet tangled under the table, Aidan finding ways of connecting with Liam he'd never imagined. Toes climbed flesh, legs pressed against each other, hands traced the delicate bone structure of ankles. They drank a lot of wine to tame the heat of the food, and by the time they'd finished eating, they were both a little tipsy.

"I usually hold my liquor better than this," Liam said, stumbling against Aidan as they walked back to Aidan's apartment. Aidan grabbed him around the waist to steady him. His hands slipped under Liam's shirt to touch bare skin, smooth and warm. "It seems awful hard to walk."

"If I make it hard for you, will you hold it against me?" Aidan asked.

Liam guffawed, and his laughter made Aidan smile too. They bumped against each other a couple of times climbing the stairs to the apartment, every touch amping up the sexual tension between them. They had to be careful not to step on the dog, who'd taken up her customary place on the doorstep.

When they stepped inside, Liam maneuvered Aidan up against the wall and kissed him. Aidan wasn't expecting it, but it didn't take him long to kiss Liam back. With his lips closed, Aidan pressed his mouth against Liam's, closing his eyes and inhaling through his nose. As the kiss continued, Aidan opened his mouth; Liam's lips tasted of wine and honey. He began nibbling at Liam's bottom lip as he felt the big man sag against him.

He lifted Liam's shirttails from his shorts and ran his hands around the big man's waist, digging below his belt. Liam's skin was so smooth, yet the texture was firm. Liam wrapped his arms around Aidan, pulling him close, nuzzling his head down to Aidan's shoulder. Then Liam's phone went off.

"I should have turned the damn thing off," Liam whispered in Aidan's ear. "Let it go."

Aidan pulled back. "No, answer it. I'm not going anywhere. As long as you're not either, we can pick up where we left off."

Liam smiled. While Aidan went to get the dog some water, Liam answered his phone. When he hung up, he said, "The girl who's picking up your stuff is on her way over. I'm going down to open the door for her. After she's finished..."

"After she's finished, you're turning off your phone."

A Night Together

Liam returned a few minutes later with a dark-eyed young woman with a short, almost punk haircut, carrying an empty backpack and a couple of flattened boxes. Aidan combed his mussed hair and figured out what he'd need to take to El Jem, and packed the rest away. Liam helped the girl carry everything down to her car, including Carlucci's suitcase and attaché. When he returned, Aidan was standing by the French doors looking out at the night sky.

"It's beautiful, isn't it?" Liam asked, coming up behind him. He nuzzled the nape of Aidan's neck, and Aidan arched his back against him, closing his eyes. Liam's lips were moist and soft, dancing lightly on Aidan's skin, and he wrapped his hands around Aidan's body and pressed him close.

"The kind of night I always dreamed of," Aidan said. Liam's dick was already hard, pressing against Aidan's ass, and one of Liam's hands snaked its way under Aidan's waistband and down his groin. Aidan shivered and took a deep breath.

"You're a very sexy guy, you know that?" Liam asked. Aidan felt Liam's short hair pressed against his ear; he inhaled the faint scent of Liam's shampoo. With his eyes closed, his other senses were magnified. He heard a truck pass outside, the floor creak as Liam shifted his weight, the low hum of the refrigerator.

Liam's hand stroked Aidan's dick, and Aidan whimpered. He wasn't about to be jerked off so quickly; he turned around to kiss Liam again. Liam's lips were just as soft and moist against Aidan's mouth as they'd been against his neck. He nibbled on Liam's lower lip, felt the big man's mouth open, his tongue dart out.

"You taste so good," Aidan said. "I can't wait to taste all of you." He lifted his right leg to rub against Liam, and Liam reached down and grabbed it, pressing it against him. The movement pressed Aidan's dick against his shorts, and from the cold wetness he could tell he'd already leaked precum.

Liam's hand wandered down Aidan's thigh, up his shorts, to stroke his groin and tease at his pubic hair. "Oh God," Aidan whispered. He couldn't believe that he was there, in that moment, his arms wrapped about this gorgeous man, ecstasy floating through his veins like blood.

Liam moved his hands from Aidan's leg to under Aidan's shirt, his thumbs rubbing gently against the bare skin of Aidan's back. Because Liam was so much taller than Aidan, and a lot of his height was in his legs, his dick pressed against Aidan's belly, while Aidan's was against Liam's thigh. "I think we're both wearing too much clothing, don't you?" Liam said, his breath so soft against Aidan's cheek.

Liam stepped back, unbuttoned his shirt, and slipped it off his shoulders. Aidan watched, his mouth open like a dog's, as Liam undid the drawstring on his shorts and let them drop to the ground, kicking them away with his sandals.

He stood there, wearing only a white jockstrap, the kind Aidan remembered wearing as a high school kid. They had been required for gym class at his suburban high school, and he'd been so embarrassed when he had to tell his mother he needed one. Just the thought of it had made his teenage dick hard, and he worried that this desire made him some kind of freak.

Aidan hated gym class, the way just thinking about the rough cotton fabric against his tender dick made him hard, the constant fear that another boy would see his boner and know what turned him on. He'd asked Blake to wear a jockstrap once, but Blake had refused, telling Aidan he wasn't there to fulfill Aidan's adolescent fantasies.

But Liam did all that without even trying. He was so handsome, so sexy, so obviously into Aidan—if that big, stiff dick peeking out of the top of the jockstrap was any indication. The fact that he reminded Aidan of his high school wet dreams was like the cherry on top of a decadent hot-fudge sundae.

Liam stepped forward a pace and began unbuttoning Aidan's white shirt slowly, staring deep into Aidan's eyes as he did. It was sweet torture, and Aidan just wanted to tear his own clothes off and roll around on the floor with Liam, but he knew it would be even better if he waited.

When the shirt hung loosely over Aidan's shoulders, Liam pushed it off so that it slid to the floor. Aidan had worn an undershirt so that he wouldn't sweat through his dress shirt, and Liam slid his big, rough hands up under the cotton fabric. Then he leaned down to sniff Aidan's armpit and inhaled deeply. "I love the smell of a man," he growled, then dragged the T-shirt off over Aidan's head.

He nestled his head under Aidan's upraised right arm and flicked his tongue over his armpit. Aidan had never known that was such an erogenous zone for him. Liam licked and nibbled at the short dark hairs there, at the tender skin, and Aidan felt weak in the knees.

Liam supported him with one hand as he attacked Aidan's other armpit. Aidan was short of breath by the time Liam was finished, his body aching for Liam's touch. Liam backed off and kissed Aidan again, his mouth musky now, slick with Aidan's sweat. Aidan felt like he was being eaten alive—and he loved it.

Aidan still wore his shorts and shoes as Liam enveloped him in another big bear hug, pressing their bodies together. Aidan kissed Liam's chin with tiny pecks until Liam grabbed his head and brought their mouths together in a deep French kiss.

Aidan groaned with desire and began fumbling with his shorts. He couldn't stand another minute with his dick so confined, with anything between his skin and Liam's. Liam took over, his steady fingers undoing Aidan's belt, the clasp of the shorts, the zipper. Free of constraints, the shorts dropped to the floor, and Aidan's dick jumped out the slit of his boxers.

"Somebody's happy," Liam said, licking Aidan's neck. Their bodies pressed together so that Aidan's dick rubbed against Liam's thigh. Aidan groaned and shivered. Liam reached down and grabbed Aidan by the bottoms of his butt cheeks, lifting him into the air, and Aidan kicked off his shorts.

There was something so sexy and almost forbidden to Aidan about wearing just his boxers, dress shoes, and socks, like he was in some porn video of a businessman getting fucked by—whom? A repairman? A professional athlete?

Maybe just a very handsome bodyguard.

Aidan slung his arms around Liam's neck as Liam carried him into the bedroom, still holding him by the butt. Aidan raised his feet and twined them together behind Liam's back. "You are just so damn sexy," Liam whispered into Aidan's hair.

He laid Aidan down on the bed, then sat at the foot, sliding off Aidan's left shoe. He began massaging the foot, pressing against the toes, the heel. Aidan shivered and bucked on the bed. Liam slid the sock off, then lowered his mouth to suck on Aidan's big toe.

He had never experienced anything like it. His breathing quickened, and he felt sensations everywhere in his body. Liam slid Aidan's right shoe off, repeating his procedure, then lay on his back on the bed, taking Aidan's dick in his mouth. Aidan shivered as Liam's mouth, warm and wet, engulfed him. Then Liam backed off, licking up Aidan's dick in long, rough strokes, using one finger to tease the sensitive area behind Aidan's balls. He began bobbing his head up and down, inhaling as he sucked, so a pressure built up around Aidan's dick.

Aidan couldn't hold out for long. He started panting and whimpering, making sounds he'd never heard himself make before. He tried to pull out of Liam's mouth before he exploded, but the big bodyguard held on until Aidan was shooting his load.

"Sweet," Liam said, licking his lips. "Just like I thought you'd be."

He scooted up the bed so his head was level with Aidan's, and they kissed once again. Aidan reached down and touched Liam's dick through the white cotton of the jockstrap. Liam had already been leaking precum in a big wet spot on the fabric.

"My turn," Aidan said, scrambling around so that he could put his mouth on Liam's dick. He started licking and kissing it through the jockstrap, and Liam groaned and bucked his hips toward Aidan's mouth. Aidan loved the feel of the ribbed fabric against his tongue, inhaling the spicy musk of Liam's groin. If this were only happening in a locker room, he thought, life couldn't be any better.

He couldn't hold out any longer; he needed to feel Liam's dick pulsing down his throat. He pushed the fabric aside so Liam's big dick popped out the side, then licked up and down it like a lollipop. Liam reached down and tousled Aidan's hair. "That feels so good when you do that."

Aidan had his mouth full, so he couldn't reply. He relaxed his throat muscles and took Liam in as far as he could. It wasn't all the way, but Liam seemed to like it. Aidan bobbed up and down, licking and sucking. Every dick was different. Some were bigger, some smaller; some had pulsing veins, others a mushroom cap perfect for chewing.

Liam's was just right. It was thick but not too thick, long but not too long. It felt like the dick Aidan had waited his whole life to suck. But good as it was, there was more to do.

He pulled back and took one of Liam's balls in his mouth, sucking it, and the bodyguard squirmed and panted.

Then the other ball. Then back to the dick. A few more long drags and Liam was ready to explode. An old bumper sticker flashed into Aidan's head just as Liam's cum rushed into his mouth. Mean people suck. Nice people swallow.

Aidan swallowed.

He pushed himself back up the bed so that he was cuddled against Liam, resting his head on the bodyguard's chest. Both of them were covered in a sheen of sweat, and as he lay there, Aidan tried to remember the last time he'd felt this kind of passion.

Had he ever felt it with Blake? He felt sure he had, years before, when they first began dating. But if he were honest with himself, those days were long past. He reached his hand down and rested it on Liam's dick. Even in its resting state it was impressive in size. "I need a few minutes to recover," Liam said. "Though it feels good to have you touch me."

His right arm stretched behind Aidan and around Aidan's shoulders. It felt so good to lie there, inhaling the bigger man's scent, letting his heart rate return to its norm. But he propped himself up on one elbow so he could get a better look at Liam's body.

"You like what you see?" Liam asked, a smile playing on his face.

"Yeah. I liked what I saw when you were showering too."

"When was that?"

Aidan had to think for a minute. So much had happened in the last few days. "Friday afternoon."

"Friday? But Carlucci wasn't shot until Saturday."

"I know. I couldn't get the image of you naked out of my head. So I went back to the bar, and that's when you showed up."

"When I mistook you for Carlucci."

"I'm glad you did. I'm not glad Carlucci's dead, the poor guy. But otherwise we might not have ever met. Certainly not ended up like this."

Aidan snuggled back down next to him, resting his hand once more on Liam's dick. This time he felt it responding. His own began to swell too.

"Think you can hold out longer in round two?" Aidan asked.

"Round two and round three," Liam said. "Even round four."

"Sounds like a challenge." He rolled over onto Liam, straddling him, dick to dick. He lowered himself carefully, so that their dicks were still touching, and began to nibble at Liam's nipple, turning it into a hard nub of flesh. He arched his back and began rubbing his body against Liam's, their sweat acting as a lubricant.

Liam did his part, sliding back and forth under Aidan, who balanced on his forearms and humped Liam's body the way he'd fucked his teenage bed, long before he'd ever touched another man. He remembered those days, when he first figured out how good friction against his dick felt, the surprise that something spurted out of its end and made his body shiver with passion.

He put those memories to use, rubbing against Liam with increasing speed and pressure until he couldn't stand the sensation on his tender dick, and both of them were moaning and panting and grabbing each other. Liam grabbed Aidan's shoulders and moved with him, howling so loud, the dog looked up from the floor in concern.

Liam came first, with Aidan just a few seconds later. Aidan collapsed onto Liam's body, and the bigger man wrapped his arms around him. "So much for round two," Aidan whispered into Liam's chest.

"Maybe we both need a rest before round three," Liam said.

Aidan slid off him and curled into his side, and they were asleep in minutes.

Departure

The next morning they woke next to each other in Aidan's bed. Liam yawned and said, "Let me teach you a little Arabic. Good morning is *sabah il-kher*, which means morning of goodness, and the response is *sabah il-noor*, which means morning of light."

Aidan tried it back to him. "Sabah il-kher."

Liam leaned over and kissed him. "Sabah il-noor. You are a good student."

"I'm accustomed to being the teacher, you know."

Liam pushed the sheets aside and rolled over on top of Aidan. "Oh yes? And what do your students do when they want to get in your good graces?" He leaned down and teased Aidan's nipple with his teeth.

"Not that," Aidan said, his body stiffening.

Liam began to lick his way down Aidan's chest. His tongue was rough, and the moisture he left behind evaporated quickly in the dry heat. As his tongue tickled Aidan's belly button, Aidan arched his back and moaned.

Then Liam's phone rang.

Aidan began to laugh. "Didn't you shut that off last night?"

Liam rolled off Aidan and reached for the phone. "Don't move. I'll be back."

Aidan looked at the clock. It was almost eight, time for them to get started if they were going to head out into the desert. He hoped that Liam might join him in the shower, but no luck. He soaped down his body, feeling the tenderness in his thighs and ass, those muscles that hadn't been used in a long time. He felt as contented as a cat.

He relished the water streaming over him. Would they be camping in the desert? Were there bathrooms and showers? He might as well enjoy these creature comforts while he could, even if he did have to enjoy them alone.

When he walked into the kitchen, hair dripping, white towel wrapped around his waist, Liam was sitting at the table. He'd pulled on his shorts, but his magnificent chest was exposed, every light brown hair glowing in the morning light. "You moved," he said.

"Somebody's got to be responsible here. You want to take a shower?"

"In a minute. My contact thinks he knows who mugged us in the souk."

Aidan leaned against the wall. "Who?"

"There's a Libyan secret service agent in town, a man named Wahid Zubran. He's been asking for favors from a man in the Tunisian police named Desrosiers."

"Is he the one who killed Carlucci?"

"Don't know. But from his description, he sounds like one of the guys we ran up against. This Zubran always wears military-style shirts with epaulets."

"Libyan?" Aidan asked. "Didn't Carlucci have a Libyan stamp in his passport?"

Liam pulled it out of his pocket. "Yup. But I don't know if there's a connection."

"The Libyans have to be after the money," Aidan said. "They knew that Carlucci was carrying that account number and password, and they killed him for it."

Liam nodded. "Quite possible. That makes it even more important that we hook up with this tribe ASAP."

"Then get your ass in the shower so we can get moving."

Liam looked at his watch. "The next train isn't for an hour. It'll only take us a few minutes to get to the station."

He reached a big hand over and tugged on the towel around Aidan's waist, which fell to the kitchen floor, leaving Aidan naked in the bright early-morning light streaming into the kitchen. Aidan's dick was already semihard, and Liam took it in his mouth. Aidan's ass clenched tight as he pushed his dick forward into Liam's mouth, and he tossed his head back and groaned. "Like that, do you?" Liam asked, pulling off for a moment.

Aidan didn't answer, because Liam swallowed him again, working his mouth up and down, suctioning, teasing the mushroom cap with his teeth. His skin was still damp from his shower, and it tingled as the breeze blew in from the open window. Liam grabbed Aidan's ass and ran an index finger between his cheeks as he bobbed up and down on Aidan's dick.

Aidan lost himself in sensation, focusing on the warm wetness of Liam's mouth, the roughness of Liam's index finger probing his ass. When his orgasm came, it ratcheted up from his groin, swelled through his heart, set every electron in his brain humming.

He slumped back against the wall as Liam pulled off him. "Guess I'll take that shower now," Liam said, standing.

"Don't you want...?"

"Consider it an IOU," Liam said, shucking his shorts and tossing them on the sofa as he walked to the bathroom. "I'll collect later."

While Liam showered, Aidan dressed and cleared up the apartment, placing the last few things he needed in his backpack. As Liam reassembled his duffel bag, Aidan took a last look around. It already looked like a place he was leaving—the forlorn sofa, rickety kitchen table, faded paint on the walls.

Things hadn't worked out the way he'd expected when he'd first walked in the apartment a week before. Then he'd been thinking he'd be in Tunis for at least a semester, teaching ESL and hiding out from the possibility of any new relationship. He'd relished the challenge of making a life in this new place, and as a consequence, everything had looked new and fresh.

Instead, his life had taken an unexpected turn. It was scary, like jumping off the high dive with your eyes closed, but he knew it was good for him. He needed to get back to that person he'd been before he met Blake, the one who was willing to take chances.

They decided it would be best for Aidan to hold Carlucci's passport since they looked so much alike. Aidan slipped the small book into his backpack and shouldered it as

Liam hoisted his duffel. He locked the apartment door and left the key with the downstairs neighbor. He said good-bye to the dog. He hoped the next tenant would take her in.

As the cab approached the modern, three-story train station, Liam leaned forward and said something to the driver in Arabic. "Police," he said to Aidan under his breath. There were two police officers stationed by the front door, scanning everyone who passed.

"Are they looking for us?"

"Don't know. Don't want to risk it, though."

The cabdriver took them past the station and around the side. Liam opened his duffel and rummaged through it, pulling out a small leather case. The driver turned and spoke to Liam, pointing at a small door set deep into the wall behind a waist-high concrete planter.

"*Shukran*," Liam said. He motioned to Aidan to get out. "Stay here," he said, positioning Aidan in the shelter of an empty city bus. "Keep an eye out for the cops."

Liam slung his duffel over his shoulder and walked around the planter to the door. He tried the handle, and when it wouldn't release, he opened the small leather case and pulled something out of it.

Liam was picking the lock, Aidan realized. He scanned the area, worried that a policeman, even an employee, would approach and challenge Liam. The side street was busy, taxis and private cars jockeying for space with pedestrians and tourists, horns blowing and lots of shouting in Arabic.

Liam waved to Aidan as he popped the door handle. Aidan hurried over, hoisting his backpack on his back, and they slipped inside to what looked like a service corridor. A door at the far end popped open, and Liam spun Aidan toward the wall and leaned down to kiss him.

Aidan was stunned. Not that he minded being kissed, but surely this wasn't the right time or place? He looked beyond Liam and saw an old man pushing a mop and bucket coming toward them. The man waved his hands and shouted in Arabic.

Liam looked at the man and scowled, then grabbed Aidan's hand and dragged him down toward the door the man had come through. The man shook his hand at them as they passed, but then turned and continued down the hall.

"What was that about?" Aidan whispered as Liam paused at the doorway, looking left and then right.

"Didn't want him to wonder what we were doing in that back hallway," Liam said. "What's the matter? Don't you want my kisses anymore?" He grinned. "The way looks clear. Let's get our tickets."

The station was busy, crowds of backpackers at the kiosks, whole families clustered on benches. Vendors sold tea, coffee, and sweets. At the ticket counter, they had the choice between first class, which had air-conditioning, and "comfort class," also air-conditioned, but with larger, more comfortable seats. Liam bought the tickets there. "We're tourists, remember? Americans go for comfort."

The train was due to leave soon, so they walked out to where metal piers the same bright blue Aidan had seen on grillwork throughout the city spanned the tracks. The train had not come in yet, so they stood back against the wall, sheltered by a news kiosk.

A single policeman patrolled the tracks, though he was more interested in a pretty young Tunisian woman in a short sundress than in who was waiting for the train. Liam's phone rang, and he turned away to take the call. Aidan heard only Liam's side of the conversation, which consisted mostly of things like "wow" and "are you sure?"

When Liam hung up, he turned to Aidan. "My buddy checked the balance of that account. It took him a while to figure out which bank it was in, but once he did, the password got him right in."

"And?"

"There's a million dollars there."

"That's a nice little relocation boost for this tribe," Aidan said.

"You bet. It's also a nice little motive for murder."

El Jem

The train pulled into the station, sweeping forward a hot, dry breeze. The Tunisians bustled into second class, while most of the tourists and backpackers placed themselves in first.

Since comfort class was so empty, Aidan and Liam had their own compartment, and as the train pulled out of the station, Aidan asked, "What made you come to Tunisia?"

"Circumstance and coincidence. Much like you. I went back to the States after my discharge, but I didn't feel comfortable there. I'd been away too long, I guess. I started looking around for someplace to go, and I got in touch with everyone I thought might be able to give me a job. I'd met the guy I work through on an operation a few years before, and he needed a bodyguard for an assignment. I came here, liked it, and stayed."

Aidan looked outside as the train moved through the outlying neighborhoods of Tunis and into the countryside. There were no fences beside the railway, and the hills were covered in bright yellow flowers.

"Don't you get lonely?" he asked. "For friends, I mean. Guys like your buddies in the navy."

"Friends turn on you," Liam said. "Don't need them." He looked Aidan straight in the eye. "So, with a name like Aidan Greene, I'm guessing you've got some Irish blood in you, but you don't look the part at all."

"Not a drop. My grandfather's last name was Grinshpun, but the immigration agent changed it to Greene at Ellis Island."

"And Aidan? That's not a Jewish name."

"In Judaism, we give kids the Hebrew names of dead relatives, so that we remember them. We carry over the first initial to whatever English name the kid gets. So I'm named after my great-grandfather, whose name was Aharon— Aaron. My parents picked an *A* name that they liked."

"Where'd you grow up?"

"New Jersey. Just outside Trenton."

"Hey, me too. Jersey, at least. Little town outside New Brunswick."

"Who'd have thought that two Jersey boys would run into each other in Tunisia?" Aidan looked out the window of the train, where a camel raced across the plain in the morning sun. "Don't have camels like that in Jersey. At least outside the zoo. Ever ride one?"

"We were doing an operation in—well, let's just call it an Arab country—and the only way to get from point A to point B was by camel. Camels are not the most well-mannered creatures around. They fidget and gurgle and chew all the time and eat whatever they can get hold of, even the water bags."

Aidan sat back in his seat, waiting for Liam to go on. "Camels can turn their heads completely backward, even though they have the same number of neck vertebrae as humans. When they sit down, they bend their front and back legs completely underneath their bellies and rest flat on the ground."

"Do you think we'll get to ride them?" Aidan asked.

Liam laughed. "It's not something to look forward to. Even with lots of padding, those saddles hurt your butt after a while." They talked about camels, and Liam told a couple of funny stories, and then Aidan opened the guidebook to El Jem to see what they might expect. It was a popular tourist destination, with a Roman coliseum where gladiators had fought centuries before, and that was good; it meant there'd be a lot of Americans and Europeans around, and they could fit in.

The conductor came around and collected their tickets. He looked Liam and Aidan up and down, and for a moment Aidan worried that the police had circulated their photos. Then he recognized the look in the conductor's eyes and followed his gaze. He was checking out Liam's dick, outlined against his khaki shorts.

Aidan looked the conductor in the eye and licked his lips. The man's face reddened, and he fumbled the tickets back to Liam and hurried from the compartment. "What was that all about?" Liam asked.

"You've got to work on your gaydar," Aidan said, laughing. "Either that, or wear looser shorts." He rested his hand on Liam's dick and gave him a knowing look.

Liam blushed almost as much as the conductor had.

The farther they got from the city, the more dust that flowed around the train, so the empty land was hard to see in too much detail. The train hooted as they passed small settlements or individual Tunisians trekking through the desert.

Miles of olive groves lined either side of the train tracks as they approached El Jem. The air outside was hazy, but Aidan could make out the massive bulk of the amphitheater, said to have once held thirteen thousand people. He wondered where they had all come from.

Leaving the train station in El Jem, they both had to don sunglasses and ball caps, not only to protect from the sun but from the fine sand blowing in the air. Liam approached a young Tunisian, and in Arabic he asked where he could find a pharmacy, miming a problem with his stomach. The guy was very helpful, giving directions to two pharmacies. The one near the coliseum, he said, was the best; the pharmacist there spoke some English.

"Sounds like our guy," Liam said to Aidan. He slung his duffel over his shoulder, and Aidan hitched up his backpack. He kept the guidebook open to the page with the map of El Jem to add to their authenticity, but the coliseum was easy to spot, towering over the city.

It was late morning by then, and the sun was high in the sky. The air was torturously hot, and they tried to stick close to the buildings to take advantage of the little shadow. The area around the coliseum was busy, cars and trucks navigating the narrow street, only an occasional date palm providing a bit of extra shade.

As they neared the pharmacy, Liam swiveled his head, trying to see if there was anyone watching. "That's our place," he said, nodding to a single-story white stucco building. "I'll stay outside. You go in and see what happens."

"Should I ask for the goldsmith? What was his name?"

"Don't know. His wife didn't tell you?"

Aidan shook his head. "Guess I'll have to wing it." It felt good to say that and believe it. With every day he was getting back to the man he'd been before he settled down, the one willing to take chances and see what life held.

He adjusted his pack and pushed open the door to the pharmacy. Two men in white coats stood behind the counter. Both were in their late twenties, though the one with a customer appeared a few years younger. The older of the two was writing something when Aidan stepped up to him. "You speak English?" he asked.

"Yes, how I can help you?"

Aidan didn't want to pull out Carlucci's passport; that seemed too obvious. Then he remembered the amulet, which was still around his neck. "I have a rash here," he said, opening his shirt to expose the amulet. He hoped that the man would recognize it for what it was, a token from the goldsmith's wife.

The pharmacist looked up, and when he recognized the amulet, Aidan saw fear rise in his eyes. "Is it serious?" Aidan asked.

"Yes, very serious," the pharmacist said. Aidan saw the younger man look up at him and then look out the front window toward Liam. He looked at Aidan again and then walked behind the older man, opening a door into the back of the building.

"It is very dangerous for you," the pharmacist said to Aidan in a whisper. He pushed a piece of paper toward Aidan, covered in strange characters, a weird mix of squared letters that looked like the bastard child of the Greek alphabet and mathematical symbols. "My friend says you should take this. Now you must go, fast."

Aidan took the paper from him and turned toward the door. Behind him, he noticed the younger pharmacist had returned from the back with a much-older man. He recognized the older man and his shirt with the epaulets.

Aidan pushed out the front door at a run. "We have to get out of here. It's the man from the souk, that Libyan."

Liam took off, and Aidan struggled to keep up with him, his backpack swaying on his shoulders and banging him in the ass. Behind them they heard the door of the pharmacy slam open, and shouting in Arabic.

Liam led them on a zigzag path, darting between trucks and down alleys. Though Aidan didn't turn around, he had the sense that the two men were following them; he heard their footsteps, the occasional shouts of people behind them.

The bulk of the amphitheater loomed ahead of them. "In there," Liam said, pointing. "Maybe we can lose them."

They rushed past souvenir stands and stores selling crafts and antiques in the plaza around the amphitheater, and the smell of harissa from the food stalls made Aidan's mouth water and reminded him that they were overdue for lunch.

Liam hurried through the entrance to the amphitheater, Aidan right behind him, and then made a sharp turn past the small museum, toward the underground passages and vaults where Aidan had read that prisoners and animals were kept in Roman times. It was cool down there, the air smelling of mold and dust. The sweat on Aidan's back chilled as they darted around corners, pausing to listen behind them. Aidan heard sounds of angry Arabic.

Aidan's heart was pounding, and he knew he couldn't run much farther. He gasped for breath as Liam pulled him into a tiny space between two stone pillars, where they were sheltered from the main aisle. Aidan heard the two men approaching, and the sound of a bullet dropping into the chamber of a gun echoed against the cold stone.

Bus Ride

Aidan dropped his pack to the ground, and he and Liam stood with their backs to the cold stone wall as the two men who had been chasing them rushed past. The older one was still berating the younger one, and they didn't notice the two Americans huddled in the niche. As soon as they'd passed, Liam put his finger to his lips and moved back the way they had come.

Even straining, Aidan couldn't hear Liam make a sound. He tried to imitate Liam's soft footfalls without much success. They rounded a corner and surprised a group of German tourists, and there was much guffawing and jollity as the men in the group wanted to pat Aidan and Liam on the back and try out their basic English.

When they escaped, they returned to the entrance, where they rounded a corner to where a big tour bus was parked with the door open. A Tunisian man with a clipboard stood next to the open door. "Hurry, please," he said to them. "We are ready to be leaving."

He made motions pushing them into the bus, and Liam stepped up into the cool interior, Aidan right behind him. The bus was only about half-full, and he moved to a pair of empty seats toward the back. He motioned Aidan to the window seat and then sat beside him.

Aidan looked out the window and saw the two men from the pharmacy, the young one in the white coat and the older one with his epaulets. They rushed past the bus and turned down an alley. Aidan took a deep breath and tried to calm his racing pulse.

"Did you get anything from the pharmacist before you left?" Liam asked.

"Just this." Aidan dug into his pocket and handed Liam the page with the strange characters. "Mean anything to you?"

"Looks like Tifinagh. The written language of the Tuareg."

"Can you read it?"

Liam laughed. "I skipped Tifinagh when I was in the SEALs. I know a little bit about a lot of things, but this isn't one of them."

The Tunisian tour guide shepherded the last Americans on the bus, a middle-aged couple with matching digital cameras around their necks, and then closed the door behind him. "Now we go to Matmata," he said to the passengers. "You have seen the movies *Star Wars?*"

Several voices chorused yes. "We will see where movie was filmed," he said. "And we will stay the night in the hotel. You will enjoy, yes?"

More yeses.

"Matmata's south of here," Liam whispered to Aidan. "So we might as well relax and enjoy the ride." He reclined his seat, stretched his long legs in the aisle, and tipped his ball cap down over his eyes.

Aidan stared at him. How could he sleep after all they had just been through? He wanted to poke Liam in the side, demand that he sit up with Aidan and go over every step of what had happened to them in agonizing detail. But within minutes, Liam's chest began to rise and fall in a regular rhythm.

Might as well get comfortable. He reclined his seat too, turning on his side so that his foot was just touching Liam's. He thought back to that kiss in the bus station hallway, the way Liam had spun him around so easily, how comfortable it had felt to fall into Liam's arms, no matter where they were. He shifted a little in the seat as his dick pronged up against his shorts, closed his eyes, and drifted to sleep himself.

Sometime later, Aidan woke up and stretched, and his movement woke Liam. "Where are we?" Liam asked.

"Just outside a town called Gabes," Aidan said. He looked out the window; every so often, he could catch a glimpse of the Mediterranean, sparkling in the distance. As they pulled into town, the tour guide, whose name they discovered was Belghasem, recommended that they stop at the bakery across the road to try a gazelle's horn, a pastry filled with honey and nuts.

"This is delicious," Aidan said. Liam was reviewing the map in the shade of the bakery's awning. Belghasem was inside the bakery with the driver and a few of the passengers; the others had fanned out through the town in search of postcards and souvenirs. "You think we should stay with the bus or slip away while no one's looking?" he asked Liam.

"We don't know how far Zubran's contacts go," Liam said. "He knows we were in El Jem, so he may have figured out that we're heading into the desert for a rendezvous with the tribe. He may have some of the train and bus stations down the line watched. If we stay with this group for a while, we'll stay under his radar."

"Fine with me. I'm getting to see the country." Despite the momentary panic of being chased through El Jem, Aidan was enjoying his little adventure.

Belghasem came out of the bakery and announced, "We will take a small walk now, to stretch your legs. Through the Souk el Henna in Jara. That is old quarter of city."

Aidan looked at Liam, who shrugged, and they trailed along behind the guide. Aidan's favorite stall was roofed over with transparent plastic, with baskets in many shapes jumbled everywhere. The rest of the market reminded him of an outdoor flea market, selling all kinds of junk. He bought several packages of locally grown dates; who knew when they would get to eat again?

One of the specialties of the area was the production of henna, and two of the women on the tour opted for henna tattoos. Aidan was watching when he spotted a police officer patrolling the edge of the market. He elbowed Liam.

"It's very hot," Liam said to Belghasem, fanning himself. "We're going to go back to the bus."

"Very good, very good," Belghasem said, nodding. "We will leave soon."

"No use risking trouble," Liam said as they slid back through the market to the broad, sun-drenched street where the bus was parked near the tall, square minaret of the local mosque. They saw a single police car crawling down the street but managed to stay in the shadow of a stand of palm trees.

Matmata

As the tour bus approached Matmata, Aidan awoke to watch the drive through the arid and rocky Berber hills, where tribesmen had excavated cave dwellings centuries before. Belghasem told them that thousands of people still lived in those homes, and that one of the largest was their hotel, the Sidi Driss. "Was the home of Luke Skywalker in the *Star Wars* cinema," he said. "You will see movie pieces in hotel. Outside scenes filmed near Tozeur, far to west, but this place his home."

When the bus pulled to a stop at the hotel in Matmata, Liam woke, yawning once and then looking around him. "We'll let everyone else get off first," he said. "See all the tour buses? We'll fit in easily, and we should be able to find someone who can read the Tifinagh message the pharmacist gave you."

"Do not worry about all tourists," Belghasem said as people began getting up and gathering their bags. "All buses will leave in one hour; then you have city all to yourselves!"

Liam and Aidan looked at each other and laughed. So much for fitting in. From the outside, the Hotel Sidi Driss looked like nothing special, a squat building with souvenir vendors out front. They waited until everyone else had gotten off the bus, hoping to slip away, but Belghasem was still waiting for them at the bus's door, and he shepherded them into the lobby.

"Is best you stay here," he said. "Men who look for you will not find you."

Liam and Aidan looked at each other. So Belghasem had seen that they were being chased in El Jem and offered them the refuge of the tour bus. Aidan vaguely remembered running past the bus on their way into the amphitheater; Belghasem must have noticed them then. "Thank you," Aidan said.

As they walked in, it seemed like they had stepped into another galaxy far, far away. The reception area was a cave with a low ceiling and walls plastered with *Star Wars* stickers. To their right, an enormous Darth Vader tapestry hung on the wall, while to their left was a passageway to a courtyard.

While the tour passengers checked in, Liam and Aidan explored the adjacent courtyard, hoping to escape from Belghasem's watchful eye. "Why do you think he let us on the bus if he knew those men were chasing us?" Aidan whispered.

Liam shrugged. "He's probably going to hit us up for money for the bus ride as soon as the rest of the people have checked in."

The first courtyard was like the center ring of a coliseum but in miniature. The walls around them shot up at least twenty feet, with arched passageways leading to more caves and corridors. For a moment, Aidan forgot he was underground; the very top of those soaring walls were at ground level, meaning that they were standing in an enormous pit.

The next courtyard was decorated with large plastic facades covered in weird knobs and metallic objects. The palm tree in one corner of the courtyard was hidden under a long plastic tube designed to look like a space-age duct. The plastic set pieces were flimsy, designed to be filmed and not touched. Aidan was astonished that so much of it was still in place, not sold on eBay as soon as the filmmakers left.

Belghasem appeared behind them. "Many houses here built like this," he said. "Because desert temperatures, they go up and down much."

Gently but deliberately, he led them back to the main lobby so that they could check in—but against Liam's expectations, he didn't seem to want anything from them other than that they settle in. They had no choice but to step up to the desk, where a young Tunisian man greeted them in English. "Welcome to Matmata. May I have your name, please?"

Liam spoke to him in Arabic, and though Aidan didn't understand the words, he got the meaning. The clerk saw Aidan's lack of comprehension and answered Liam in English. "We have one room available," he said. He looked at them and smiled. "But there is only one bed. I believe that will be acceptable?"

Aidan's gaydar started going off like mad. Well, what do you know? he thought. He smiled and said, "That will be just fine."

The clerk smiled. "I am very happy," he said. "I am called Abbas. I will show you to the room myself."

He led them back through the courtyard, off to a side hallway, and opened a door before them. The only thing in the cave was a single bare lightbulb and a bed, but after their adventures of the morning, it looked just fine.

"We are very happy to have you here at the Sidi Driss," Abbas said, smiling again. "I am very happy you are here."

Aidan slipped his arm around Liam's waist, and Abbas grinned again. He had a gold front tooth that glinted in the light. Liam slipped him a few dinars, and he and Aidan entered the room. "No lock," he said. He didn't look happy about that. He looked at Aidan. "I didn't figure you for the public-display-of-affection type," he said. "You have to be careful with stuff like that in this country."

"Abbas is gay," Aidan said.

"That's just the way Tunisian men are."

Aidan shook his head. "Nope. Gay."

Liam raised his eyebrows, but Aidan didn't think the topic needed any further discussion. While Liam thought about their next step, Aidan set out across a few courtyards to find the restroom. The facilities were very rudimentary and not very sanitary. It probably wouldn't have bothered Liam, but Aidan was discovering that he very much preferred his creature comforts. He'd enjoyed the air-conditioned train and the comfy tour bus, and if at some point his tender butt was going to end up on a bumpy camel for a long ride, he didn't think he'd like it.

By the time Aidan returned to the room, Liam was ready to go out into the village and look around for someone who could read the Tifinagh message the pharmacist had given Aidan.

They hiked up and down the hills that made up the village, past a few cafés and souvenir stalls. By then most of the buses had left, and there were few people around. Most of the shops had already closed, and the street reminded Aidan of a movie back lot after the filming was over.

Many of the local men, young and old alike, were wearing the long, hooded cloak that Obi-Wan Kenobi had worn. For a while Aidan thought they were part of the general *Star Wars* theme, but he realized that they were the traditional Berber cloaks he had read about in the guidebook, and that George Lucas's costume designer had simply ripped them off for the movie.

Liam approached anyone they saw, speaking in Arabic, but either no one understood him or no one wanted to help. They stopped at a kiosk selling handfuls of roasted sunflower seeds to local children. The vendor offered them tea and some seeds, which were still piping hot, freshly scooped from the roasting pan. But he simply stared at the Tifinagh writing as if he'd never seen such a thing before.

By the time they made their way back to the hotel, it was just before six o'clock, and it was pitch-black. Aidan was feeling discouraged, until they walked back into the lobby and saw the desk clerk.

"I have an idea," Aidan said to Liam, pulling him off to the side of the claustrophobic room. "You still don't believe that Abbas is gay, right?"

"So?"

"So I'm going to see if I can charm him into helping us," Aidan said. He hesitated. "It may take more than charm," he continued. "I'll take care of him, if that's what he wants—but he might prefer you instead. If that's the case, are you willing to do it?"

Liam looked at him in the flickering light of the cave. "I thought you were a picket-fence kind of guy," he said. "The kind who just wants romance and monogamy and a house somewhere." Aidan could see the laughter in his eyes. "You'd have sex with a stranger just to get information?"

"Wouldn't you?"

"Hasn't come up yet," he said. "But I guess so."

"You slept with me to get me to go to the souk with you," Aidan said drily.

"Nope. I slept with you because I wanted to. Because you charmed me. Because you have the ability to keep on surprising me, and I like that." He gave Aidan a gentle swat on his butt and said, "Go on. Work your magic. Let me know if you need me to pitch in."

Aidan walked across the room to Abbas, who smiled again. For a moment Aidan did think about kissing him, wondering how that gold tooth would taste against the tongue. A barista at his favorite coffee shop in Philadelphia had a tongue stud, and Aidan had fantasized about kissing him. "You are liking our hotel?" Abbas asked.

Man, it had been a long time since he'd flirted with a guy, not counting Liam—where it had seemed almost effortless. Maybe he really was a picket-fence kind of guy, he thought, and faltered. But they needed to get that message deciphered, and all their other efforts in Matmata had been a washout. So Aidan said, "Yes, very much. Tunisian people are so friendly." He smiled. "And the men so handsome."

Abbas blushed, his dark skin deepening a bit more. "I have a problem," Aidan said. "A guy in the last town we visited gave me this piece of paper with these funny symbols on it, and I'm dying to know what he wrote."

"Funny symbols?" Abbas asked.

Aidan nodded. "Somebody told me it was Tifinagh?" He deliberately mispronounced the word—though he probably would have said it wrong even if he hadn't tried.

Abbas smiled again. "Ah, you are in great luck. My mother's family are the *Kel Tagilmus*, the people of the veil. You would call them the Tuareg."

Aidan nodded, his hand resting on the counter between them. "Tifinagh is our alphabet," Abbas said. "If you show me, perhaps I can help you read."

"That would be great." Aidan pulled the paper out of his pocket, unfolded it, and handed it to the desk clerk.

Abbas scanned it, then looked up at Aidan, curiosity in his eyes. Aidan looked back at him in what he hoped was a combination of helplessness and flirtation. But he might have just looked confused.

Abbas said, "It is both a man's name and location and a warning."

"A warning?"

"It says that you must be very careful, that there is danger all around you."

Aidan remembered the men who had attacked him and Liam in the souk, and who had chased them through the streets of El Jem, and shivered. He hoped that the pharmacist had been able to get away from those men himself.

"I know," he said.

Abbas looked at him once more, then at Liam in the background, and nodded. "You are to meet a man named Ifoudan, who—how do I say this—he takes camels across the desert?"

"Yes, I expected something like that," Aidan said. "Does it say where I find this man?"

"In the camel market at Remada," Abbas said. "A town south of Tataouine. We call it the Green Heart of the Desert. It is surrounded by a forest, the trees from the north. Not like an oasis." He studied Aidan's face for a moment. "You are to be there the day after tomorrow."

"Shukran," Aidan said.

He crossed the courtyard to Liam, who suggested dinner in the hotel's bar area. After the waitress, a pretty, young Tunisian woman, took their order, Liam said, "What did the desk clerk say? Are you meeting him later for a roll in the sand?"

Aidan was surprised to hear a note of jealousy in Liam's voice. He filed that away for further consideration. "Nope. He just translated the note for me."

The waiter poured wine for them. "Really? What does it say?" Liam asked.

"We're going south." Aidan repeated what Abbas had said. As he was finishing, the waitress delivered a platter of *briq* as an appetizer, a folded, crispy crepe with a lightly cooked egg inside that had to be slurped quickly. Liam and Aidan laughed at each other's attempts to eat the deliciously sloppy mess.

Liam ate in silence for a few minutes, then said, "I've been thinking. Maybe it would be best for you to stay with the tour rather than come with me. You'll get back to Tunis safely that way."

"But I thought you needed me to pretend to be Charles Carlucci with the Tuareg."

Liam shrugged. "I'm bringing them the account information. I'll figure something out if there's a problem."

Aidan's first reaction was that Liam was dumping him. He didn't know why that bothered him so much. After all, Liam had known Aidan was going back to the States as soon as they returned to Tunis. This relationship, if that's what it was, was only for the short term.

The waitress cleared away their dirty dishes and returned a moment later with a platter of lamb couscous with copious amounts of fiery harissa sauce and French bread.

As she served them, Aidan realized that if he left Liam behind in Tunis after everything was finished, he'd be the one doing the dumping. But if Liam sent him back there before the adventure was over, it would be like getting dumped again. Blake had kicked Aidan out of his life, and Aidan wasn't about to let another guy do that to him so soon afterward.

"I signed on for the whole trip," he said when the waitress left, cutting in to the rare, pink lamb. Blood dripped off the edge of his knife. "I'm not quitting now."

"Are you forgetting the Libyan intelligence agent who grabbed us at the medina and then chased us from the pharmacy? This isn't a pleasure trip, Aidan. You're in over your head, and I don't want you getting hurt."

"You may be taller than I am, Liam, but I'm not in over my head, not yet. You seem to think I'm some kind of nitwit who needs babysitting. But I've been holding my own here so far."

"I don't think you're a nitwit at all. On the contrary, I think you're a smart, brave, resourceful guy. But—"

Aidan didn't let him finish. "If I'm so smart and brave and resourceful, then you need my help. End of story. This lamb is delicious, isn't it?"

Liam laughed. "Did you boss your boyfriend around like this?"

Aidan shook his head. "Nope. But maybe if I had, I'd still be in Philadelphia. This is the new Aidan Greene. Get used to it." He kicked off his right shoe and stretched his leg out so that his foot grazed Liam's leg.

Liam responded by grasping Aidan's foot and bringing it higher up his thigh. Aidan slid back in his chair as Liam guided his foot, up, up, until a beatific smile graced his face.

Hidden Dangers

Dinner at the Sidi Driss was a lot better than the run-down accommodations. They sat under the stars, and it was magical—just the kind of romantic date Aidan loved. He only had to ignore the Libyan intelligence agent pursuing them and the realization that one man had already died because of the account information they were carrying.

Belghasem stopped into the bar to make a few announcements. "Tomorrow we go early morning to a *ksour*, very lovely, interesting trip. We spend night in Tataouine."

Liam called him over and asked about the itinerary. After Tataouine, which Belghasem said was interesting, very lovely, the tour would cross the desert toward Douz and the Chott el Jarid. After a few more stops, they would return to Tunis.

"I guess we'll stick with the tour as far as Tataouine," Liam said when Belghasem left. "From there, though, we'll have to find a way to get to Remada."

Two of the men from the group had bought light sabers in the market and staged a mock battle near the restaurant entrance. "I want to do that," Aidan said.

"I'm afraid not," Liam said. "We don't want to call too much attention to ourselves."

"You're no fun."

"You didn't say that last night," Liam said with sly grin.

After the waitress had tempted them with dessert, Aidan said, "I don't think I've ever been in a place with so little ground light. I want to go out and look at the stars. I'll bet we can see the Milky Way."

"Since I had to deny you a light-saber battle, I guess we're going," Liam said. They walked out of the hotel's front door, and after a couple of moments they had left behind the town. Liam wrapped his arms around Liam and whispered, "I can make you see stars."

They kissed, and maybe it was the darkness or the lack of any other stimulus like street sounds, but everything about the kiss seemed magnified. Liam's lips were already familiar, but tonight they tasted like dinner, the spicy harissa, the rare lamb, the sweetened coffee they had finished the meal with. Aidan turned his head to the right, and Liam nibbled at his lower lip, then moved to his chin. Every kiss, every bite, sent shivers through Aidan's body, directly to his dick.

The sky overhead was a magnificent canopy, more stars and constellations than Aidan had ever seen before. Liam pulled back and pointed out those that he knew, the ones he had learned to navigate by. To Aidan, they looked almost like 3-D, and he kept wanting to reach out and touch them. A shooting star blazed across the sky, and he knew he should make a wish—but at that moment, it seemed like he had everything he wanted.

Walking back toward the hotel, Liam gently pushed Aidan up against a rough stucco wall and kissed him again. The bodyguard's chin was rough, a five-o'clock shadow blossoming there and on his cheeks, but Aidan welcomed the sensation. The sandpaper feel of Liam's beard was an amazing counterpoint to the soft moistness of his lips.

Aidan's dick pressed against his pants, and as Liam pressed their bodies together, he could feel that Liam was hard too. "I could get used to this," Liam said in a whisper, right into Aidan's ear. In response, Aidan lifted his leg and wrapped it around Liam's butt, pulling him even closer.

"I think we'd better take this back to the room," Liam said. He backed away, and Aidan felt a moment of physical longing as their contact was released. He didn't want to wait to walk back to the hotel; he wanted to pull his clothes off, offer his naked body to Liam right there in this darkened alley, lit only by the stars above.

He'd never felt so much sexual abandon, not even in his younger days, traveling Europe and moving from job to job and guy to guy. He'd had plenty of sex, from a quick roll with a Polish laborer on the floor of a London squat to sucking an elderly Frenchman in the grand bedroom of a fabulous, high-ceilinged apartment just off the Champs-Elysées in Paris. He'd kissed men in the lavender fields of Provence, in the men's room of the Monte Carlo Casino. He'd been fucked by Yugoslavs, Italians, and Czechs; fucked the asses of Chinese political refugees and Nigerian street vendors.

It had all been fun, in retrospect, even the incidents that hadn't worked out so well, like the time in Brussels when a businessman's wife had surprised them in bed and chased Aidan, bare-assed but clutching his pants, down a long spiral staircase. He'd spent a night in a small country jail in a remote Swiss canton, been surprised by the jailer in the middle of the night as he sucked his cell mate, and been kicked back on to the street in outrage.

But none of it compared to the feeling he had with Liam. A single glance, the lightest touch, was enough to get him hard. It seemed like there was a continual wet spot in his boxers where his dick leaked against the fabric. When he had Liam in his arms, he never wanted to let go.

He scrambled to keep up with Liam's long strides through the darkened town, then as they navigated the hotel corridors back to their room. Once there, the moment had passed. While Aidan relaxed on the bed, Liam sat next to him, poring over a map of Tunisia. Aidan spent some time with his guidebook, discovering that the ksour were fortified adobe structures built by the Berbers to store their grain. Around eleven, Liam yawned. "Guess we should get some rest," he said.

"Really?" Aidan looked up at that sexy body as Liam stood next to the bed and peeled off his shirt and shorts. "That's what you want? Rest?"

Liam laughed. "You have something else in mind?"

"I could think of something."

Liam dropped his boxers and stood naked before Aidan. Aidan remembered seeing Liam showering behind the Bar Mamounia, and how he'd believed there was no way he could even touch a body so perfect—the beefy biceps and triceps, the six-pack abs, the narrow, tapered waist, the tree-trunk thighs. Liam's dick stiffened as Aidan watched, and Aidan scooted across the bed to take Liam in his mouth where he stood.

His dick tasted so good, filled Aidan's mouth, and banged against the back of his throat. He longed to grasp Liam's ass and pull him even closer, but his gag reflex was acting up, and he had to twine his fingers together in a trick he'd learned years before, to calm it. Liam seemed to be enjoying Aidan's actions; then suddenly he put his hands on Aidan's shoulders and said, "Don't move."

There was something strange in his tone, so menacing and unexpected in the middle of sex. Aidan stopped, Liam's dick in his mouth, and then Liam backed away very carefully.

"What...?" Aidan began as soon as his mouth was free.

"Ssh," Liam said, holding his finger to his lips. Slowly he turned and moved around the bed, behind Aidan. Disobeying his order not to move, Aidan twisted around on the bed to watch him, and then he saw it.

A scorpion clung to the wall, just about even with Aidan's head. He backed away as Liam picked up the guidebook and then, in a quick motion, slammed the book against the scorpion and the wall.

The loud *thwack* startled Aidan, even though he'd been expecting it, and he nearly fell off the side of the bed. Liam pulled back the guidebook, and the scorpion fell to the ground dead. Using his T-shirt, Liam picked it up and walked to the door of the room. Aidan got a great view of his tight butt, lightly dusted with light brown hair, as he looked out into the hallway.

Aidan saw him bend to the ground and felt a tremor of anticipation rush through his body. Liam was so damned gorgeous. They might only have one more night together, but Aidan was sure as hell going to make the most of it, scorpions or no. Regardless of what happened in Tataouine or Remada or even back in Tunis, Liam McCullough was his for the time being.

Liam dropped the dead scorpion outside the door as if it were a used room-service tray, and then shook out his T-shirt. He turned back to Aidan, closing the door behind him.

Liam's erection was gone, but Aidan knew he could make it come back. He stood and slowly lifted his T-shirt off above his head, exposing his flat abs, dusted with fine dark hair. He heard Liam catch his breath.

Looking directly into Liam's eyes, Aidan unbuckled his belt and unfastened his shorts and let them drop to the floor. He was already barefoot, so all he was left wearing was his boxers, and his stiff dick was tenting them. Liam reached across, putting one hand on each side of Aidan's waist, pushing the boxers down as they kissed.

Both of them were fully hard by then. Aidan resisted the urge to fall into Liam's arms, instead maneuvering his hips so that his dick slapped against Liam's. "That's the way you want to play it?" Liam said, his voice husky.

It became a sword fight, each of them slapping at the other. Liam grabbed his dick at the root and swung it against Aidan, and they battled until Liam couldn't resist any longer. He grabbed Aidan and pressed him close, lowering his head so they could kiss as they embraced.

Aidan's pulse raced at the heat Liam's body threw off. He loved the way his chest hair feathered against Liam's smooth skin, the way his hands fastened onto Liam's shoulder blades.

He pressed against Liam so hard, it was like he hoped they could meld into one being.

"I want you inside me." Aidan panted into Liam's chest. "Oh God, I want you in me so bad."

Liam took hold of Aidan's shoulders and turned him around so that Aidan faced the stone wall. Aidan spread his legs, reached out to the wall, and pressed his cheek to the cold stone. "You're lucky I was a Boy Scout back in Jersey."

"Always prepared?" Aidan asked.

"You bet. Our troop leader was my friend Barry's uncle, and he gave us all kinds of useful advice. Like always have a condom on you, because you never know when you'll get lucky."

"Are you lucky tonight?"

"Oh yeah," Liam said as Aidan heard a spurt of lube and felt Liam's finger, cold and wet, snake into his ass. "And so are you."

Liam kissed Aidan's back, from shoulder blade to shoulder blade, as his index finger explored Aidan's ass. Aidan was lost in the sensation, loving the contact between their bodies. He'd never felt this sense so strongly before, wanting another man inside him, wanting them to be so connected.

"Take a deep breath," Liam said, kissing Aidan's neck and using his hands to spread Aidan's ass cheeks wide.

The pain shot through Aidan's body as Liam's dick entered him. He couldn't help crying out. Blake thought anal sex was too messy, so they'd hardly done it over their ten-plus years together, no matter how much Aidan had longed for it. And Blake's dick had been slimmer than Liam's, and shorter too.

"Sorry," Liam said. "I don't want to hurt you."

Aidan gritted his teeth and bucked back against Liam. "Oh God, just fuck me, please."

The pain turned to fire as Liam moved slowly in and out of Aidan's ass. He felt the head of Liam's dick banging against his prostate, and he began to pant and sweat. He pushed back from the wall, Liam inside him, and then turned to the bed. Liam's dick popped out as Aidan knelt on the bed, raising his butt in offering.

"That is such a sweet ass," Liam said. He followed Aidan, kneeling behind him on the bed. Holding his dick, he aimed it at Aidan's hole and bucked into him. He was sweating too, a fine sheen covering his body as his chest heaved.

As good as it felt, Aidan thought it could be better. "No, it's still not right," he said. "I want to be able to look at you."

He pulled away from Liam, feeling a momentary pang of emptiness as Liam's dick left his ass, and sat back on the bed. He leaned far back against the pillows and opened his legs wide, pulling them back toward his shoulders. "Now," he said. "Come fuck me."

"With pleasure," Liam said, and he knelt down on the bed in front of Aidan, guiding his dick back toward Aidan's ass. It took a minute to get the position and the rhythm right, and then their eyes were locked together as Liam pistoned into Aidan's ass.

Both of them were panting heavily as Liam grabbed Aidan's dick and started jerking it, timing his strokes to the movement of his dick in Aidan's ass. Then Liam couldn't hold out any longer, and he howled as his ejaculation shook his body.

The pressure pushed Aidan over the edge as well, and he shot ribbons of cum into Liam's fist. Aidan grabbed Liam's shoulders and pulled him down.

"I'm too heavy for you," Liam protested, trying to back away.

"You're just right," Aidan said, pressing down to keep Liam in place. "This is just right."

Checkpoint

Wednesday morning, Aidan awoke with a piss hard-on and tried to creep out of the bed without disturbing Liam. "Where are you going?" Liam asked, grabbing his leg with a strong hand. Then the fingers of that hand moved up Aidan's leg, tickling his thigh and dancing across his groin.

He pulled Aidan toward him, taking Aidan's stiff dick in his mouth, and Aidan's body was racked with exquisite torture. The piss-proud dick didn't want to give up its load, and Aidan writhed and gasped until Liam pulled off. "You've got me hard now too," he said. "Where's the bathroom in this place?"

They grabbed shorts, and Aidan led the way back to the toilet he'd found the night before. There was just the one, so they shared, standing next to each other and aiming their streams into a trough along the floor. It was a sensual pain, forcing the urine out of their stiff dicks, and as they were finishing, Liam leaned over and kissed Aidan.

Aidan had made love in better places, and worse, but right then he wanted to be nowhere else than in that rudimentary stone bathroom. He leaned down to suck on Liam's nipple, and the bodyguard arched his back and moaned. "We shouldn't." He gasped. "Anyone could…"

Aidan ignored his protests. He spit in his hand and reached into Liam's shorts. As he sucked the big man's nipples, he jerked his cock. "You are such a bad boy." Liam panted, but he did nothing to stop Aidan. "I'm going to have to punish you."

"Really?" Aidan pulled back from sucking, retreated his hand from Liam's shorts. "How?"

"Oh God, don't stop," Liam said.

"Talk to me, then," Aidan said, grabbing Liam's dick, slick with saliva and precum. "Tell me what you want to do to me."

He bent back to Liam's nipple again. "I should take you over my knee," Liam said, gasping between words. "Smack that beautiful ass of yours until it's red. Then smother it with cream and pry apart those round, ruby-colored cheeks so I can fuck you..." He gulped as Aidan bit his nipple. "Fuck you till you scream."

With a strangled cry, Liam shot off in Aidan's hand.

Aidan backed away at last. "I might just take you up on that," he said. Despite the pressure of his dick, stiff to the point of aching, he backed away, then slid out the door of the restroom.

The shower was in the small room next door to the toilet—a nozzle stuck out from the wall, with a drain in the floor. Aidan was standing under the flow, soaping himself, when the door opened and Liam slid in. "I thought I locked that," Aidan said.

"Like a lock can keep me out," Liam said. He was naked but for a towel wrapped around his midsection. Liam reached down to Aidan's belly and grabbed a handful of lather, which he transferred to Aidan's dick. "You're not the only one who can take charge around here," he said, leaning down to kiss Aidan.

He kept his mouth fastened firmly on Aidan's as he rubbed his hand up and down the length of Aidan's dick. It didn't take long before Aidan's dick was spurting cum just a shade darker than the soapy lather around it.

They finished their shower, then breakfasted on sugar crepes in the restaurant of the Hotel Sidi Driss. As Aidan was checking out, Abbas slipped him a piece of paper with four words in Roman script and what he assumed were the same words in Arabic script. "If you need help in Tataouine," he said. "My cousin Nailah, she will help you."

Aidan thanked him. He wanted to say something—that there was a larger world out there, that there were places where Abbas could live more openly—but Liam was waiting impatiently at the front door, and all Aidan could do was smile and tell Abbas to be happy. He stuffed the paper in the pocket of his Windbreaker and forgot about it as he hurried toward Liam.

The other passengers on the tour had begun to look familiar, and many of them greeted Aidan as he got on the bus. A few minutes later they pulled out for the road to Medenine, where they would make a turn south to Tataouine. The Medenine road led farther east to Tripoli, Libya, and Aidan was reminded of how close the border was, just a couple of hours away.

That reminded him of the Libyan intelligence agent who had attacked them in the souk and chased them in El Jem. Where was he? Would he be able to pick up their trail?

Looking out at the expanse of sand and scrub, it wasn't surprising that the tribes could cross these borders so easily. And that meant that the Libyan and his thugs could do the same.

The Tuareg tribe was out there somewhere, waiting to meet with Aidan and Liam and get access to the bank account that would provide them with a permanent home, schools, and computers, and other things they would need to succeed in the twenty-first century. And once they delivered the information to them, Liam and Aidan would return to Tunis.

Aidan didn't want to think that far ahead. He looked outside the bus window, reminding himself once again that this was an adventure, that there was a whole world out there to appreciate.

The road was lined with kiosks selling plastic jugs of cheap Libyan gasoline or hanging freshly slaughtered sheep on ceiling hooks. The horizon stretched on for miles, the sky a cloudless light blue. There was not a hint of a breeze to ruffle the fronds of the occasional date palm or the leaves of a wizened olive tree.

Farther south, they reached a police checkpoint. A single officer stood in the middle of the highway, waving the bus to the side of the road. He boarded the bus, speaking with Belghasem and reviewing his paperwork.

Liam was on alert. "If he compares our passports to the names on that list, we're in trouble," he said in a low voice. "Do you still have Carlucci's passport?"

"I do. But it's in a hidden compartment in my backpack," Aidan said. "I don't think they'd be able to find it, even if they searched."

"You ever been searched by the police?"

"Yup."

He looked at Aidan. "I want to hear about that. Later."

In the meantime, the guard and Belghasem were arguing in Arabic, but Liam and Aidan were too far back in the bus for Liam to eavesdrop. Finally Belghasem shrugged and motioned to all the passengers. "You will all please to get off the bus," he said. "So that this police officer may talk with you. Please to have your passports available."

"Do you think the police know our names?" Aidan asked Liam.

He shrugged. "Hard to say." Aidan saw him surveying the area carefully, but beyond the checkpoint were miles of empty desert. There was nowhere to go, even if they could cause enough of a distraction to slip away from the police officer.

There were twenty passengers in all; Aidan had plenty of time to count as they huddled in the small shade offered by the bus. Liam and Aidan were the youngest, though there were a few couples in their forties. Most of their fellow passengers were older, probably late fifties or sixties. The women outnumbered the men. They didn't seem to know each other, so it was probably a group tour organized out of Tunis rather than one that had come from the States.

Only about half were American; the rest were either French, German, or Australian. They spent the next ten minutes or so waiting as the officer went from person to person, examining documents and comparing them to what Belghasem had given him.

"What should we do?" Aidan whispered to Liam. "If he doesn't find our names on that list?"

Liam shrugged. "There's nothing that we can do now. We see what happens. Worst case, he calls someone to take us back to Tunis, and we figure out what to do from there."

That wasn't the kind of news that either reassured Aidan or helped his heart rate return to normal. Sweat began to drip from his forehead and pool under his arms. It was sweltering, even in the shade of the bus and even though it was still relatively early in the morning. There was no breeze, and the only movement of air came from an older American woman fanning herself with a paper flyer.

"It is not to worry," Belghasem said to the group. "This police is concerned about your safety. We will be continuing to the ksour very soon."

When the officer finally came to them, Aidan smiled and handed the officer his passport, as he'd seen everyone else do. The officer scanned it, flipping through the pages, which were mostly empty. Blake and Aidan had taken a couple of overseas trips, mostly to England or the Bahamas. Aidan wasn't worried about what the policeman would see there—he was worried that the officer wouldn't be able to match the name on the passport to one on his list.

And yet he did. Aidan saw him make a check at the bottom of his page, and he handed the passport back.

As the officer moved on to Liam, Aidan got a glance at the list. Sure enough, his name and Liam's had been handwritten at the bottom of the page. By Belghasem? He must have gotten the names from the desk clerk. Somehow, Abbas and Belghasem were working together to help them. Aidan didn't understand what was going on, but he felt better.

Aidan was still worried about Liam. Even if he didn't call himself a soldier of fortune or a mercenary, it was possible that the Tunisian government saw him that way. In any case, he was an American living in Tunis, and that was curious enough on its own to warrant additional scrutiny.

The other passengers stirred restlessly. It was so hot, and they were all eager to get back into the air-conditioned bus. There wasn't even anything to look at, just miles of empty desert.

Liam stood impassively as the officer reviewed his passport. The officer said something in Arabic, and Liam shrugged. "I'm sorry. I don't understand," he said.

That was curious. Aidan knew that Liam spoke Arabic; he'd heard him use it enough times. "You live Tunis?" the officer asked in English.

Liam nodded.

It was clear the officer wanted to ask Liam more questions, but the language barrier was frustrating him. For a moment Aidan thought the officer might enlist Belghasem as an interpreter, but he shrugged and handed the passport back to Liam.

Belghasem smiled broadly and said, "We may now continue. Everyone back on the bus, please."

Aidan waited until he and Liam were back in their seats and the bus had started off again before he said anything. The air-conditioning was a blessed relief after the heat of the desert, and Aidan fanned himself and said in a low voice, "Our names were on the bottom of his list."

"I noticed," Liam said. "Curious."

"Abbas must have done it," Aidan said. "He's the only one who saw our passports at the hotel."

"Guess your flirting paid off," Liam said and grinned.

Ksar Ouled Soltane

"So now, tell me about being searched by the police," Liam said as the bus rolled forward.

Aidan shrugged. "It was nothing, though it was scary at the time. I was traveling in France with my friend Alex, right after college. We both had ESL jobs lined up in Nice, and we thought we'd see the country first. So we bought France Rail passes in Paris and took off."

He looked out the window, remembering that summer. He'd had a massive crush on Alex, who was straight, and he'd spent three weeks in close quarters with the guy, trying not to betray the fact that he had a constant hard-on. "Alex had done a semester abroad at the University of Grenoble, at the edge of the Alps, so we stopped there on our way south."

"I know Grenoble. I spent a couple of weeks there, tailing a guy we thought was a terrorist."

"Was he?"

Liam shook his head. "Nope. But we didn't know that until we'd watched him for a while." He poked Aidan in the side. "Get back to your story."

"We stayed with this guy named Jean-Pierre, in an apartment in this little town called St. Martin d'Heres. We were running short on cash at that point, and he had a scam we played into. We went to this doctor and said that we'd lost our prescription for sleeping pills, and he wrote one out for each of us."

"Let me guess. Quaaludes?"

Aidan nodded. "Jean-Pierre sold them to other college kids by the pill. Alex and I each pocketed a couple hundred bucks, and we were about to leave for Nice when the police swooped in."

"Ouch."

"Yeah, I said that a couple of times during the cavity search," Aidan said drily. "Like I would have stuffed pills up my butt for safekeeping."

Liam laughed. "And I thought you liked guys poking around up there."

Aidan gave him a look that tried to be a frown but ended up in a smile. "Only certain guys." He couldn't help laughing. "Fortunately there wasn't anything on the premises, so they let us leave."

Once in Nice, Aidan had found a French boyfriend, and he'd distanced himself from Alex, who had set himself up in a flourishing little business, recruiting American tourists to get him pills and then sending them up to Jean-Pierre in Grenoble for sale, until he was arrested and deported six months later.

They looked out the bus window as they passed through Tataouine on the way to Ksar Ouled Soltane. As they drove, Belghasem lectured, telling them that ksar was the singular, and ksour the plural. He pointed out several ksour, which looked like ruined forts on the sides of hills and mountains.

The Berbers built them around former strongholds known as *ka'ala*, which they used to protect themselves and their foodstuffs from marauders.

Aidan's heart was light when they got off the bus at Ksar Ouled Soltane. He was in an exotic country, sightseeing on a gorgeous day with a handsome, charming man, and over the last few days he'd had the best sex of his life. What was not to be happy about? They had eluded the Libyans at the souk and the pharmacy. Soon they would meet up with a Tuareg tribe and deliver them a precious gift. The world was full of joy.

The first courtyard reminded Aidan of the adobe villages outside Taos, New Mexico. Ksar Ouled Soltane had the same color of dried mud, the same arched doorways and staircases. Trailing off the bus, they followed Belghasem around the corner, then down an alleyway into a remarkable adobe courtyard. To the left and right were vaulted *ghorfas*—grain storage areas—stacked two or three on top of each other. Adobe stairs suspended in midair led up to each ghorfa, while wood beams jutted out at the highest levels, allowing villagers to bring up goods on pulleys.

The group followed the perimeter of the ksar, admiring the workmanship of the ghorfas and their accompanying stairs. Belghasem told them that this ksar was over five hundred years old; despite being abandoned, it was in remarkable condition.

Liam and Aidan walked up the stairs on different ghorfas, trying to get a better view of the ones across from them. "You're enjoying yourself, aren't you?" Liam asked.

"You bet. This place is phenomenal."

"I'm glad you came along with me. When I'm on a job, I'm focused on my objective. I can't afford the distractions. I've been in this country for nearly three years, and I've never seen it like a tourist."

They had a beautiful view of the rough, barren countryside. The ksar was located on a hillside, so they could see anyone approaching the granary from miles around. Several tour buses and taxis huddled around the entrance.

As Liam scanned the area, Aidan watched a young couple get out of a taxi. There was no reason why he should recognize them; they were Arab, and the woman wore a filmy veil over her head and shoulders. But something about the man was familiar; the way he held himself reminded Aidan of someone.

He racked his brain trying to figure it out. Someone from Tunis? From the hotel in Matmata? A man Liam might have spoken with in the town? Aidan said, "See that couple down there? Do they look familiar to you?"

Liam was instantly alert, which impressed Aidan. "There is something about them," Liam said. "Not the woman, but the man." He shrugged. "We're too far away to see much, but we'll keep an eye out for them."

Belghasem led most of the group off through a passageway into another courtyard behind a small group of Italian tourists; Liam and Aidan soon followed. Inside was another plaza of ghorfas, but much more spectacular. They were stacked four levels high, dozens of them, with each side of the plaza at least one hundred feet long. It was quite a sight. The Italian tourists were having tea at a small café as a thin young man sold drawings of the ksar.

Liam began speaking in Arabic with the young man, translating for Aidan. The man's name was Ziyad, and he was from the village but hadn't been allowed in the ksar when he was a child because it was reserved as a meeting space for adult members of the tribe. They gathered in the ksar once a week to discuss community members and socialize. Once he was older, he was allowed to set up his small shop selling snacks, trinkets, and artwork.

Aidan was only half following the conversation, killing time until they were ready to return to the bus. He looked across the long plaza and saw the young couple from the taxi enter. They were laughing and holding hands, and Aidan was pleased for them. Probably honeymooners, and he remembered the way Liam had held him the night before after he'd dispensed with the scorpion.

There had been such tenderness and passion in his touch. After they had spent themselves, Liam had talked about what it was like to be gay in the military. "*An extra level of vigilance,*" he'd said. "*I couldn't let anyone get to know me because I had such a big secret to keep.*"

Maybe that was the source of his distance, Aidan thought. After spending so much time with Liam, under such stressful circumstances, Aidan felt he'd told him everything about himself that there was to know, and yet Aidan hardly knew anything about Liam beyond some basic facts. Would he ever get the bodyguard to open up? Aidan wondered if perhaps Liam knew how limited their time together was going to be, and was determined to avoid being hurt.

After Liam dozed off, Aidan had wondered about that. Liam was such a big, strong man, and yet Aidan could tell that there was something vulnerable deep inside him. Aidan looked over at him with affection and then saw the young couple once again, this time close enough that he could see the man's face.

It was the pharmacist's assistant from El Jem. He didn't appear to have recognized them, so Aidan turned his face away and leaned forward to Liam, who was laughing about something with the art seller. Aidan whispered, "That couple we saw getting out of the taxi. They're just behind us."

Aidan felt Liam stiffen, as if his senses had all gone on alert. "Do you recognize them?" he asked in a similar whisper.

"The man was behind the pharmacist's counter in El Jem," Aidan said. "He chased us with the Libyan man."

"How the hell could they have tracked us?" Liam stole a glance over Aidan's shoulder. "You're right," he said. "I don't know the woman, but that's one of the guys we saw out of the bus window. You think they realized we were on that bus?"

"I don't know. Could it be a coincidence?"

"Whatever it is, we've got to get out of here," he said.

Hookah Hookup

Aidan watched the young couple as they walked past. The man who had pretended to be the assistant pharmacist kept stealing glances at them, so he knew that he and Liam had been recognized. His pulse began to race, and his throat dried up. His quiet life in Philadelphia started to look pretty good.

When the older man from the souk had passed the bus in El Jem, Aidan had looked out the window and seen his face. He had looked implacable, like he would continue to hunt them down until he caught them. And now here was that other man, following them into the ksar.

Aidan looked at Liam. The bodyguard was on full alert, and that scared Aidan more than anything. He could see the soldier in Liam—and that reminded him just how ill-prepared he was for anything military. He hadn't even been a Boy Scout, as Liam had.

Belghasem stood up. "My group, you will come back to the bus now, please."

Aidan knew that they had to do something to distract the couple so that they couldn't see where he and Liam went or whom they were with. Around them, several passengers got up. A nice woman from Pennsylvania thanked Ziyad, who had sold her a drawing of the ksar. That inspired Aidan.

"Ask Ziyad to keep that couple busy," he whispered to Liam. "Then we can sneak back to the bus without them seeing."

"Good idea." Liam turned back to the young man and said something in Arabic. Ziyad smiled, and Liam gave him a few dinars. Then Ziyad got up and walked over to the young couple, offering to show them his paintings, and while they were occupied, Aidan and Liam stood and hurried back the way they had come. It wasn't until they were safely in the bus that Aidan realized he was sweating madly.

Liam was still on alert, watching the exterior of the ksar until the driver closed the bus door and pulled out. Aidan saw him looking back, trying to determine if the couple had come out to watch them depart, or if the older man was lurking somewhere on the grounds.

Aidan settled into his seat, sweat dripping from his forehead and under his arms. He didn't know how many more of those narrow escapes he could survive. "How could they have tracked us? I thought we dumped them in El Jem."

Liam shrugged. "They know we're heading south. It was likely that we'd show up somewhere along the route. We don't know how many places they've staked out where they've missed us."

"We haven't seen the girl before, have we?" Aidan asked.

"Don't think so. She could be a local they picked up for camouflage."

"So what do we do?"

"Hope we stay lucky." Liam tugged on the brim of his ball cap.

Aidan was staring out the window, wondering what that meant, when he saw a brown cloud on the horizon. "At least we'll get some rain," he said to Liam, motioning outside. "See that cloud?"

"That's a sandstorm."

Aidan watched in fascination. One minute he was looking across the dunes, the ksar receding in the background, and the next they were engulfed in swirling sand. The driver pulled the bus over, and Belghasem said, "Sandstorm will pass quickly. Please to stay in your seats."

"I'm glad we're not out in that," Aidan said, nodding his head toward the window.

"We may end up in one like it," Liam said. "The desert's a dangerous place, in more ways than one."

Not the kind of reassuring words Aidan needed to hear then. The sound of the sand pelting against the metal of the bus was worse than any hailstorm Aidan had heard back in Philadelphia, and he could even feel some fine sand flying around the inside of the bus. He put his hand over his mouth to avoid breathing it in. He felt comforted, being protected inside, next to Liam.

The storm passed, and after a short drive, they arrived at the Hotel La Gazelle in Tataouine. It wasn't four-star, but it was less rustic than the Hotel Sidi Driss and had en suite bathrooms. Aidan hoped the room was scorpion free, but then again, it was still Tunisia.

The lobby was decorated with the beautiful tiles Aidan had seen throughout Tunisia, and he wondered if he would be able find a shop that sold them and take a few home with him. Then he remembered that he didn't have a home to go to.

The desk clerk wasn't as gay-aware as Abbas had been, and he slotted them into a room with two narrow twin beds. Aidan wasn't going to argue the point.

"We need to be extra careful," Liam said as they sat down to dinner in the hotel restaurant. There was a "tourist menu," but Liam insisted on ordering à la carte, rattling off a list of dishes in Arabic. When the waiter had left, he continued. "We're going to have to rent a taxi tomorrow to keep going south. According to the map, it's about eighty kilometers to Remada, but I'm hoping that the taxi drivers are accustomed to Americans with a lot of cash to throw around."

As they ate, Aidan reconsidered his decision to accompany Liam all the way to the meeting with the Tuareg. Seeing the pharmacist's assistant at the ksar had really spooked him. Was continuing the trip a foolish idea? Was he ignoring the danger just to stay around Liam, because he was handsome and charming and great in bed?

Liam must have known what Aidan was feeling, because he said, "You can stay with the tour if you want. Belghasem will look after you, and you'll get back to Tunis in a couple of days. You can stay in my house behind the bar until I get back."

Aidan thought about everything they had been through. Was he a handicap to Liam—someone who might slow him down? Aidan didn't think so. He'd recognized the pharmacist's assistant. He'd had some good ideas. Liam was strong and resourceful, and Aidan was sure he could manage on his own. True, Aidan wasn't a trained soldier. He didn't speak Arabic, and he didn't have Liam's strength or grace.

But he had proved to himself over the past few days that he could keep his head in a crisis, that he could think fast and react instinctively. And despite the danger they had gone through, he felt like he'd crammed more living into the past few days than he had in all the years he'd spent with Blake. And he felt a more powerful attraction to Liam than any he'd ever felt before.

He didn't want to walk away, face the chance of losing Liam and losing this rediscovered sense of what he could do. He wanted to stay with Liam and help him. "I'd like to keep going," he said. "As long as you feel I won't get in the way."

"Aidan." Liam looked at him. "I'm not Blake. You're never going to be in the way when you're around me. But it could get dangerous. We're up against a guy who has some significant resources. We don't know what else he's capable of."

"Let's see. He's capable of shooting Charles Carlucci and attacking us in the souk. He's capable of following us this far. I'd say that gives us a pretty good place to start."

Liam laughed. "I have never met anyone like you, Aidan. On the outside, you seem like such a lightweight—you know how to cook and arrange flowers; you look like you read the *New Yorker* and have your shirts custom made. But underneath that very attractive facade, there's a smart guy with a wild heart. Why do you keep that covered up?"

"Maybe because it's never been valued before." Aidan smiled. "So, on to Remada tomorrow."

After the meal was over, Liam ordered them each a hookah. "I haven't used one of these since college," Aidan said, looking at the glass pipe and its accompanying hose.

"It isn't intoxicating. It's a mix of tobacco and herbs. Very relaxing."

"I suppose we could both do with a little relaxation."

Others around them were smoking, and the atmosphere in the little restaurant was close and convivial. Aidan felt a pleasant sensation rising in his stomach, snaking trails through his brain. With those sensations came a heightened sense of touch, so that when Liam's leg brushed against his, an electric jolt went right to his groin.

He could tell from Liam's lazy smile that he felt it too. "Shame there are two beds in the room," Liam said.

"We can push them together." Aidan stood up. "The sooner the better."

They raced up the stairs to their room, taking them two at a time, laughing and knocking against each other. Once inside the door, Liam took Aidan's hand and pulled him close. They kissed without the frantic urgency they'd felt before, taking their time. Aidan explored Liam's mouth with his tongue—the hard surface of his teeth, the slight roughness of Liam's tongue, feeling no urgency, just this overwhelming desire to know everything about Liam he could.

Liam pulled him down onto one of the single beds, lying on his back fully clothed, like a country ready to be explored.

Aidan leaned over him, nibbling Liam's full, bee-stung lips, licking his tongue along the edge of Liam's chin. Liam simply looked up at him with a beatific grin.

Aidan would be the first to admit he wasn't the most dominant man in bed; he could reply with passion when passion was offered, but he usually preferred a strong man to set the pace. That was one of the most erotic things about Liam; he set the erotic agenda and swept Aidan along with him.

But the hookah had changed him from master to servant; he was more relaxed than Aidan had ever seen him, the most happy, submissive bottom. The change took Aidan by surprise, but once he'd figured it out, he took it as his own challenge—to rise to the occasion, top this sexy Adonis until he drowned in the same passion Aidan felt.

Sitting back, his legs on either side of Liam's body, Aidan unbuttoned the bodyguard's shirt and slipped it to the side. He cupped Liam's pecs in his hands, weighing them, then leaned down to take the right nipple in his mouth. Liam groaned as Aidan nibbled and bit the sensitive nub. Aidan felt so strong and powerful then, knowing he had the big man totally under his control.

He toyed with the other nipple for a while, then kissed and licked his way down Liam's chest, taking his time. He licked the treasure trail of light brown hair that led from Liam's pecs down to his belly button as Liam ran his hands through Aidan's hair, petting him, eyes glazed with lust and affection.

Feeling like he was moving in slow motion, Aidan unbuttoned Liam's shorts and spread them open. He wore

another of the jockstraps that drove Aidan crazy, and his stiff
dick angled up against the ribbed white fabric. He buried his
face next to Liam's dick, licking at the edges of the pouch, his
tongue snaking under the fabric to tease Liam's sensitive
groin.

Liam thrust his hips up, trying to get his dick toward
Aidan's mouth, but Aidan ignored it, pushing down Liam's
shorts so that he could lick and kiss the big man's thighs.
"You're killing me." Liam groaned.

Aidan said nothing, just looked up and smiled. He traced
one lazy finger over Liam's hips, and he giggled. "That
tickles," Liam said, squirming under Aidan. He reached up to
unbutton Aidan's shirt, but Aidan swatted his hands away.
"I'm in charge here," he said, and Liam laughed.

"You think that's funny?" he said, backing away. He
stepped back off the bed, leaving Liam lying there half-
dressed, like a lust-choked odalisque in the harem of a gay
sultan. He began a slow, seductive striptease, undoing his
shirt one button at a time, sliding it off his shoulder, then
replacing it. Liam reached up toward him, but Aidan stayed
where he was, swaying gently to an unheard rhythm.

He slipped the shirt off, twirled it on one finger, then
whipped it toward the empty bed. He didn't know where
this persona had come from, this sexual tease, but he loved it.
He undid the top button of his shorts, let them slip a bit
down on his hips, thrusting forward. His dick was so stiff, it
hurt, pressing against the fabric, but he held back from
dropping them, rotating his hips as if he were in a nightclub,
throwing his head back and closing his eyes, just feeling the
rhythm and the sense of anticipation.

"Aidan," Liam said, and it was almost a whimper. "I miss you."

Aidan opened his eyes and smiled. Liam had shucked down his shorts and slid away his shirt so that he lay there nearly naked on the bed, only the white jockstrap against his golden skin. Aidan undid the last buttons holding his shorts in place, and they slipped to the floor, leaving him only in his boxers.

The ones he'd chosen that morning had a pattern of palm trees—a design he'd always found so phallic, the stiff trunks and the cluster of coconuts just under the fronds like a dick with nuts clustered under a thatch of pubic hair. He put his hands on his hips and thrust forward a few times, then turned around, dropping his waistband and teasing Liam with glimpses of his ass and crack.

"If you don't get over here, I'm going to blow my load without even touching myself," Liam warned in a throaty growl.

Aidan turned back to him, slid his shorts to the floor, and jumped back onto the bed, attacking Liam's throat with kisses as his stiff dick banged against Liam's belly. He worked his way back down Liam's chest, faster this time, pushing aside the jockstrap and teasing down the cowl of Liam's uncircumcised dick.

Liam whimpered, and Aidan bobbed up and down on his dick for a moment, then pulled back. "What?" Liam asked. "Why did you stop?"

"Just messing with you," Aidan said, grinning. He turned sideways so that his dick was at Liam's mouth and groaned himself as Liam slid his lips around the mushroom tip. Aidan felt like the fog around him had cleared as he sucked Liam's dick, moving faster and faster.

Liam groaned, and Aidan slowed down, licking Liam's dick, nibbling at his cowl, teasing the tip of Liam's dick with his tongue.

Liam worked on him at the same time. He went all the way down on Aidan's dick, then pulled slowly back off, sucking deeply. He nosed into Aidan's pubic hair, and Aidan giggled. "What?" Liam asked, pulling off for second.

"That tickles," Aidan said, letting Liam's dick slide out of his mouth. He grabbed Liam's ass, inching his index finger around the hole, and felt Liam's body clench, then relax. He eased more of his finger in, continuing to suck.

Liam shot off first, his body convulsing, a few tiny whimpers escaping from his mouth, which was still full of Aidan's dick. Aidan let Liam's dick slide out of his mouth and then focused on fucking Liam's face, bucking his ass in and out as if he were possessed. Sweat dripped down his forehead, and he howled as the force of his orgasm shook him.

Liam held him in place, cleaning Aidan's dick with his tongue. It was so sensitive by then that each swipe of Liam's tongue was an exquisite torture—he couldn't stand it, but he couldn't stand for it to stop either.

Aidan turned himself around once again so that he could rest his head on Liam's chest, and Liam wrapped one big arm around him. They drifted off to sleep.

Leaving Tataouine

When Aidan woke the next morning, Liam was already up, his reading glasses perched on his nose, and he was poring over the map and the guidebook. "It says here that the only way to Remada is by car or truck," he said. "The taxis only go back and forth to the ksour."

Aidan sat up in bed, yawned, and stretched. "So what do we do?"

"I'm not sure. The tour group is going north, so we can't stay with them. We'll look for a taxi driver who's willing to make some extra money."

They ate breakfast in the hotel restaurant, and Liam told Belghasem that they would not be continuing with the group. "You will be careful?" he asked. "The desert is dangerous place for those who do not know it."

"We'll try," Liam said.

They packed their bags and took them up to the roof of the hotel to watch the bus depart. Brisk gusts blew sand at them, and Aidan put on his Windbreaker. From there, they had a broad view of the city and the highway north. Before the bus had traveled more than a few blocks, a police car pulled out behind it with sirens and flashing lights.

"Something's up." Liam pointed a few blocks in the other direction, where another bus had been pulled over. "That Libyan agent has some clout. I'll bet they're stopping every bus out of town."

"Good thing we're not on one."

"But we're still here," Liam said. "If they're stopping buses, they may be stopping taxis and searching hotels too."

"There's one thing that bothers me." Aidan leaned back against a parapet. "If this Libyan guy has so much clout with the police, why didn't he just get them to arrest Carlucci? They didn't have to shoot him down on the street."

"Because the Libyan must be after the money," Liam said. "I don't know what he's got on Desrosiers, the police captain, to get all this help. Maybe he's promised him a cut."

Aidan shivered and put his hands in the pockets of his Windbreaker, where he found the piece of paper Abbas had given him as they checked out of the Hotel Sidi Driss. "Oh. Abbas gave me this—it's the name of his cousin."

He handed Liam the paper.

Liam scanned it. "We need to find this Nailah. This word, *soora*. It means picture. And *hina* means here."

"Could she be a photographer?" Aidan asked. "Someone who takes pictures?"

Liam pulled a tiny pair of binoculars from his duffel and surveyed the area. He'd looked about three-quarters of the way around when he said, "There. A photography shop." He pointed down an alley.

"I'll take your word for it. Let's give it a try."

Aidan followed Liam down the stairs and out the hotel's back door, where they paused as Liam surveyed the alley. It was empty except for a couple of bags of trash and a pair of feral cats skulking past.

They paused once again where the alley met the main street. A dark-skinned police officer in black slacks and a robin's egg blue shirt stood at the hotel entrance. His white gloves hung from his utility belt along with a white leather holster from which a pistol's grip protruded. He wore a black tie, with black epaulets at his shoulders.

The officer looked at his watch, then continued down the street. "Coffee break," Aidan whispered, watching him step into a storefront café.

"If they're checking all the hotels, they'll find us pretty quickly," Liam said. He pointed down the street. "There's the photo shop. We'd better hustle while the cop is still in that café."

Liam looked left and right. There were a few people on the street, but none seemed to be paying attention to them or the store. They hurried down the block and across the street. As he struggled to keep pace with Liam, Aidan scanned the street. Was the young couple out there somewhere, looking for them? The Libyan agent? Knowing that their pursuers had the power of the police at their disposal made things that much more dangerous—there was no chance that they could look to the police for help.

The dusty shop window announced that cameras were repaired, film sold, and photos developed. A new sign even promised you could download photos from your digital camera and print them there.

Liam opened the door, and they ducked into the shop, where a tiny young woman stood behind the counter. She wore a T-shirt with the name of an American band, Vampire Weekend, and her ears had been pierced in multiple places. She had a puffy cap on her head and looked like she'd have fit in just fine in New York's East Village. "Good morning," she said in barely accented English. "How can I help you?"

Liam looked at Aidan. "We're looking for Nailah," Aidan said. "Her cousin Abbas sent us."

"You know my cousin?"

"We stayed at the Hotel Sidi Driss the night before last," Aidan said. "He gave me this paper with your name on it."

He showed it to her. She read it, then looked up at them and smiled. Aidan realized that perhaps the Arabic wasn't exactly a translation of what Abbas had written in Roman script.

"You are in danger?" she asked, her attitude turning businesslike. "How can I help you?"

"We need to get to Remada," Liam said. "But there are roadblocks, and they are stopping buses and taxis."

She thought for a moment. "They are looking for you? Two American men?"

They both nodded.

Then she smiled again. "I have a solution for you."

Motorcycle Matters

"You say the police are looking for two American men," Nailah said, leading them into the back of the shop. "But they will not notice a Tunisian man and a woman in a burka."

Aidan started to protest. He didn't do drag. He never had. In the first place, he was too hairy, down to his fingers and toes, to ever pass as a woman without a lot of painful hair removal. In the second place, it had never appealed to him. He didn't want to be a woman, and he didn't want to dress like one.

But he did want to get out of Tataouine and get that account number to the Tuareg tribe, who would use the money for schools and health care. "Since I doubt they have women as tall as you in this country, I guess that puts me in the dress," he said to Liam.

"I'm sure you'll look lovely," he said.

"That is not the point," Nailah said. She handed Aidan what looked like a polyester funeral shroud, though it was a hideous shade of light blue, brassier than the color of the iron railings in Tunis, darker than the policeman's shirt. "You may have to, how you say, bend down."

She gave Liam a cloak like the ones they had seen men wearing in Matmata and a scarf he could wind around his head. With Nailah's help, Aidan climbed into the burka. She was so tiny that she had to step onto a stool to reach his head. The inside of the burka was claustrophobic, just a narrow slot for his eyes and a filmy veil over his nose and mouth.

It was oddly comforting at first, reminding Aidan of hiding under the covers as a kid with a book and a flashlight. But as he experimented walking around, he realized he had no peripheral vision. He kept catching the voluminous cloth on doorknobs and the edges of cabinets, and Nailah criticized his walk.

"You walk like an American," she said. "See, look at me."

She moved slowly with tiny steps, as if she were some kind of small, wary creature. Her whole posture changed—gone was the little New York gamine; in her place was a woman who looked like property. Aidan tried to mimic her, without much success. "Your shoes are wrong," she said, standing with her hands on her hips. Aidan was wearing a pair of battered Nikes. "Wait here."

"I see why Arab men like their women to wear those things," Liam said when she'd disappeared out the back door. "You look sexy."

"Get out of here," Aidan said.

"No, really. I'm imagining you naked under there, parading around. And I'm the only one who gets to see what you're hiding."

"You are seriously deranged," Aidan said, but he laughed. They flirted for a few minutes, putting aside the problems that faced them, until Nailah returned with a pair of black slippers.

"My cousin has big feet," she said. "Here, you try these."

Aidan couldn't bend over to take his shoes off or put on the slippers, so Liam had to do it. He tickled Aidan's instep, and Aidan squirmed, but Liam got the slippers on. With the burka hanging down as far as it would go, no one would notice Aidan's big American feet.

Aidan practiced walking some more, attempting to channel his inner woman, until Nailah was satisfied he could pass.

Then she appraised Liam, hands on hips. "Your scarf is wrong," she said, climbing back on her stool. She unwound the scarf, tried it one way, then another. Finally she was satisfied.

"This still doesn't solve our problem of how we get out of town," Aidan said.

"You will come with me," Nailah said. She opened the back door of the shop to a narrow alley. Aidan was reminded of the street in Tunis where he'd nearly been mugged. It seemed like he couldn't stop getting himself in trouble.

A sleek black Japanese motorcycle with yellow accents leaned against the back wall of the shop. Aidan found it hard to imagine the tiny Nailah perched on it, zooming around the narrow streets of Tataouine. "You know how to ride?" she asked Liam.

He nodded.

"There is only one road south," she said. "But if you are lucky, they are only stopping tourists."

"And if we're not?" Aidan asked.

"We don't have any choice," Liam said. "The longer we stay in Tataouine, the greater the chance that they will look here in town for us. We have to get out."

He straddled the motorcycle, and Aidan tried to get on behind him. It was pretty comical as he struggled with the long burka. He tried to hitch it up around his waist, but Nailah shook her head. "No woman would ride like that," she said. She made him sit sidesaddle and pushed and tugged at the cloth around him, draping it down so that his legs were covered.

She stacked Aidan's backpack on the shelf at the bike's rear, with Liam's duffel on top of it, then covered the lot with a ratty sheepskin and tied it all down with bungee cords striped in bright colors. For effect, she added a pair of tin cups and a leather canteen full of water.

Aidan caught their reflection in a mirror through the open door of the photo shop. With the scarf wrapped around his head, Liam looked like a typical Tunisian man. And if Aidan hadn't known he was inside that burka, he would have assumed the woman behind Liam was his wife.

"Good luck," Nailah said. "When you reach Remada, leave the motorcycle with Ifoudan. He will get it back to me."

Liam pulled out his wallet and handed Nailah a sheaf of dinars. "No, no," she said, trying to back away, but he insisted. She took the bills and folded them into her pocket as Liam gunned the motorcycle. They took off, Aidan clutching Liam's back, the hem of the burka flapping in the wind. It took Liam a few blocks to get his bearings and a feel for the cycle, and then they found the road south.

The soldiers at the roadblock were occupied with a tour bus packed with foreigners. Aidan saw the girl who had been with the pharmacist's assistant standing with them, peering at the tourists. A single soldier moved the rest of the traffic along. He glanced at Liam and Aidan and waved. For a moment Aidan thought the girl had noticed them, but she turned back to the tourists, and they sped past.

Even with the air rushing by, Aidan was sweltering inside the burka. It didn't help that he felt trapped between the bags and Liam's broad back. Liam's body heat radiated through to Aidan as his hands slipped around Liam's sweaty waist.

Aidan knew they couldn't stop until they reached Remada. Who knew what other roadblocks there might be? If he slipped out of the burka, he'd be very conspicuous, an American man behind a Tunisian.

The map said the trip was eighty kilometers from Tataouine to Remada, but it seemed like a lot longer. There was no break from the unrelenting sun, and even the river they crossed halfway there was no more than a trickle. Aidan had never been so uncomfortable in his life. The sweat had drenched him, and he'd begun to itch—under his arms, around his waist, at his groin. The burka felt like a giant blanket, and his body chafed against the motorcycle seat and against Liam. He worried he'd end up with blisters on his thighs.

A short while after they crossed the tiny river, a breeze picked up. But the relief was short-lived because the wind continued to grow, whipping tiny grains of sand around them. Aidan realized what it was just as Liam shouted, "Sandstorm," over his shoulder. "We've got to find some shelter."

"Where?" Aidan asked. There was nothing around them. Not even a tall dune. The desert stretched around them as flat as a dinner plate. Within minutes, Aidan couldn't even see more than a few feet ahead. "Pull over," he called out.

He thought Liam was about to; he felt the motorcycle starting to slow. But then they hit a sandy patch on the road and began to skid.

Wipeout

Aidan was knocked out when he flew off the motorcycle. He woke up on his back a few feet from the bike and Liam, sand in his eyes. He struggled to sit up, and every muscle and sinew in his body rebelled. It felt like someone had beaten him with a hammer repeatedly.

He wiped the sand from his eyes and looked over at Liam. He wasn't moving, and his left leg was bent beneath him at what had to be an uncomfortable angle. The bike lay on its side, its front wheel still spinning lazily. The sandstorm had passed, and the sun had returned.

Aidan looked in the other direction and was startled to find a camel staring back at him. It seemed to chew on its lips and looked about to spit at him. He rolled away and tried to stand up, getting tangled in the folds of the burka. Miracle polyester, it had survived the accident without a tear, though there was a smudge of motor oil near the hem.

Was Liam alive or dead? Was Aidan stranded in the desert with a dead lover, a broken motorcycle, a Swiss bank account number, and a Libyan intelligence agent on his trail?

Looking up, he saw a dark-skinned man on the camel, wearing a long-sleeved T-shirt and jeans frayed at the knees.

Though he had the slim, wiry body of a young man, his face was leathery.

The man leaned down and said something to Aidan in Arabic. He tried to remember the few words of Arabic he'd picked up from his guidebook, and the phrase "Mish bakalum arabee" finally came back to him. He didn't speak Arabic, though at that point he wished he did.

The man didn't seem surprised to find an American man inside the burka. He nodded, then dismounted from his camel and walked toward Liam. Aidan struggled to his feet, though his legs felt like jelly, and limped after him. From a goatskin sack, the Tuareg dribbled a few drops of liquid onto Liam's lips. He stirred and looked up. Aidan let out a huge breath as he realized Liam was alive. He wasn't on his own. Allah be praised. "Are you okay?" he asked, crouching next to Liam, his muscles crying out as he did. "Anything broken?"

Liam tested his extremities, and they all seemed to be functional. He said something in Arabic to the Tuareg man, who replied and helped him stand up. Liam held on to Aidan's arm and they followed the man to the motorcycle. Liam and the man spoke back and forth for a few minutes, peering at various parts of the cycle, and Aidan was impatient to know what was going on.

The Tuareg man picked the bike up, and Liam straddled it. He tried to turn it on, but nothing happened. He and the Tuareg switched places, and Liam bent over to tinker with the engine. As he did, Aidan saw him grimace. Liam was hunching his shoulders over as if he'd hurt his back in the crash.

The camel stood placidly a few feet away, chewing on its lip. They had slid a few feet off the road, but there was no traffic coming. After a few minutes of tinkering, Liam gave up. "It's fucked," he said. "This coping is twisted, and it can't be fixed by hand. Until it gets back in its proper place, the engine won't start."

The Tuareg began to speak rapidly in Arabic, and Liam listened, stopping him a couple of times for what Aidan assumed was clarification. "Bilal here says that his tribe is a short way behind him. His brother has tools and may be able to help us."

"That's great," Aidan said.

"I think we ought to camouflage ourselves while we wait," Liam said. "We don't know who might come down this road."

Bilal had a goatskin and a couple of tent poles on the back of the camel, and he and Liam constructed a shelter, Liam stopping now and then to stretch or flex his shoulders. With the three of them sitting in front of the bike, it was well hidden. The camel sat down next to them once they were settled, adding to the illusion.

"How are you, really?" Aidan asked. His own body ached, but already he was feeling better, more able to put pressure on his legs without limping. He had drunk from the canteen and rubbed a couple of sore muscles.

"I'll survive," Liam said. "I've been hurt a lot worse on operations." He dug in his pack and pulled out two tiny packets of aspirin. "Take these," he said, handing two tablets to Aidan. "Don't sit in any one position too long."

Aidan took the tablets with a little water and sat back under the tent. A couple of cars and a truck passed by on their way south while they waited. Bilal shared some dates, and Liam and Aidan dozed in the shelter of the tent. Aidan woke later in the afternoon to hear a buzz of Arabic voices. When he looked up, he saw several Tuareg men clustered around the motorcycle.

The man with the wrench appeared to be Bilal's brother. With Bilal and Liam, he managed to pry the damaged coping out of the way of the engine and get the bike started up again. By then it was late afternoon. Liam and Aidan thanked the Tuaregs.

"Shame we don't even know the name, or the tribe, that we're looking for," Liam said as the Tuaregs packed up. "I asked Bilal if he knew a Tuareg tribal leader who went to school in Tunis. He said he had heard of such a man, but he and his family are from a different tribe."

"Would have been too easy," Aidan grumbled. "Let's get back on this damn bike." He hopped on the back, sidesaddle once again, doing his best to arrange the light blue cloth to camouflage his hairy legs, then grabbed Liam's back once more as they took off for Remada.

As they approached the outskirts of the town, the two-lane road broadened, divided by a median strip. Aidan was surprised at all the trees. There was actual shade in parts, especially as the road curved and buildings sprung up. Even though he'd looked at the guidebook in Tataouine, he hadn't realized how different Remada would be. It wasn't just an oasis, although there was one on the far side of town. It was like finding a town in the middle of a forest.

His sense of discomfort intensified as they drove into town, past the four-story square minaret, the oddly shaped war memorial with red flags sticking out. There were soldiers everywhere, and Aidan worried that any one of them could have pictures and be on the lookout for two Americans. The arched gate to the army barracks was at the top of a set of steps, dark blue wood surmounted by whitewashed stucco in odd, pointy shapes.

There were few women anywhere, only men and young boys playing in the pitiful shade offered by a few palm trees and a couple of buildings. Aidan wished that he could understand Arabic script; seeing so much of it, often accompanied by the red Tunisian flag of star and sickle moon, made him nervous.

Liam stopped the motorcycle at the far edge of town, where men leaned against the walls of a stucco building and smoked cigarettes, a cluster of tents in front of them, a group of camels just beyond. "This looks like the place," Liam said. "You stay here while I see what I can find out."

"Be careful." Aidan watched Liam walk toward the market and again was amazed at how he was able to blend into his environment. His whole walk changed—instead of the confident stride of an American tourist, he walked slowly, almost lazily, nodding occasionally to men he passed.

Soon Aidan lost track of him in the crowd at the camel market. He sat down next to the motorcycle in what he hoped was a submissive female posture and waited. He worried that because there were so few women on the street, he might stand out, but instead the men who passed ignored him.

He realized the burka was a sign that he belonged to some other man, and to accost him would be to court trouble. That was one good thing about the disguise.

It was cooler in town than it had been in the desert, and there was some shade from a one-story brick building. Aidan was still miserably hot and sweaty, and he wanted nothing more than to strip off the clumsy burka and burn it.

An hour passed as he waited for Liam. He yawned and thought of dozing off when he saw the pharmacist's assistant and the girl. They walked so close to him that he could hear them speaking in Arabic, though he couldn't understand what they were saying.

His disguise worked; they had no idea he was there, under the light blue burka. He didn't know what to do, though. Should he get up and follow them? He didn't think he should leave the motorcycle alone, and he was worried that either he'd get lost and separated from Liam or that the couple would discover his identity.

They walked toward the camel market, and Aidan stressed even more. What if they spotted Liam there? His disguise was just an illusion—some clothing, an attitude. Anyone looking for him would be able to spot him.

The Camel Market

Liam did not return until the sun had dipped below the rooftop behind Aidan on Wednesday afternoon. "I found Ifoudan," he said. "He's leading a camel caravan out into the desert. He has plans to meet the Tuareg chief, Ibrahim, in a couple of days at an oasis along his route. We have to go along with him."

"I saw that young couple from the ksour," Aidan said. "They're here in Remada. They walked right past me."

Liam said nothing, just led him back into the market, rolling the motorcycle, and introduced him to a slim, young Tunisian man. "This is Ifoudan," he said.

The Tunisian looked at Aidan buried inside the burka and smirked. "He says we will be too obvious here, that we have to come back after sunset," Liam continued. "He suggests we go to the hammam."

"What's that?"

"Turkish bath. We can stay there for a couple of hours, then come back."

They left the motorcycle with Ifoudan and followed his directions out of the market to a small stucco building with ornate Arabic script over the doorway. Liam took him by the arm and pulled him behind the building. Liam slipped off his heavy cloak and said, "Let's get you out of that getup."

It was a blessed relief to have the polyester burka pulled over his head. But as he looked at himself, he realized he was as sweaty and grimy as Liam, who had patches of dried sand on his legs and deep sweat stains under his arms. Liam's face was red, his light brown hair plastered down to his scalp.

When they walk inside, Aidan was assailed by humidity and the scent of lemons. They crossed a tile floor, and Liam handed a few dinars to an old man who stood behind a pile of towels.

The man gave them each a rough white cotton towel and motioned them toward the locker room. "What do we do?" Aidan whispered as they walked inside. There were hooks on the wall and a low bench, but nothing more.

"We strip," Liam said. He began to peel off his dirty clothes.

"Here?" Aidan squeaked.

"The old man's wife will wash our clothes while we bathe. Come on, get naked."

Aidan turned his back on Liam and began to unbutton his shirt. Liam laughed. "Modest, are we?"

Aidan kicked off the black slippers Nailah had given him, and dropped his pants and boxers. His hard-on stood away from him, pointing toward the sky. "Something about locker rooms," he said sheepishly as he turned to face Liam, who was naked himself.

Liam's ample cock, though, was still soft, nestled in a bush of brown pubic hair. "You are a horny bugger, aren't you?" Liam asked. He tried to wrap the tiny towel around his waist, but there was no way it was big enough. Finally he gave up and gathered his and Aidan's clothes. "You go on into the steam room," he said. "I'll take these out to the old man and then join you."

Aidan watched Liam's sexy butt walk out of the locker room. He still looked as mouthwateringly handsome as he had that first day behind the Bar Mamounia. Aidan couldn't believe he had held that gorgeous ass in his hands, that his tongue had penetrated Liam, that Liam's beefy dick had been inside his ass, making him feel more complete than he ever had.

He held the towel in front of him as he walked into the steam room, trying to think of math problems as he had when he was a teenager embarrassed to be turned on by the bodies of his naked classmates. It worked a little.

The steam room was small, hardly bigger than their hotel room the night before, and it was lined with beautiful blue and white tiles. There were benches around three sides, with a drain in the middle of the floor. The room was empty, and the steam was hot and lemony. Aidan spread his towel on one bench and lay down on his back.

He closed his eyes, luxuriating in the clean steam. He was half dozing when he felt fingers gently caressing his chest. He looked up in alarm.

"I hate it when you sneak in like that," he said to Liam.

"Sorry, couldn't resist. You look so sexy there."

"Mmm. You're not bad yourself."

Liam stood in front of him, and his cock finally reacted as Aidan's did. Aidan reached out for it, but Liam backed away. "Not in public," he said.

"Come on. We're all alone here."

"But someone could come in at any minute. We'll have plenty of time to fool around in private."

Aidan snorted. "Then go over to the other side of the room." He closed his eyes and lay back on the bench.

He must have dozed as all the fear and the toxins of the past few days oozed out of his pores. He woke to find Liam standing over him once again.

"The old man delivered our clothes and showed me the showers. Time for us to go."

They sluiced off the sweat and grime and then stepped into their clothes, now clean and crisp. Even the light blue burka had been laundered and pressed. Liam didn't think it was necessary for Aidan to climb inside it, though, which was a blessed relief. A short while later, they were back at Ifoudan's place in the market as dusk was falling.

"You wait here with Ifoudan while I take the motorcycle where it has to go. Then I'll come back, and we'll stay here tonight, then leave in the morning."

"Here? In the market?"

"Sorry, Hilton hasn't come to Remada yet," Liam said. "Don't worry; sleeping here will be a lot better than sleeping in the desert, which starts tomorrow night."

"You make this sound so glamorous," Aidan said.

"There's still time to back out. You don't have to do this. I'll give you money, and you can get a taxi back to Tataouine.

You can get a bus there to Gabes and then take the train back to Tunis."

Aidan shook his head. "Nope. I signed on for this trip, and I'm going to see it all the way through."

"We'll talk about it more when I get back. I don't think you fully understand what's coming yet."

"Drive carefully," Aidan said.

Aidan watched Liam get on the motorcycle. He'd given up wearing his Tunisian head scarf, and Aidan worried that he would be too visible. But he was just taking the cycle a few blocks away, and he'd return on foot. He promised he'd only be gone a few minutes.

Ifoudan had pitched another of those goatskin tents, and Aidan went inside it to pass some time reading the guidebook. After half an hour or so had passed and Liam still had not returned, he got fidgety and left the shelter of the tent to examine the camels, a ball cap pulled down on his head. He hoped he looked like an average tourist.

Each camel had a traditional Tuareg saddle with a high back and front. There were thick ropes around their necks used for steering. They also wore little packets around their necks that reminded him of the gris-gris he'd seen in New Orleans.

For a while, he watched Ifoudan negotiating with a buyer, though he had no idea what they were saying. It looked like the camel didn't either, or at least it didn't care. Its long tongue hung quivering out of the side of its mouth, something the guidebook told him had to do with mating, showing off to potential females. Maybe he was trying to show he could retain a lot of water, since Aidan had read that they could go for up to three months in the winter without water.

When Ifoudan tried to bring him over to the buyer, the camel groaned like Chewbacca from *Star Wars*. Ifoudan forced the camel to its knees, and the other man climbed on. He had tanned, aged skin and a short white mustache, and a khaki green cloth strip was tied to form a loose hood over his head. His beige, billowy robe ended slightly above his sandaled feet.

If it was possible to look graceful on a camel, the man accomplished it. Aidan knew he'd look much worse when he had to ride, but he watched closely to see how the leathery man balanced himself, how he used his feet on the ropes to exert pressure and direct the camel. After riding around for a while, the man dismounted and began examining the camel, looking at its legs, its tail, its teeth.

The camel didn't like the attention, making more of those Chewbacca noises, and Aidan would have found it almost comical if he weren't worrying about riding one himself and about why Liam hadn't yet returned.

When another hour had passed, Aidan started to get anxious. What if the police had arrested Liam? What if the pharmacist's assistant and his girlfriend, whoever they were, had spotted him? Suppose he'd been shot or killed? What was Aidan supposed to do?

Ifoudan spoke no English, so Aidan couldn't even ask him where he'd told Liam to take the motorcycle. And that posed another problem. Suppose he had sent Liam into an ambush? Suppose he was working with the Libyans?

Aidan didn't want to leave the camel market, because he wanted to be there if Liam came back—*when* Liam came back. But it was frustrating to wait there. He watched the setting sun lengthen the shadows in the market, and worried.

Going for a Ride

Ifoudan concluded his negotiation with the white-mustached man, and the man led the camel away. Then Ifoudan turned to Aidan and, using hand signals, asked if he wanted to get on a camel.

What the hell? Aidan thought. He'd have to do it the next day, and he might as well get in some practice. Ifoudan led him to a camel sitting on all fours behind his tent, and from his hand motions, Aidan deduced that this was a female and more gentle. Even on the ground, though, the saddle was very high, and Aidan couldn't figure out how to climb into it. Ifoudan had to get behind the camel and mimic leaping on from behind.

Easier said than done, of course. When Aidan made it, he found the saddle was too small for him, and he felt pinched from front and back. Ifoudan noticed and said something in Arabic, which Aidan assumed meant this was not the saddle he would be using in the desert. That was a good thing.

At a signal from Ifoudan, the camel rose up on its back legs, pushing Aidan forward. Unlike riding a horse, where the horse's head comes up in front of you, there was nothing on the animal to hold on to.

At every moment Aidan was afraid he would tumble to the ground, but he managed to lock his thighs on to the saddle and grab hold of the high part in front of him, hoping desperately that the saddle would stay put on the camel. It was a weird perspective; the hump dropped down in front of him, and the neck and head stretched out ahead.

It wasn't that bad once he got settled. He tried to get his legs into the ropes the way he had seen the older man do, which made Ifoudan laugh. Once the camel was standing, Ifoudan let him have a moment to get his balance. His butt was uncomfortable; the saddle was hard, and he wondered if the Tuareg had ever discovered the concept of padding. After a minute, Ifoudan picked up a walking stick and began moving ahead of the camel, every once in a while adjusting the ropes around the camel's face.

Meanwhile Aidan was rocking back and forth like a sailboat in a heavy current. He was afraid he'd either fall off or throw up, but he gritted his teeth and tried to feel the camel's movement through his body. He'd taken riding lessons for a year as a kid, and so he began to get comfortable. At least he stopped feeling nauseated and stopped worrying about falling off.

The view was very different from the top of the camel. Aidan could see the whole of the market, the random tents, the small groups of camels. Beyond, he could see a little of the city, including many palm trees. Liam was out there somewhere, though Aidan didn't know where. He strained for a glimpse of someone of Liam's height, of his build or coloring, but as he'd already seen, the bodyguard was a master at fitting in.

Eventually Ifoudan led Aidan back to his tent, and with more of those Chewbacca noises, the camel slid to its knees and Aidan was able to jump off. His butt was sore and his legs ached, but he felt good about his first ride. A vendor came by selling some kind of stew and flatbread, and Aidan bought dinner for himself and Ifoudan. They sat on crossed legs in front of his tent as the sky darkened.

Aidan kept looking around for Liam, and it seemed like Ifoudan was trying to reassure him, but Aidan couldn't understand any of it. When night fell, Ifoudan pulled out a clay griddle, lit a fire, and put flatbread on top of it, grilling it and then filling it with tomatoes, peppers, and some kind of seeds, then folding it over like a pita pocket.

He handed Aidan a bottle of warm soda called *Boga*, which tasted like 7-Up, and they sat quietly as the market closed down around them and the stars came out. When it was fully dark, Ifoudan cleaned up, then rolled out two sleeping mats and lay down on one of them.

Aidan lay on the other but couldn't sleep. The night air was cooler than the day but still warm, and around them he could hear the sounds of camels, a man's laughter, some quiet music. Where was Liam? he kept wondering. Was he coming back? Was he even alive?

Aidan had only met him less than a week before, but already he felt more connected to the ex-SEAL than he'd ever felt to Blake. Despite all logic, he'd been imagining a future with Liam, the two of them going back to Tunis and then... What? Aidan didn't know. But he knew it would be hard for him to give up what he'd felt with Liam.

Aidan woke Thursday morning to the smell of food, his stomach grumbling. Liam was nowhere in sight. Crawling out of the tent, he mimed a question to Ifoudan, but the Tuareg shook his head.

Around them, the market was shutting down, the vendors and their camels preparing to depart. Where was Liam? Why hadn't he come back the night before? If he wasn't dead, Aidan was going to kill the big guy for worrying him so much.

Ifoudan began assembling his caravan. Nearly a dozen other Tunisians, mostly men, but including two older women, were going to accompany them, along with several dozen camels. Ifoudan was waiting for something to happen, and while he and Aidan stood around, he began pointing out the parts of the camel.

He'd point to the hump and say, "*Sanaam.*" Aidan repeated the word, nodding. And so he learned that the foot was called *farsam*, the nose was *khashm*, and the tip of the tail was *shabib*. There were more, but Aidan didn't catch them all. The way this desert adventure was shaping up, knowing the parts of a camel in Arabic might come in handy.

When a police officer appeared, Ifoudan engaged him in a lengthy, animated discussion. Where was Liam? Aidan worried. Liam could understand the Arabic, whereas Aidan felt lost. Not only had the bodyguard abandoned him, but what if this police officer was here to arrest him? What if Ifoudan had turned them in? What if Liam hadn't returned the night before because he'd been arrested?

Aidan looked around for a place he could go. But where? Without his burka, he was visible as an American. The town was so small, and so isolated, that even if he did manage to slip away, he'd be caught.

So he stayed, rooted in place by a combination of fear and resignation. When Ifoudan completed his discussion, the officer turned and strode away. Ifoudan motioned Aidan to get back onto the camel he'd ridden the day before, with a bigger saddle, and Aidan was filled with relief—but a new uncertainty.

Should he go along with the camel caravan? He had Carlucci's passport with the account number. Could he hand the passport, with the account information inside it, to Ifoudan and trust that he would give it to Ibrahim? He didn't know anything about Ifoudan and couldn't speak his language. How could he be sure that Ifoudan would do what Aidan asked?

Aidan thought about what Carlucci's money could do for the tribe. Schools and health care, a chance to settle in one place and build a community. His own fear and discomfort seemed to matter very little in the face of the good that he could do.

He shrugged and mounted the camel, which Ifoudan called Ruby. He'd given up the burka, wrapping himself in a cloak Ifoudan supplied. Aidan knew he wouldn't pass for a Tuareg, but it would protect him from the desert sun. Groaning with displeasure, Ruby rose, and Ifoudan led her into line.

Craning his neck around, Aidan saw two people, a man and a woman, approach Ifoudan and carry on some kind of negotiation. He couldn't tell what was going on because Ruby swayed back and forth restlessly. He did see some money change hands, and then Ifoudan led the couple toward a camel.

The woman climbed easily onto it, and Ifoudan tied a bag to the back of the saddle. Ifoudan handed the man the ropes, but he could not seem to master handling them, and watching him, Aidan had to laugh. He hesitated to laugh too much, though, because he didn't want to bring bad camel karma on to himself.

It was only when the man had finally gotten the camel turned around to walk toward the rest of the caravan that Aidan saw the his face clearly, if only for a moment. It was the pharmacist's assistant.

Momo

After he left the camel market, Liam took a quick run around Remada. He'd hoped that Ifoudan would say that the Tuareg tribe was on its way into town, but instead the camel herder had indicated they would have to travel several days with the caravan to meet at an oasis. Liam knew that he and Aidan were not prepared for such a long trip.

Because he had gone on many desert missions during his time with the SEALs, he knew they needed a compass, water, sunblock, and food. He had a gun strapped to his leg, but he had no extra rounds for it, and that could present a problem if they were attacked.

Remada was too small to supply everything he needed, and any purchases he made would be sure to draw attention. His disguise was good enough when passing on the bike, but up close he was sure his American nationality would be noted. And then whoever came around asking would know what he was planning.

There was no choice but to make a quick run to Tataouine. By then the roadblocks should have come down, and he'd be able to sneak into the town, buy what he needed, and get back on the road.

He looked up at the sun. It was already late; he'd have to hustle to return before it was too dark to travel. He thought about going back to the camel market to let Aidan know what he was doing, but didn't want to waste the time. If everything worked out, he'd be back before Aidan had time to worry.

The trip north was quicker than the trip south, maybe because Liam pushed the bike harder, maybe because there was less weight on it. He reached Tataouine about an hour before sunset and went to the market for the ammunition he needed. That was his most pressing concern; everything else would be easier to find.

He shopped quickly and efficiently, buying a battery-operated GPS unit, energy bars, and sunblock. But no matter whom he asked, there was no ammunition for sale.

He couldn't head out into the desert to face unknown danger without extra rounds for his gun. And he worried that if he didn't get out of Tataouine soon, he'd never make it back to Remada. As it was he was pushing his luck; the desert was a dangerous place after dark, with sudden sandstorms and little or no passing traffic. They'd been lucky once that day; he couldn't count on the luck holding.

He remembered Nailah, the girl in the photo shop, and left the market, riding through the narrow streets to find the shop again. He got there just as she was pulling shades down on the front windows. "You have not left yet?" she asked. She took a quick look out at the empty street, then said, "Bring the bike around to the back. You never know who is watching out here."

She closed and locked the door, and he rode down to the end of the street, rounding the buildings and traveling back up the alley. "Where is your friend?" Nailah asked in Arabic when she opened the back door.

"He is in Remada. I had to come back for supplies."

"What do you need?" She looked at him, at the bags piled on the back of the bike. "Wheel the bike inside here."

As soon as he had brought it inside, she closed and locked the back door as well. "You are in some kind of trouble, aren't you? The police were all over town today, looking for two Americans." She gave him an appraising glance. "Is it that they know you and your friend are lovers?"

Liam was surprised and uncomfortable. He had passed for straight for so long that he'd taken it for granted that no one knew he was gay. Was it Aidan? Was he too demonstrative? Had the clerk at the hotel written something in the note?

"Well?" Nailah asked, and Liam realized she was waiting for an answer.

He didn't want to tell her about the Libyan agent, the Tuareg tribe, the million dollars. The more people who knew what he and Aidan were doing, the more chances there were that the wrong people would find out. But Nailah had given him an easy out; just admit that he and Aidan were lovers, that someone didn't like them. "My friend is a little too…friendly," he said. He struggled to remember the Arabic word for *flirting* and couldn't. "We were in a bar," he said, trying to keep as close to the truth as possible.

He remembered meeting Aidan in the Bar Mamounia. He had resembled the photo Liam had of Charles Carlucci, fit the general body type. But there was something more, something that had drawn Liam to him, an almost electric connection that had sparked between them.

Nailah was waiting for more. He embroidered a bit. "Another man, he liked my friend. My friend said no. The man turned out to be an officer. He was angry, and he reported us to the police."

Nailah nodded. "And now they are following you. What do you need?"

He leaned down and unstrapped the pistol from around his ankle. "I need ammunition for this."

Nailah stepped back, surprised at the gun. But she regained her poise, pursed her lips, and thought as she hurried to the front of the store, turning out all the lights. When she returned to Liam, she said, "You must come with me." He felt awkward following her out into the alley; she was so much smaller than he was, it was like walking with a child.

She led him through a maze of darkening streets, and he began to worry. What if she intended to betray him? After all, he didn't know anything about her other than that her cousin had been helpful to him and Aidan in Matmata. But then he remembered her willingness to lend them the motorcycle based only on a note from her cousin. Even so, he remained on alert as they stopped at a single-story house, where Nailah rapped on the door.

An Arab man opened it a moment later, wearing only boxer shorts, yawning, and scratching his head. "Nailah, my little desert flower," he said in lazy Arabic. "I was just getting out of bed. But I will get back in for you."

She put her hand flat against his belly and pushed past him, motioning for Liam to follow. "This is Momo," Nailah said, introducing Liam. "If you want something illegal in Tataouine, you come to Momo."

"You flatter me, Nailah," Momo said. He turned to Liam. "Who are you?" he asked in English.

"Lee Morris," Liam said, reaching out his hand to shake, adopting a hearty American personality. "Nailah here says you can get me some ammunition for this." He pulled the gun out of his pocket and laid it in his palm.

"Whoa," Momo said, backing away. After a moment, though, he stepped back toward Liam, looking at the gun. "May I?"

Liam never liked to hand over a gun to a stranger, but he had removed the bullets and had them in a side pocket. "Sure."

Momo took the Glock and examined it. "Nine millimeter?" he asked, and Liam nodded.

"I know a man. But it will cost you."

Liam shrugged. "What's money?"

Momo named a figure that was less than Liam had expected, and Liam pulled out a wad of dinars from his pocket. He counted out the bills and handed them to Momo. Liam experienced a slight frisson as their hands touched; despite his growing feelings for Aidan, he was only human, and the Arab was a fine specimen, especially wearing only a pair of tight boxers that belied a growing dick.

Liam wasn't sure if the growth was due to him or to Nailah, but the only thing that mattered was the ammunition. As soon as Momo had the money in his hand, he turned and walked over to a sagging armchair, then grabbed the baggy pants that lay on top of it. He pulled them on, then a white T-shirt with stains under the arms. His dark hair was tousled, his beard grown in for a day or so. Liam was pleased that once the man had his clothes back on, he was no longer that attractive.

"I'll be back," Momo said, walking to the door.

"I'll come with you," Liam said.

"No, you won't." Momo turned back to him.

"You have my money."

"Nailah, tell him."

"Momo works alone," Nailah said. "You can trust him."

Liam looked from Momo to Nailah, then back. He shrugged. "How long?"

"I'll be back as soon as I can." He leaned down and kissed Nailah on the lips. Liam didn't think she liked it much. Then Momo walked out.

"We might as well be comfortable," Nailah said, taking some dirty clothes from another chair and throwing them on the floor, then motioning Liam toward it. "Do you want some tea?"

"Is Momo your boyfriend?" he asked.

She pursed her lips together. "Momo is a slob. He's rude, he has no job, and he treats women like they are animals."

Liam laughed. "So it's a yes?"

Nailah laughed too, showing a row of tiny white teeth. "He is good for some fun sometimes."

"And you trust him?"

She nodded. "He has a feeling for people. He knows you are not the kind of man he can cheat."

"I'll take your word for it. And yes, I'll have some tea, if there's a clean glass."

Momo's kitchen was filthy, but Nailah began to clean as she waited for the water to boil. Liam even helped, scrubbing the tabletop as she washed the pile of dirty dishes in the sink. By the time the water had boiled and the tea had cooled enough to drink, the kitchen was much cleaner, though it was far from sparkling.

As he sat down, Liam was struck by the resemblance between Nailah and Aidan. It wasn't physical; Aidan was quite a bit taller than Nailah, and though he had a Mediterranean complexion, hers was darker. But it was about attitude. He could see Aidan behaving in much the same manner—coming in and taking charge, cleaning up, looking after his man.

This must have been what Aidan's life was like in Philadelphia, taking care of Blake, feeling attraction and at the same time an almost palpable sense of being unappreciated. For a moment he considered the possibility that Aidan would stay in Tunis after their adventure in the desert was over. That Aidan would stay with him, looking after him, making love with him in his bed.

Liam had never been one for domesticity. He'd preferred the adventure of the navy, the chance to see the world, to explore everything it had to offer. Since coming out of the closet and leaving the SEALs, he had experimented sexually with men. First back in Jersey, in furtive encounters at Xrated bookstores, then even venturing into a couple of clubs in New York.

Once in Tunis, he'd found men more available than he'd expected, both Tunisians like Abdullah and the occasional visiting foreigner, sometimes tourists, sometimes businessmen. There was one oil executive he'd seen on several visits, until the man mentioned a wife back in Houston. That was a mood killer for Liam.

Nailah started asking questions about the US, and Liam told her where he was from, described New York and San Diego. Then they talked about music. Liam kept looking at his watch as time passed. When Momo had been gone for an hour, he said, "How long do you think he'll be?"

Nailah shrugged. "Momo lives on his own schedule. But don't worry, he will be back."

Liam looked out the tiny window in Momo's kitchen. Night had fallen with its customary suddenness; there was no way now that he would be able to get back to Remada that night. If he rose at first light and sped down the desert road, would he be able to catch Ifoudan before the caravan left? What would Aidan be thinking when Liam failed to return?

Another hour passed, and Liam could not contain his restlessness. It was strange; through dozens of missions with the SEALs, he had been able to put aside his fears, relax, wait for the action to start. But he could not help thinking of Aidan, concerned about him alone with the camel driver, knowing that Aidan would be worrying about him.

The erotic tension of thinking about Aidan, combined with the fear that Momo might have decamped with his cash with no intention of returning, made him jittery. He found some oil and a cloth in Momo's kitchen, and he took apart the Glock, cleaned it, and loaded it with the ammunition he had. When the door opened another hour later, he reflexively pulled the gun out and pointed it.

"Hey, don't shoot," Momo said, holding up his hands. In one hand he carried four boxes of bullets for the Glock.

The relief washed over Liam. He was so happy he wanted to kiss someone—but the person he wanted to kiss was Aidan, and he was in Remada.

"You can't go back out on the desert road at night," Nailah said as if she were reading his mind. "It will be too dangerous. You will have to stay overnight."

"I'll go back to your shop," he said. "Then I can leave at first light."

"Momo will walk you back there," she said, handing the Tunisian man her key ring. "And then he'll come right back here." She smiled at him, and he kissed her.

"Can't he just stay here?" Momo asked. "I have a sleeping bag. And we'll be quiet, I promise."

"We won't be quiet," Nailah said. She ran her hand along his side, up under the dirty T-shirt. "But we can't get started until you get back."

"Come on," Momo said.

The man slipped through the shadows like a ghost, and Liam had to move quickly to keep up with him. It seemed to take only minutes to return to the photo shop, which Momo unlocked with a flourish. "There are some cushions in the front," he said. "When you leave in the morning, just close this door, and it will lock."

As Liam was looking around the back room, relieved to see that the motorcycle and its cargo were still there, Momo slipped away down the alley.

Was he going back to Nailah? Liam hoped so, hoped that the man would not make a detour past the police station, for example, to report that the American the police were searching for could be found at the back of the photo shop.

Liam knew Momo's type, though. He wouldn't go to the police without something definite; otherwise the police would arrest him for a handful of petty crimes.

Still, it wouldn't be good to let his guard down. He found the cushions and set himself up in the front of the store, where he could keep an eye on the street through a gap in the shades. He knew that he could not afford to sleep.

The Caravan

Aidan kept hoping to see Liam return, even as the caravan assembled and set off into the desert. He didn't know where they were going or how long it would take to get there, and he didn't know what he would do when they arrived. How would he communicate? He hoped that the tribal leader, Ibrahim, could speak English or at least French.

How would he return to Tunis? From the little he understood, the caravan was continuing across the desert after the rendezvous with Ibrahim's tribe. What if the tribe was returning to the desert? Where would that leave him?

And who the hell were those people following him, the pharmacist's assistant and his girlfriend? Since he'd seen the young man with the Libyan intelligence agent, did that mean they were agents too? How dangerous were they?

Aidan had a lot of time to think as the caravan moved across the desert. They soon left Remada behind, and all around them were trackless miles of desert. How could Liam ever find him, if indeed he was still alive?

The thing that surprised Aidan most was that the desert was not flat. He had always pictured a desert as a kind of beach stretching for miles in every direction. But instead they went up over small rises, threaded their way through narrow passes between hills of sand, and only occasionally passed through flat areas.

After a few hours, they stopped at a small tree, and the women of the caravan—and a few of the men, because there were so few women—laid out blankets and prepared a lunch of dried fruit, dates, and dark flatbreads. The men cooked lamb and rice over a fire of sticks.

Aidan accepted food from an elderly woman, avoiding the young couple and eating by himself in Ruby's shadow. When they began traveling again, they crossed stretches where not a blade of vegetation was visible, then to a deep, narrow channel that water had long ago carved through the sand. Though it was dry, the first camel balked about stepping over it, and Ifoudan had to force the beast to cross.

Once he did, the others followed, eager to keep up with the group. After nearly four hours, they reached a small oasis called Borj Bourguiba, just a couple of buildings, a few palm trees, and a tiny spring. Looking at the guidebook, Aidan could see that they had been heading southwest toward the Grand Erg Oriental, and that there was a road from Borj Bourguiba back north, where it connected with the main road toward Tataouine. From Ifoudan's actions, Aidan assumed they were stopping there for a while to wait out the heat of the day. He stayed on Ruby until Ifoudan came over and tugged on her ropes, getting her to kneel to the ground. Then Aidan helped put up the goatskin tent.

His lack of sleep the night before, combined with the oppressive heat, made him drowsy. He crawled under Ifoudan's goatskin tent, stripped to his boxers, and fell asleep on the mat.

He didn't know how long he dozed. He thought he was still dreaming when he felt Liam's body behind him. Aidan struggled to stay in the dream. Liam wrapped his arm around Aidan and kissed the back of his neck. Aidan didn't want to turn to face him, because he was afraid he would wake to find himself alone again in the middle of the desert.

Then Liam whispered, "I'm glad to see you," against the back of Aidan's neck.

From the pressure of Liam's hard-on against his ass, Aidan didn't need words to tell him that. He couldn't resist anymore; he turned to face Liam and opened his eyes.

Liam was there, wearing only his white jockstrap, the head of his dick peeking above the waistband. "Man, I'm glad to see you too," Aidan said, leaning across to kiss Liam. Then he pulled back. "Where the hell did you go?"

"Once I knew we were going into the desert, I realized we would need some stuff," he said. "I took the motorcycle back to Tataouine to buy it, and it was too dangerous to come back at night, so I couldn't leave until this morning. By the time I got to Remada, you had already left."

"You came out here on the motorcycle?"

He shook his head. "Ifoudan left a camel for me. I've been riding all morning to catch up with you."

Aidan scooted close and rested his head on Liam's chest. Liam wrapped an arm around his shoulders. "I was so worried about you," Aidan said.

Liam leaned down and kissed the top of Aidan's head. "Sorry, sweetheart. It couldn't be helped."

Aidan looked up. "You called me sweetheart." It was the first endearment he'd heard from Liam.

Liam looked as surprised as Aidan. "You don't like it?"

"I like it." Aidan leaned forward to Liam's bare chest and took Liam's left nipple in his mouth.

"And I like that." Liam groaned, arching his back.

Aidan felt his dick stiffening, knew the same thing was happening to Liam. "Can we?" he whispered.

"We have to be quiet," Liam said. He reached under the waistband of Aidan's boxers and took his erection in his hand. Aidan shivered at the feel of that rough hand against his tender dick. He pushed aside the pouch of Liam's jockstrap and wrapped his hand around Liam's dick. They kissed, each of them stroking the other.

Aidan kept repeating that endearment in his head. Sweetheart. Liam had called him sweetheart. That simple word excited him even more than Liam's body next to his, Liam's hand on his dick. It was as if a big, gaping hole had opened in his chest, emotion pouring out like lava.

The sleeping mat was just barely wide enough for the two of them, the sand hard beneath it. Liam lifted one leg over Aidan's so that they could nestle even closer together. Aidan couldn't look down to see his dick or his hand on Liam's dick. He just felt his dick bubble over with precum, felt Liam's doing the same, both their shafts slick, friction exciting both of them.

Kissing Liam while getting jerked felt awesome—Liam's lips, chapped from the long trip in the sun, warming Aidan's, both of them pressing against each other. Aidan wanted to open his mouth and swallow Liam whole. Electricity surged through his body, and he worried that he'd set off sparks in the dry desert air.

He bit his lip to keep from making noise as a monster orgasm racked his body and cum spurted out of him into Liam's hand. Only a moment later, Liam came too.

"Big mess," Liam said, but he was laughing. He grabbed a ragged piece of cloth, poured a little water on it from a bottle, and they cleaned up, Liam adjusting his jockstrap, then pulling his shorts on. Aidan was sad to see any bit of that beautiful body covered up.

Liam turned to Aidan's bag. "You have a guidebook with a map, don't you?"

Aidan sat up, stuffed his dick back into his boxers, and pulled the bag to him. "I'll get it." He fished around inside, finding it buried under a couple of dirty T-shirts. He should have asked the old man at the hammam to have his wife do a full load for him.

He handed the map to Liam. "Do you know where we're going?"

"Rough idea. Ifoudan wants to avoid the border crossing at Dehiba; he knows a place we can get through between there and Bir Zar. Then we're heading to an oasis along the Shurshut River to connect with Ibrahim's tribe."

"So we'll be in Libya," Aidan said, looking over his shoulder and following the progress of his finger.

"Sounds like it."

"And where do we go after we hook up with Ibrahim?" Aidan asked, sitting back. "When we're at this oasis in the Libyan desert?"

Liam shrugged. "Ibrahim's people will have to go somewhere to access the bank account numbers. We'll stick with them until we can find a way to get back to Tunis."

"But what if they're going back into Libya?"

"Logically speaking, they can't. They've got to get into either Tunisia or Algeria in order to make use of the money."

Aidan wasn't sure that a Tuareg tribe would act in a way that Liam considered logical, but he held his tongue. It sounded like as good a plan as they were going to have.

"We have another problem," Aidan said.

"What's that?"

"Remember the pharmacist's assistant? And the girl he was with at the ksar?"

"How could I forget them?"

"They're here. On the caravan."

"What? Are you sure?"

Aidan nodded. "I was already up on Ruby when they showed up. I didn't know what to do, so I just tried to avoid looking at them."

"Ruby?"

"My camel. Ifoudan calls her Ruby."

Liam laughed. "Every year, a camel gets a new name, based on how old it is. Your camel's name is actually *rubii*, which means she's six years old."

The way he pronounced it, it sounded a lot less like a sparkly gem—but Aidan preferred his way. "The camel's name is not the problem," he said. "The pharmacist's assistant and his girlfriend are."

"I'll talk to Ifoudan," Liam said. Aidan went back to sleep on the mat, and sometime later Liam joined him, snuggled against him. When he woke again, the sun had fallen low on the horizon, and Liam was in front of the tent talking in Arabic to Ifoudan.

Aidan stretched, dressed, and found a palm tree to pee behind. As he walked back to Ifoudan's tent, he surveyed the other travelers. Most were men, several of them responsible for a long line of camels loaded up with goods. The pharmacist's assistant and his girlfriend seemed to be traveling with an older couple, and they worked with them, helping clean up the campsite and load the camels.

Aidan caught the young man looking at him and looked away. Who were they? Had they killed Charles Carlucci? All Aidan remembered was a man on a motorcycle. Could it have been the pharmacist's assistant? If he was Carlucci's killer, that must mean he was after the password and number to the million-dollar Swiss bank account. Which Aidan was carrying.

Aidan was still worrying about the young couple as he leapfrogged over Ruby's back and took his place in the caravan line. When he looked over at Liam, on his own camel next to him, the bodyguard was smiling. "You continue to surprise me," Liam said. "How'd an English teacher from Philadelphia learn to mount a camel so smoothly?"

"Natural grace," Aidan said. "What can I say? I do physical things well." He smiled at Liam and winked.

Liam laughed out loud. "You do indeed."

Ifoudan no longer needed to lead Ruby; Aidan had gotten comfortable enough that he could manage her on his own. Instead Ifoudan took his place at the head of the caravan, and at a barked command in Arabic, the camel train began to move.

Liam kept his camel next to Aidan's, apart from the rest of the caravan, so they could talk. "Any ideas on who the pharmacist's assistant really is?" Aidan asked.

"Not a one," Liam said.

"I've been thinking about it. I think they must be the ones who killed Carlucci. Remember? It was a young guy on a motorcycle."

"There are a lot of young guys on motorcycles in Tunis," Liam said.

"But this is the only one who's been following us. They must know what Carlucci was carrying, and know that we have it."

"But if they know that, why didn't they take it from Carlucci? Remember, that guy on the motorcycle sped away."

"I don't know," Aidan admitted. "Maybe they weren't trying to steal the money—they were just trying to keep the Tuaregs from getting it."

"Then why haven't they tried to kill us?"

"They did, at the souk."

Liam shook his head. "If they'd wanted to kill us, we'd be dead. Or at least, you'd be dead. If one of them had pulled a gun or a knife, I might have gotten away—or I might not have."

"So what did they want?"

"I wish I knew. Maybe they learned about the money after Carlucci was dead—and killing him without securing the money first was a screwup."

Night was falling, but the caravan continued to move forward. "They came after us at the souk," Aidan said. "That means they knew Ibrahim was connected to the gold merchant. And the pharmacist."

"You think maybe they want Ibrahim?"

"Maybe they think they need him to access the money."

"And they've been following us so that we'll lead them to him," Liam said.

"Which we're about to do."

They rode along in silence. As the sun sank and the sky darkened, stars became visible. Aidan couldn't see Ifoudan anymore, just the outline of the camel in front of him and Liam next to him. It was creepy out there in the darkness, knowing that the pharmacist's assistant and his girlfriend were back there somewhere in the caravan, waiting for their chance. To do what? Kill them?

Aidan realized with a shudder that it might come down to killing them before they could kill. Fortunately he was riding alongside a trained soldier.

"Liam?"

"Yes, Aidan?"

Aidan lowered his voice. "Have you ever killed anyone?" As he waited for a response, he listened to the sounds the caravan made as it moved—the clanking of merchandise, the occasional snort from a camel.

"Four times," Liam said softly. "Every time you do, it takes something out of you. I'm not sure how much I have left to give up. I won't do it again unless I absolutely have to."

"I hope it doesn't come to that," Aidan said, but he had a feeling it might.

Through the Night

Aidan had piled some of his dirty T-shirts under his butt, so he was moderately comfortable as the caravan crawled through the desert night. "I'm going up to ride alongside Ifoudan," Liam said late in the evening.

"What if I get separated from the caravan in the dark?" Aidan asked. He hated how needy he sounded, but the desert was creepy with only the starlight above. "What about the pharmacist's assistant and his girlfriend?"

"Camels are pack animals. Ruby is going to follow the camel in front of her, no matter what. And as for our entourage, I don't think they'll try anything while we're moving."

"That's comforting."

Liam rubbed the side of Aidan's leg. "You'll be fine. I have faith in you."

Then he was gone, and Aidan was alone with his thoughts, remembering Blake, Philadelphia, and so many other details summoned by the darkness and his sense of isolation. What if someone else had replaced Aidan as soon as he'd left town? Suppose there was someone new sleeping in those three-hundred-thread-count sheets Aidan had bought during a vacation in France, brewing Blake's coffee in the espresso machine Aidan had custom ordered from Italy. Inhaling the scent of Blake's lime aftershave.

Looking up at the stars, Aidan realized it didn't matter. Blake had been a jerk; he'd used Aidan and then dumped him. Aidan didn't want to go back to him. If he and Liam made it back to Tunis and it was clear whatever they shared had come to an end, he'd go back to Philadelphia but not to Blake.

An uproar broke out at the front of the caravan. Men were shouting in Arabic, and camel hooves were thudding against the sand. The camel in front of Ruby took off at a gallop, and Ruby followed. Aidan clutched the saddle and bent forward, the camel behind them hot on their heels.

The desert air, still hot long after sunset, rushed past him. Aidan was disoriented by the way Ruby's head and neck seemed to disappear from in front of him, by the rough bucking. He gripped the camel's flanks with his legs and grabbed handfuls of neck fur.

The rush was over suddenly, like a carnival ride that stops without warning. Ruby nosed her way to a trough of water, making a place between two other camels. Aidan was just catching his breath when Liam appeared, whacking Ruby on her flanks. She lifted her head from the trough, water dripping from her jowls, and glared at him, making a loud cry that demonstrated her displeasure.

But she went to her knees, and Aidan jumped off. "What happened?" he asked Liam, his legs grateful for the solid desert below them. His hands were shaking, and he was having trouble catching his breath.

As soon as Aidan was off her back, Ruby stood up again and returned to drinking. "When a thirsty camel smells water, it rushes for it," Liam said. "The lead camel smelled the water and took off, and the rest of them followed."

Aidan took a couple of deep breaths and stuck his shaking hands in the pockets of his shorts. "Look at her drink," he said. Ruby had her head down to the trough, and she was gulping like it was the last water she'd ever get.

In the background, Aidan heard several of the men singing. "They sing because they think it helps the camel drink," Liam said. He took Aidan's arm and led them away from the drinking camels and the rest of the caravan.

"Did you learn anything up there with Ifoudan?" Aidan asked.

"When we stop in the morning, I want to take a closer look at the cargo," Liam said. "We're supposed to be taking materials out to a school and hospital, but Ifoudan says there are weapons in some of the packs."

"Did he have any idea who our entourage is?"

Liam shook his head. "They just showed up in Remada and bought a camel. He's going to nose around the old couple they're traveling with."

While they waited, Aidan asked how troughs of water showed up in the middle of the desert, and learned that the ancient Romans had set up these watering stations to capture rain. "The camels need water every couple of days in the summer," Liam said. "If they start to dehydrate, their humps waste away, their eyes fill with tears, they start to moan, and they lose their appetite."

"That's sad," Aidan said, imagining Ruby crying.

"Well, that's why the Tuareg take good care of them."

Aidan's butt ached and his thighs were sore, but when the camels finished drinking, he jumped back on Ruby, laughing to himself as he imagined Blake staring at the maneuver with his mouth open.

Liam rode at different places, sometimes with Aidan, sometimes with Ifoudan, sometimes with others. They kept moving until a few hours after sunrise, then stopped at what appeared to Aidan to be a random spot in the desert, pitched the tents, and rested the camels.

Aidan couldn't imagine how Liam still had the energy to go snoop around after riding all night, but he did. Aidan lay down on the sleeping mat in Ifoudan's tent, massaged his sore thighs, then fell asleep.

He woke sometime later, still alone, to a sharp smell— acrid sweat mixed with spicy harissa. He looked up and saw Liam's shadow outside the tent. *I can move as quietly as he can.* Aidan crept to the front of the tent.

He was stunned to discover, after he jumped out, that he had landed not on Liam but on the pharmacist's assistant. Aidan got a good look at his face, and then he wriggled out of Aidan's grasp and ran away.

The experience reminded Aidan of a mouse he'd discovered in the kitchen of Blake's town house. Surprise, fear, then anger raced across his brain. The bitter smell of the man's sweat lingered in the air as the sound of his racing footsteps faded.

Aidan looked around. The little encampment was quiet; everyone was dozing through the heat of the day. Everyone, that is, except the pharmacist's assistant and Liam, who was out somewhere doing something.

He went back into the tent and sat on the sleeping mat. The pharmacist's assistant could have killed him while he slept—but he hadn't. Aidan felt sure the man hadn't been inside the tent, but he checked the hidden compartment in his backpack just to make sure. Carlucci's passport, with the account number and password in its minuscule script, was still there.

He lay back down on the mat. Worry and fear swirled through his brain, but his exhaustion and the heat overtook him, and he dozed until Liam woke him a few hours later. "What time is it?" he asked, yawning.

"Close to dusk." Liam sat down cross-legged beside Aidan.

"Where's Ifoudan?"

"He's looking after the camels. The man doesn't seem to need much sleep." He tapped his fist against Aidan's thigh. "Unlike you. Just sleeping the day away while I'm out gathering information."

"I have some information of my own." Aidan sat up and told Liam about catching the pharmacist's assistant snooping around.

"Did he say anything?"

Aidan shook his head. "I think he was as surprised as I was. He slipped away from me and ran."

"I don't know what those two are up to," Liam said. "They joined the caravan at the last minute in Remada, and they don't know that older couple they're traveling with. The girl's Tuareg, but the guy's not. His name is Hassan, and hers is Leila."

"Hassan was working at the pharmacy, but I don't think he's really a pharmacist. I was thinking about how he acted when I walked in. He didn't seem to know anything, and he was always asking the pharmacist questions."

"Of course," Liam said. "Now I remember. When my contact told me about this guy, this Wahid Zubran, he mentioned that he had a protégé in his office—the son of his mistress. That must be Hassan."

"And the girl?"

Liam shrugged. "They must have recruited her in Tunis."

"Maybe she's from another tribe," Aidan suggested. "Maybe her tribe doesn't want this other one to get the money."

Liam chewed his bottom lip. "It's a possibility." He got up and walked to the front of the tent, looking around, then came back, speaking in a lower voice. "I checked out the cargo Ifoudan was telling me about. There's an awful lot of weaponry going out to a place that's supposed to be a school and hospital."

"What kind of weaponry?"

"AK-47s. M-6s. Bundles of dynamite. A couple of antipersonnel mines."

"Maybe it's a prison, and the weapons are for the guards."

"You have a way of putting the most positive spin on things," Liam said, laughing.

"Well, excuse me, Mr. Doom and Gloom. Maybe there's a secret military base in the middle of the desert, and we're bringing in weapons to stage an armed insurrection."

"Equally creative," Liam said with a smile. "Unfortunately there's an equal possibility that's the true story. Or that the truth is somewhere in between."

"The truth is always somewhere in between."

"I need to know who they are and who they work for," Liam said. "I have an idea. Wait here."

Before Aidan could protest, Liam had slipped out of the tent.

Aidan crawled over to the entrance, but by the time he got there, Liam had disappeared. The sun was very bright, and not a single cloud marred the expanse of light blue sky. Funny how such a beautiful day could have so many dark undercurrents, he thought. Back in Philadelphia, he'd loved sunny days and clear, cloudless nights. They made him think the world was safe and beautiful. Now he wasn't so sure.

Liam was back before Aidan had had a chance to imagine too many horrible deaths for him. "Let's see what we've got," Liam said, holding up a worn leather wallet. "Whatever this guy is, he's not a professional spy. Stealing his wallet was way too easy."

"Unless he wanted you to steal it," Aidan said.

"You've watched too many movies." Liam opened the wallet and started flipping through the cards in it. "Well, well. Our friend is a cultural attaché."

"What's that?"

"Sometimes it's a person who organizes things like art exhibits and poetry readings and receptions for visiting dignitaries."

"And other times?"

"Other times it's a cover for covert operations or military intelligence," Liam said. He looked through the rest of the wallet. "His name seems to be Hassan el-Masri, but that could just be an alias."

"How do we figure out what the truth is?"

Liam yawned. "The truth is, I'm beat. I need a power nap before we start moving again." He smiled at Aidan. "It would sure help me nod off if I was cuddled up with you."

"I'm here to serve," Aidan said drily, but he lay down on the mat, and Liam stretched his long body behind Aidan's, one arm casually draped over his chest.

Liam fell asleep almost immediately, but Aidan still had too many thoughts running through his head. If Hassan el-Masri was really an intelligence agent, where was his backup? Could Leila be another agent just pretending to be his girlfriend?

Or was it possible that they were operating outside the scope of his authority? Maybe they were chasing down the money in the Swiss bank account as a nice little nest egg, something to kick off their married life together. How far would they go?

And then Aidan fell asleep.

Meeting with Ibrahim

When Aidan woke, the sun was setting and Liam was gone, though he returned a few minutes later. "I gave our friend his wallet back," he said. "Minus his ID, though." He held up the plastic-coated ID card.

Within a short time, the caravan was moving again. Just as the last embers of the sun flared on the horizon, they passed the ruins of a Roman fortress. Aidan wished they could stop and explore, and for miles afterward he wondered what life had been like so many centuries before, when that fortress had been built.

He tried to imagine being a Roman soldier a thousand miles from home, baking in the desert heat. Surely it must have been just as sandy then, just as hot, just as isolated. Were there tribes in the desert then who launched attacks on the fortress? Did the soldiers take comfort from each other? Did they love each other as fiercely as Achilles and Patroclus?

Once again they moved through the night, climbing rises and threading through narrow passes. Aidan was getting accustomed to Ruby's swaying motion, and though the saddle was still hard under his butt, he didn't ache as much. Though the air was warm, it was dry, and he didn't sweat.

Liam spent some time riding next to him and some time with Ifoudan. At one point Liam announced that they had crossed the border into Libya. "We did?" Aidan asked.

"Sure, didn't you see the border guards?" Liam laughed. "Seriously. There aren't any borders in the desert, but Ifoudan is good at navigating with the stars. Between him and my GPS, I figured out we were in Libya now."

"Libya's not exactly friendly toward Americans, is it?"

"No. But I doubt we'll be in this country that long. Ifoudan says we meet Ibrahim's tribe at the next oasis. And then we'll join up with them, turn around, and head back to Tunisia."

Aidan wasn't sure it would be that easy, but he didn't say anything. Liam faded back into the night, and Aidan rocked gently on top of Ruby and tried not to think. Shortly after sunrise, they crested a tall dune, and Aidan saw a group of palm trees ahead. He was tired and achy and his throat was dry, so he wasn't sure if it was a mirage or not. At least not until they got closer and he saw the cluster of tents and a couple of camels grazing.

This time the camels were better behaved as they approached the water. None of them got loose or galloped forward, and Liam returned to Aidan's side to guide Ruby toward some thorny shrubs. "Can she actually eat that stuff?" Aidan asked as she went to her knees, her neck stretching out so she could nibble.

"Her lips have some stiff hair that protects them from the thorns," Liam said. "And her mouth and stomach are adapted to chewing and digesting that stuff."

"Better her than me," Aidan said, hopping off her back. She ignored him to focus on the greenery in front of her. "Is this the place?" he asked. "Is that the tribe we've been looking for?"

"That's what Ifoudan says. I'll know for sure soon." Aidan helped Ifoudan set up his tent while Liam went off to look for Ibrahim. The sand around them was scattered with fossilized shells and pieces of red sea coral, and Aidan realized with a start that the whole plain must have once been covered with water, either an inland sea or an arm of the Mediterranean. He marveled at what small creatures humans were in the grand sweep of time and the desert.

When Liam returned, he said, "Ibrahim is eager to meet the most beneficent Charles Carlucci. You ready to play the part?"

"Well, if he doesn't know Carlucci is dead, he probably isn't prepared to make small talk about Charlie's wife and kids. I think I can manage it."

"No time like the present."

As they walked, Liam said, "Remember, I'm your bodyguard and translator. If you don't know what to say at any point, just say something, and I'll wing it."

Aidan felt a surge of adrenaline through his body, replacing the weariness that had accumulated during the long camel ride. His butt hurt and his lips were dry, but he was ready for action.

They approached a large goatskin tent with three women and two men underneath it. "The young one with the scar on his cheek is Ibrahim," Liam whispered.

As they had rehearsed, Aidan stepped forward, bowed, and said, "My name is Charles Carlucci, and I am here to greet the *Amenokal* of this tribe."

The young man stood and stepped forward to shake his hand. "Hello," he said in English. Then he continued in Arabic, and Aidan looked to Liam.

"The Amenokal apologizes for being unable to communicate with you in your own language. He hopes you will forgive him, but his only languages are Arabic, Tamashek, and French."

"No apologies are necessary. I am honored to be welcomed."

They went through some more formalities, including the offer of seating and green tea. Ibrahim inquired about their journey and asked how they were holding up under the heat.

Aidan wanted to get to the reason why he and Liam had struggled through the last week, being ambushed in the souk, running through the streets of El Jem, then enduring the long camel trek into the desert. It was frustrating to suffer through these formalities. After a long speech by Ibrahim, Liam said, "The Amenokal asks if we have brought something for him."

He looked confused, though, so Aidan asked, "Is something wrong?"

"He used the words for trading," Liam said. "So it appears he has something to give us."

"I hope it's not a goat," Aidan said. "Or his firstborn daughter."

"I don't know."

Aidan opened his wallet and pulled out a piece of paper on which he had carefully written the account number and password, and handed it to Ibrahim. "You know what to do with this?" Aidan asked.

Ibrahim nodded even before Liam had finished translating. "He says he has friends from school who will help him access the money," Liam said. "I guess that means the pharmacist and the goldsmith."

Ibrahim must have recognized the word "pharmacist," because he began talking rapidly. Liam had to ask him to slow down and then launched into his own monologue in Arabic, first telling Aidan that he was filling Ibrahim in on everything that had happened.

Ibrahim looked at Aidan and spoke. Liam said, "He asks who you are, if you are not Carlucci. I told him that Carlucci was dead."

"What should I say?"

"Tell him the truth."

Aidan explained that he and Liam had seen Carlucci killed, and that because Aidan looked somewhat like him, Liam had asked him to help carry out Carlucci's mission. He pulled the eye charm on its chain from around his neck, which he hadn't been able to return in El Jem, and handed it to Ibrahim. "Will you see that this goes back to your friend the goldsmith?"

Ibrahim nodded. Then he spoke, and Liam looked at first confused, then nodded; then his face turned grim.

"What?" Aidan asked. "What's he saying?"

Liam held up his hand so that Ibrahim could finish. When he did, Liam took a deep breath, then sighed. "This is worse than I thought," he said.

"What? What's worse?"

He turned to Ibrahim and spoke, Ibrahim nodding. Then he said, "Let's go back to our tent. I told Ibrahim we will come speak with him later."

Ibrahim was eager to jump up and shake Aidan's hand again, and though Aidan was worried about what Liam wasn't telling him, he felt relieved that they had carried out their mission.

When they returned to Ifoudan's tent, the caravan leader was there, fast asleep on his own mat. Aidan yawned, and in a low voice Liam said, "We should both get some sleep."

"But what did Ibrahim tell you?" Aidan asked.

"Sleep now," he said firmly. "We'll talk later."

"But..."

"The only butt I want is yours, up against me." Liam pointed toward the sleeping mat.

I could argue, Aidan thought. But he was tired now that the adrenaline from meeting Ibrahim had drained away. And there were worse things in the world than curling up with a handsome, sexy guy behind him, even if the lack of privacy prevented them from doing anything fun.

Aidan thought he'd probably lie awake again, savoring the feel of Liam's body against his or wondering what Ibrahim had said that had upset Liam, but instead he dozed off. When he woke a few hours later, the tent was empty.

The wind had blown up while he slept, and there was a film of sand over everything. All he'd had to eat since the previous oasis were some dates he'd kept in his pocket and the green tea served by Ibrahim's tribeswomen. He was starving, and he had to pee.

He was careful, peering out of the tent in case Hassan el-Masri or Leila was lurking around. It was the heat of the day, and everyone appeared to be sleeping, so he crept out to the edge of the encampment and found a private spot.

When he'd finished, he walked back, following his nose back toward Ibrahim's camp. Something smelled delicious.

He found a young woman in Ibrahim's tent, stirring a pot over a small fire. As soon as Ibrahim spotted him, he jumped up and said, "Hello! Hello!"

Aidan answered him in French. His command of the language wasn't great, but at least he could say more than he could in Arabic. Ibrahim was delighted that they could communicate, and he started asking a lot of questions about Aidan's life and what he was doing in Tunisia.

"Are we in Tunisia?" Aidan asked. "Or Libya?"

"These borders mean little to us."

Aidan tried to be careful in what he said, because he didn't know if he could trust Ibrahim, at least not until he heard what the Amenokal had told Liam that had upset him. Aidan said that he was an English teacher and that he had come to Tunis to teach. That he had enjoyed seeing the country as they traveled south.

Ibrahim asked about America, and Aidan told him about Philadelphia. It reminded him of the dialogues he had had to memorize in French class—"*Les États-Unis sont un grand pays*," or "The United States is a big country."

The woman, Ibrahim's sister, served them big, sloppy plates of food, which they ate with their fingers. Aidan wondered where Liam was. He'd grown accustomed to his periodic disappearances, but he still liked the feeling of having Liam close.

Ibrahim was busy eating, so Aidan didn't have to worry about following his conversation and translating in his head. The food was delicious, though he couldn't identify anything in it beyond the couscous. When they finished, Ibrahim's sister served dates rolled in coconut, and Aidan thought he'd never tasted a sweeter dessert.

But still, he worried. Where was Liam?

Aidan Makes a Suggestion

After he'd eaten, Aidan made his way back to Ifoudan's tent. Just before he got there, Liam accosted him. "Where have you been?" he asked. "I've been searching for you."

"I went over to Ibrahim's tent, and he gave me something to eat."

"You shouldn't have left without telling me where you were going."

"I would have—except you'd disappeared on me."

Liam's body language relaxed. "I was worried about you. After what Ibrahim said—"

"Which you still haven't passed on to me," Aidan said.

"I haven't told you because I'm not sure what to do yet."

"Then talk to me," Aidan said. Liam looked skeptical. "Come on. You must know that the best way to figure something out is to talk it out."

"You're a great guy, Aidan. You have a lot of unexpected qualities. But you're not a soldier, and you've never been a soldier."

"I have two ears and a brain. And it doesn't look like there are any other SEALs, or former SEALs, around for you to brainstorm with. So you're stuck with me."

He sighed. "I guess you're right. Let's find a shady place where we can talk."

Ifoudan was tending to the camels, so they climbed back under his tent. "What did Ibrahim tell you? What made you so upset?"

Aidan could see Liam thinking, trying to figure out how to phrase what he had to say. He said, "The money we brought? It wasn't just a charitable donation. Ibrahim had some information he was selling to Carlucci's foundation."

"What kind of information?"

"You know the caravan is going on from here to some kind of school and hospital in the desert, right?"

Aidan nodded. "And you were wondering why we're delivering so many weapons to a school."

"Well, I know why, now. It's not just a school; it's a military training facility called the Tagant School. Tagant's the Tuareg name for one of the desert regions."

Liam leaned back against the sleeping mat. "It sits on an ancient underground site, something the Bedouins built centuries ago as a way station. There are caves there with ground water. The school and hospital are on the ground level, but the Libyans are training soldiers underground. This is the first time Ifoudan has been out this way, so it's a big surprise to him."

"Okay. Why would Carlucci's foundation want that information?"

"They're pretty right-wing," Liam said. "I did some research on them before we left Tunis, and I was surprised that they cared about setting up a school for a migratory tribe. Most of what they fund is related to national security and antiterrorism."

"Why would Ibrahim's tribe deal with them? Why not just give the information to the CIA?"

"Probably because the CIA wouldn't give them a million bucks. But Carlucci's foundation would. And then they could pass the information on to the government."

"So where does that leave us? Do we just turn around and pass that information back to Carlucci's foundation and let things go forward?"

"I don't trust them. And I want to know more before I pass any information to anybody."

"Let's go back and talk to Ibrahim again," Aidan said.

"I need more than just his say-so. I need to see for myself."

Aidan thought about that for a moment. "So you want to stay with the caravan until they get to this place. You, an American. You think you'll be able to get into this school and what? Take pictures? Pretend to be a tourist? Then what? You think you'll just waltz away?"

"I told you, I haven't figured it out yet."

"And what about Hassan and Leila?" Aidan asked. "Don't forget, they're on our tails. And if you're right and he's really a spy, then there could be a whole contingent of people after us."

"Yes, I'm aware of all the problems. Maybe if you came up with something positive to say, we could start making a plan."

"Me? I'm the one without any military training, remember? I'm the one you didn't even want to tell about all this."

Aidan realized they were both getting angry, and that wasn't going to help anything. "I'm sorry. It's just things seem to have gotten a lot worse."

"Tell me about it."

They sat there in silence for a while. Aidan didn't know what Liam was thinking, but it was probably something like *How did I get myself into such a mess?* Aidan knew that was running through his own head. His little adventure had taken a darker turn.

But there was no point in fretting over the past. The important thing was to move forward. And if they had to do that in small steps, then they would.

"What do you think about me volunteering to go in there as a teacher?" Aidan asked. "I mean, it's what I do. I teach English as a second language. Even terrorists have to be able to communicate, right?"

Liam smiled. "That's a good idea. But it's got some flaws. First off, they're going to be suspicious of a guy just wandering in off the desert looking for a teaching job. And second, you wouldn't know what you're looking for inside."

He reached over and squeezed Aidan's hand. "But I appreciate your willingness to volunteer."

They sat there for a while, holding hands in the tent, and Aidan wished like hell that he could pretend this was just a fun sightseeing trip. But it wasn't. He and Liam hadn't even been able to get onto the camel caravan without being followed.

That thought spurred an idea. "We have to get rid of Hassan and Leila," Aidan said. "With them lurking around, you won't be able to get anything done. We have to disable them somehow, get them off our tail."

"True that. But how do we do that?"

A plan started to form in Aidan's head. "There are bound to be guards at this Tagant School, right?"

"Bound to be."

"And you said there's a lot of military stuff in the cargo?"

"Yes."

"Suppose you liberated something, like a bomb or something, and planted it with their luggage. Then when we get to the facility, you or Ifoudan or someone reports them to the security there. We could put a suspicious spin on it— they just showed up at the caravan and tacked on. And without his ID, nobody's going to believe either of them. At least not for a while."

Liam leaned forward and kissed Aidan on the lips. "You are a genius. As a plan, it still has a couple of rough edges, but it's a great start." He lowered his lips to Aidan's neck and nuzzled there. "I'll have to find a way to thank you."

Aidan caught his breath as his dick stiffened. "I'm sure you can manage that."

Liam's hand rubbed across Aidan's dick through the fabric of his shorts. "Ifoudan's smoking a hookah with friends. He won't disturb us."

"If he does, maybe he's interested in a threesome," Aidan said.

Liam grabbed Aidan's dick and squeezed. "I'm not sharing you with anybody."

Aidan's breath caught in his throat, and he arched his head back. Liam's fingers were busy unzipping Aidan's shorts, and then he bowed his brush-cut head down and took Aidan's dick in his mouth.

Aidan thought he would never get tired of that feeling, of this connection with Liam, the warm moistness of Liam's mouth on his dick. Liam licked Aidan's dick from the root to the mushroom tip, the way a dog laps up water.

Liam squirmed around so that he was lying flat next to Aidan, who sat cross-legged on the mat, Liam's head at his crotch. Aidan stroked Liam's hair and shoulders as he bobbed up and down on his dick.

Why the fuck, he thought, was he out in the middle of the desert with this man? Aidan wanted Liam in a luxury hotel, not a dimly lit tent redolent with the smell of the last meal and just a hard, sandy floor. He wanted a luxurious king-size bed with three-hundred-thread-count sheets, fluffy down pillows, and air-conditioning. He wanted to be naked with Liam, their bodies rolling around in the throes of lust.

Liam's teeth nipped at the sensitive tip of Aidan's dick, and he came back to the present. His guts were boiling, and he was having trouble catching his breath. He was here, in this moment, with this man. His dick ached for release, and he teetered on the edge of pleasure.

He looked down at Liam and realized, with the suddenness of a desert sandstorm, that he'd fallen in love.

And wasn't that the most dangerous situation of all? He turned so that he was lying on the mat next to Liam, his face at Liam's dick. He ran his hands over Liam's muscular calves and thighs, making his assault on Liam's dick. He swallowed Liam all the way down, then backed off, sucking as he went. Slowly he began a rhythm like that, swallowing down and then sucking up.

Liam's index finger tickled its way between Aidan's ass cheeks and into his hole, magnifying the sensations running through Aidan's body. It was followed by a second finger stretching him, making him squirm on the thin mat.

Aidan couldn't hold back any longer, his brain flooded with endorphins and his body assaulted front and back. He squeezed his lips tight around Liam's dick as his body shattered with the power of his orgasm.

He was rewarded a moment later with Liam's release as he shot a hot, salty load down Aidan's throat. Liam's body shook as he ejaculated, and Aidan grabbed his ass cheeks and held on.

It was a big mess—sand, sweat, and cum mingling, the two of them clasped together in an awkward dick-to-face embrace. But Aidan thought he'd never been happier.

A Traitor Revealed

"Ibrahim's tribe is leaving tonight for Tunisia," Liam said when Aidan awoke from their postsex nap. "I think you should go with them."

"We've had this discussion before," Aidan said, yawning. "I'm staying with you."

"No, the discussion we had before was about you staying until we met up with the Tuareg tribe. And I agreed with that because we had an exit strategy in place. We don't have that anymore."

Aidan sat up. "So that's it? You just want to get rid of me?"

"Aidan. I just want you to be safe."

"Well, maybe I'm tired of being safe. Maybe I'm tired of being told what to do, of doing what somebody else wants all the time."

"Don't be a drama queen. You said it yourself. You don't have any training in combat or espionage."

"And you admitted that I've been good to have around when things get tough. If you get into that facility, and especially if you get caught, you need someone on the outside who knows what's going on."

Liam didn't answer for a while.

"Liam?" Aidan asked.

Liam turned to face him. "I love you. I didn't mean to, and I don't know how it happened, but I do. And I want to protect you."

Aidan leaned up and kissed Liam's scratchy cheek. "That's sweet. And I love you too. Which is why I'm not letting you do this by yourself."

Liam tried a dozen other arguments, but Aidan wouldn't be moved. So when the caravan continued toward the Tagant School, Aidan was on Ruby, Liam riding beside him.

They noticed that the girl, Leila, had remained with the Tuareg tribe at the campsite, though Hassan was still with them. "Good," Liam said. "That'll make it easier to get Hassan out of the way, if he's alone."

Aidan looked back over his shoulder at the Tuareg tents just once, afraid, like Lot's wife, of turning to a pillar of salt. What was he doing, insisting on staying with Liam? Aidan had no training that could be useful. He could prepare couscous, rake the desert sand into neat patterns. He couldn't creep around silently like Liam, use a gun, knock a man out. He'd been lucky at the souk when he'd disabled Gold Tooth by grabbing his crotch. But that had been a fluke.

In his heart, though, he knew he was doing the right thing. He had been too scared to defy Blake, afraid that any dissension would be grounds for a breakup. And see where that attitude had gotten him? He also felt a fiery determination, stronger than anything he'd ever felt before, to look out for Liam, to protect him, even though Liam needed protection less than any other man Aidan had ever met.

This had to be love. Not just lust—that would have evaporated the first time things got crazy. If he were following his dick, he'd have run as soon as Wahid Zubran and his thugs attacked them in the souk. But instead he'd gotten himself in deeper and deeper.

When they halted with the rising sun and pitched their tents, Liam slipped away. Aidan was dozing as the bodyguard returned to the tent. "I liberated a few items from the stuff heading for the school," he whispered, sliding down behind Aidan. "Three grenades and a Soviet-made handgun. Just before we get to the school, I'll slip them into Hassan's bags."

Aidan was too restless to sleep. "Tell me what you know about this place," he said. "This school."

"Ibrahim didn't know much," Liam said, leaning down to wipe the sand from his feet. "He's taken people from his tribe there for medical attention, and they saw things that didn't belong. He wondered why they needed so many soldiers to protect schoolchildren and medical personnel."

"Reasonable question," Aidan said.

"Foreign visitors come in by helicopter and four-wheel-drive vehicles. Some of them stay for a long time, but they never show up as either teachers or patients."

"So how did he connect with Carlucci?"

"The Tuareg pass tribal leadership through the mother. So his mother's brother was the Amenokal, or leader, of the tribe before him. His uncle decided Ibrahim needed to know more about the outside world, so he sent Ibrahim to a boarding school in Tunis, where he met up with the pharmacist and the goldsmith."

Aidan turned to face Liam. "Go on."

"The goldsmith found the Counterterrorist Foundation online and made the first contact with them. Carlucci investigated the information, thought it was credible, and made the deal."

Liam yawned. "Let's get some sleep," he said, pulling Aidan close to him.

They rode for another two nights, sleeping during the heat of the day. At the last rest stop, Liam slipped the grenades and the gun into Hassan's canvas bag, hoping that by burying them at the bottom, the Libyan wouldn't notice them.

Aidan and Ruby halted at the top of a low rise, keeping their place in line as the caravan came to a halt at the Tagant School. Aidan shifted position, rearranging the T-shirts under his butt and pulling down the brim of the safari hat Liam had lent him to shade his eyes from the sun. He wore what had become his regular costume in the desert: one of Liam's long-sleeved T-shirts to protect his arms from the sun and a pair of Liam's loose cotton drawstring pants, so that his calves wouldn't chafe against Ruby's hide as she trekked through the desert. On his feet he wore sneakers and socks.

Ifoudan left his position at the head of the caravan and walked alone up to the gate in the barbed-wire fence. The complex was larger than Aidan had expected: a single building, one story tall, with various courtyards and wings, and sentry towers at the corners. The whole facility was the size of two or three city blocks.

As Ifoudan entered the camp, Liam left the head of the caravan and climbed up to stand by Aidan. Liam was dressed for the desert too in a long-sleeved T-shirt and another pair of loose cotton pants, though they clung to his body in a way that made Aidan shiver when he looked too closely.

Hassan sat on his camel just a few hundred feet ahead. His head slumped forward, and Aidan thought he was dozing. Ifoudan walked back out through the gate a few minutes later, accompanied by a pair of guards.

The three men moved slowly toward the caravan, and Aidan's heart rate quickened at the possibility that Ifoudan might betray the operation, or that the guards would believe Hassan and pull him and Liam in for questioning.

The three men stopped in front of Hassan, and Ifoudan began speaking and gesturing, pointing at the man. The two soldiers with him held their guns ready.

Hassan woke with a start as Ifoudan grabbed the ropes of his camel and brought her to her knees. The soldiers pointed their guns at him and demanded that he dismount. "Salaam aleykum," Aidan heard him say as he climbed off the camel with difficulty. He started to speak in Arabic, but the first soldier quieted him.

Aidan noticed Liam's posture stiffen as he focused on the conversation between the men. Hassan began speaking again, and the soldier swung his rifle, hitting Hassan on the shoulder. While the first soldier held his gun on Hassan, the second one grabbed his bag and tore it open. After rooting around for a moment or two, he pulled out the grenades and the gun. He said something in Arabic.

Though Aidan couldn't understand the words, he could interpret well enough. The soldiers were accusing Hassan, who looked first angry, then confused. Then the first soldier turned to the old couple and began speaking. Aidan felt a momentary pang of guilt at involving them—but then, he didn't know they were innocent, after all. They could have been in cahoots with Hassan and Wahid all along.

The first soldier spoke into his radio, listened for a moment, then said something to his colleague.

Hassan started to argue, but the second soldier pulled out a coil of rope and tied his hands behind his back, then pulled him to his feet. A troop of six soldiers came out of the gate, marching up the rise to where the old couple cowered and pleaded, and they were bound as Hassan had been. Ifoudan accompanied the soldiers, the old couple, and Hassan el-Masri into the Tagant School. "That went as we hoped," Aidan said to Liam as he watched them walk inside.

"It was a good plan," Liam said. He patted Ruby on her flank. "Come on. Let's get camp set up."

They joined the rest of the caravan in putting up tents in the shadow of the rise a short distance from the entrance to the Tagant School and settled down to wait. Liam and Aidan sat on the sleeping mats inside Ifoudan's tent. Aidan was exhausted from the long trek through the desert night, but he was sure there was more they were supposed to do. "What happens now?" he asked.

"They'll need men to carry the materials into the facility," Liam said. "Ifoudan is going to let me join the laborers. That gets me inside."

"But what if the soldiers figure out who you are?"

"I'll have to be good at my camouflage," Liam said.

Aidan remembered watching him change as he'd moved away in Tunis, going back to his house to check for surveillance. Liam had been able to modify his body language and blend in with the crowd. But could he do that under close supervision?

"What can I do?" Aidan asked.

"Wait here." Liam opened his bag. "This is a satellite phone. I have a number programmed in. If anything happens to me, call that number and tell the man on the other end everything you know."

"Who am I calling?"

"My former boss. Colonel Hardwick. SEAL Team 12 is based in Sardinia right now. He can call in an assault if we need it." He handed Aidan the phone. "Once you make the call, you've got to get the hell out of here. Stick with Ifoudan, if you can."

Liam looked out of the tent. Ifoudan was still inside the school, and the caravan could not begin unloading and transporting the goods until he returned. "Let's get some rest," Liam said, lying down on the mat.

Looking at him, Aidan finally understood what they were up against, how much danger they were both in. "I'm scared, Liam."

"Come here."

Aidan sat on the mat, and Liam pulled him down and curled his body against Aidan's. "You've been amazing so far," he said. "Much smarter and braver than I ever would have imagined. I wish you'd have listened to me and stayed with the Tuaregs, but you're here now. You just have to stick it out a little longer."

"This Colonel Hardwick. Is he the one who kicked you out of the SEALs?"

Liam licked his lips. "He didn't have a choice. He was just following policies."

"Did you know it was going to happen?"

Aidan felt Liam's breath on his back, the bodyguard's leg curled against his. "I couldn't keep on hiding anymore. In the end, that was more important to me than being a SEAL."

"I can't imagine how hard that must have been. Losing everything like that."

"You went through that yourself. When Blake kicked you out."

"It's not the same. Sure, I lost a lot. And I probably overreacted by getting out of Philadelphia and coming here. But I didn't lose who I was."

"I didn't either," Liam said. He snuggled against Aidan, and they both slept.

When they woke at dusk, Ifoudan still had not returned. "What do you think is going on?" Aidan asked. "Are they blaming Ifoudan for bringing Hassan here?"

"I don't know, but I'm starting to get worried. The plan was just for Ifoudan to notify the guards. I didn't expect them to take him in too. Or that old couple."

"They helped him and his girlfriend," Aidan said. "The friend of my enemy is my enemy too."

"That one of the English phrases you teach your students?" Liam asked, and the ends of his mouth twitched toward a smile.

"Why don't you get a fire started," Aidan said, smiling back. "When Ifoudan gets back, he's going to be hungry."

The Desert by Moonlight

By the time Ifoudan crested the rise, helping the old couple make it the last few steps, Liam had built a fire, and Aidan had begun preparing dinner. Liam rose and met Ifoudan, and they moved to the side of the encampment to talk.

Aidan had learned to use a couscoussière in one of his gourmet cooking classes back in Philadelphia, and he had a decent meal prepared by the time Liam and Ifoudan returned to the fire. Aidan had stripped down to one of his own T-shirts and a pair of shorts; Liam had replaced his T-shirt with his leather vest.

"So?" Aidan asked Liam. "What happened?"

They used pieces of flatbread to scoop up the couscous as Liam said, "The old couple turned on Hassan. They made it sound like he forced the girl to befriend them, and that she escaped with Ibrahim's tribe."

"That's not good," Aidan said. "She could be spying on Ibrahim, and he won't realize it."

"That's a problem we can't deal with at the moment. Once we figure out what to do with our current situation, we'll think about how to get word to him."

"What about Hassan? Is he in custody?"

"He wasn't a very cooperative prisoner," Liam said, smiling. "He kept insisting that he was an intelligence officer, but he had no ID to prove it."

"Not even his ID as a cultural attaché."

"Exactly. He demanded that they call Wahid Zubran in Tripoli. The soldiers still hadn't agreed by the time Ifoudan left."

"So they didn't try to arrest Ifoudan?" The camel herder looked up from where he sat across from them at the mention of his name. Liam smiled and nodded, and Ifoudan went back to eating the couscous.

"In talking to her, Ifoudan discovered that the old woman is a distant relation on his mother's side," Liam said. "He felt he had to stay to make sure she and her husband were all right."

"*Kweiss*," Ifoudan said, holding up a piece of the flatbread with couscous piled on it.

"That means good," Liam said.

"Shukran," Aidan said to Ifoudan, and the camel herder smiled, showing a gap-toothed grin, his gold tooth winking in the firelight. "That means thank you," Aidan said to Liam, smirking.

Liam poked Aidan in the side, and they wrestled good-naturedly. Ifoudan said something in Arabic to Liam, who laughed and said, "Shukran."

He turned to Aidan and said, "Ifoudan says he will clean up. He suggests we might want to go for a walk together in the moonlight."

"Shukran," Aidan said to Ifoudan.

Liam was sure-footed, even climbing the dunes in the half-light, and when they got farther from the camp, the darkness around them was complete except for the canopy of stars above. Aidan noticed that Liam was carrying a sleeping mat with him and asked, "Are we going to sleep out here?"

"Maybe not sleep," Liam said, and though Aidan couldn't see his face, he could tell by the tone of Liam's voice that he was smiling once again.

They walked for a while and then climbed another rise. From the top, they could see the firelight of the camp, and then, farther, a few electric lights at the Tagant School.

"Ifoudan says that they have a generator," Liam said. "And an air-circulating system. There is a central courtyard and a dormitory building for the trainees. The soldiers sleep in a different wing, and the officers in a third. There is also a row of offices and a couple of detainment cells."

"Ifoudan was busy," Aidan said. He leaned up against Liam, his head resting on the bigger man's shoulder. Liam wrapped his arms around Aidan, holding him close. It felt so good to Aidan standing there. He shut out everything else, all the danger and uncertainty, and focused on the feel of Liam's body against his, feeling Liam's heart beating against his chest.

Liam used his index finger to position Aidan's head, then leaned down to kiss him. Liam's lips tasted like the couscous they'd had for dinner, hot and spicy. Aidan wondered how he would ever go back to kissing a man whose mouth tasted like breath freshener.

He felt Liam's dick swelling, pressed against the top of his groin, and wanted to drop to his knees right there and take it in his mouth. But no, he wanted more than that. He wanted Liam in him; he wanted to be impaled on Liam's dick out there in the middle of the desert, wanted to claim this man for his own no matter what happened the next day.

He stepped back from the kiss, took Liam's hand, and led him down the back side of the hill, where they would be sheltered from the camp. He spread the sleeping mat on the hard sand. In the glow of the full moon, Aidan kissed Liam once again and slipped his leather vest away. He wished that Liam were still wearing the nipple rings he'd been wearing in the shower that first time Aidan saw him; he longed to tease and play with them.

Liam ran his fingers under Aidan's T-shirt, then pulled it over his head. The desert air was still warm but dry, and there was no hint of a breeze on the back side of the dune. They pressed their bodies together once more, skin on skin, and Liam groaned. "I didn't know we'd be out here so long," he said. "Or I'd have been better prepared."

"For infiltrating the school?" Aidan asked, leaning back to look at him.

"For this," he said. He put Aidan's hand on his crotch, where Aidan felt his big dick hard and pulsing. "I'd have brought more condoms. I used my last one in Matmata."

"Before I met you, I hadn't had sex with anyone other than Blake for eleven years," Aidan said, pressing down on Liam's dick through the light cotton fabric. "He was a fanatic about health, so he insisted we get tested for HIV every year."

"Wasn't that insulting?" Liam asked, speaking to the top of Aidan's head. His breath feathered Aidan's fine hair.

"Either he thought that you were cheating, or he knew that he was."

Aidan shrugged, leaning more into Liam. "Blake did so many little things like that, I gave up worrying about them. But the point is, I'm healthy."

"My last HIV test was negative," Liam said. "And since then you're the only man I've been with." He paused. "I've never had unprotected sex in my life."

"There's always a first time," Aidan said. He slid his body against Liam's so that their dicks rubbed against each other.

"I wish I had some lube," Liam whispered in Aidan's ear. "I don't want to hurt you."

"We'll have to make do," Aidan said. "Saliva works just as good as K-Y if you're properly motivated."

"I'm motivated, all right."

Aidan undid his shorts and slipped them and his boxers to his feet. He kicked off his sandals too and stood there naked against the desert air.

"You are so handsome," Liam said. "Sometimes when you're sleeping, I just want to sit there and watch you. Your hair's a little mussed and you're smiling, and you remind me of one of those angels painted on a church ceiling."

"There's nothing angelic about me," Aidan said. He turned his back to Liam, bent over, and pulled his ass cheeks apart. "You see this pose on church ceilings?"

"I saw it in those porn magazines I used to jerk off to before I met you," Liam said, his voice husky. He undid the drawstring on his pants and dropped them, peeling off his jockstrap too.

Aidan got down on his hands and knees, doggy-style, and Liam joined him on the sleeping mat. He began to use his tongue on Aidan's ass, licking up and down, then curling his tongue like a miniature dick and using it to penetrate Aidan's hole.

Aidan shivered as Liam's stubbled chin passed against his sensitive butt cheeks. He adjusted his balance to spread his legs as far as they would go, and Liam kept licking and kissing and tonguing his puckered asshole. Aidan felt warmth flowing through his body. His ass opened to Liam's probing tongue, and he felt like throwing his head back and howling with pleasure.

"If this is too much for you, just say so," Liam whispered, positioning himself behind Aidan. He put one big, rough hand on each of Aidan's hips and tried to guide his dick to the mark. He'd just gotten the tip inserted when the sand shifted below Aidan and his right knee dropped an inch or two.

Liam lost his balance too, and the force of gravity drove his dick deep into Aidan's ass, much sooner than he expected. Aidan exhaled with a stifled whimper. "Sorry," Liam said.

"Don't pull out," Aidan said. "Just fuck me, please."

He was surprised at the note of passion and desperation in his voice. But Liam obliged, getting himself set again, then pushing in and pulling out of Aidan's ass. The desert around them was so quiet, the air so heavy and soft, that it felt like they were in another world, just the two of them together.

Aidan had never felt such intimacy before—Liam's skin against his, Liam's unprotected dick invading his ass. His arms started to hurt, his back to ache, and rough grains of sand pressed against his legs, but none of it mattered. Just Liam's urgent need matching his own.

Liam rubbed a sandy hand against Aidan's back, and Aidan said, "Ouch!"

Liam leaned down to kiss his back. "Better there than"—he spat into his hand and moved it to Aidan's stiff dick—"here."

Aidan moaned with pleasure as Liam's hand began to jerk him. The bodyguard established a rhythm, pushing faster and faster into Aidan's ass as he rubbed Aidan's dick. Aidan closed his eyes and focused on sensation, the hard-packed sand under his hands and knees, the brush of Liam's pubic hair against his ass, the distant scent of camels, and the sound of one of them moaning.

"I love you, Aidan," Liam whispered as his dick slid deep into Aidan's ass, then pulled back. "I've never felt anything like this before, and it scares the shit out of me."

"People go their whole lives without feeling like this." Aidan panted. "Don't be scared of it. Just take it in."

"I'm supposed to tell you that," Liam said, laughing. "Take it in, baby. Take everything I've got to give you."

"I am," Aidan said. "I'm...I'm...gonna come." He howled, letting himself go completely, and as his body was overcome with the power of his orgasm, the involuntary contraction of his ass pushed Liam over the edge.

"Oh Jesus." Liam moaned, his body shaking as he spurted up into Aidan's ass. He wiggled around inside for a bit, Aidan panting and whimpering, then pulled out, and the two of them collapsed together to the sleeping mat.

Aidan took a couple of deep breaths, resting on his side. His ass was tender, and he didn't think he could rest on it, at least not for a few minutes. It wasn't the best sex he'd ever had, but it was pretty damned close. He preferred a bed to the sand and wished they didn't have the specter of the next day looming over them.

Liam turned on his side too, offering his back to Aidan, who snuggled close, wrapping one arm around Liam's chest. They lay there in the velvet darkness for a long time, just cuddling together.

Aidan wondered then what it might be like if he and Liam returned to Tunis together. Would everything they had felt, shared, fade away? Tears welled in his eyes, but he forced them back. He had always looked too far ahead at the expense of living in the moment. But now the moment was all he and Liam might have, and he was determined to enjoy it. He nestled his head against the pile of their discarded clothing, his body pressed close to Liam's. He stopped thinking and just felt.

By the time they got back to Ifoudan's tent, the caravan leader was sound asleep, and they stretched their mats out and went to sleep too. The next morning, Ifoudan was up at first light, organizing the men to begin carrying the goods from the caravan into the facility. The camp outside was noisy as camels lowed and men called to each other in Arabic.

Liam stretched and reached for his clothes. "Remember what I told you," Liam said, kissing Aidan. "If I don't come back by dusk, make the call."

"You'll come back," Aidan said and wished he believed it.

The Tagant School

Liam followed Ifoudan through the entrance gates to the Tagant School and Hospital, second in the line of men leading camels to the inner courtyard, where they would be unloaded, the materials carried inside. All his senses were on alert as he observed everything from the posture of the guards to the thickness of the walls.

One wing of the complex was used as a boarding school for tribal children, and another housed a clinic where any passing Tuareg or other tribesman could get medical attention. Boys and girls played in separate groups in the courtyard, supervised by a male teacher in a white shirt and pants. A man in hospital scrubs crossed the courtyard and entered a single-story building with ocher-colored shutters on the windows.

The line of men and camels passed by the children, and Liam noticed guards with rifles positioned around the facility's outer walls. Ibrahim had been correct in wondering why so many guards were necessary for a school and hospital so far from civilization.

Liam wore a blue cloak he'd borrowed from Ifoudan, the better to blend in with the other men, and began to sweat underneath it. But he continued following Ifoudan, conscious that there was a line of men and camels behind him, and all he had to do was stay inconspicuous to remain unchallenged.

Ifoudan stopped before an elaborate Moorish-style archway. "We must unload the camels here and carry the cargo into the building," he announced in Arabic, then organized the men. Three began unloading the camels, passing the cargo to the rest. With Ifoudan in the lead and Liam behind him, the porters walked through the arch and into the lobby of what could have been any nondescript office building in Tunis.

The inside of the building was surprisingly cool after the heat of the desert. As they walked down a wide corridor lined with offices, Liam felt the movement of cold air around him, and when he passed a doorway that led to a staircase to the lower level, he realized that the air handlers were bringing cool air up from below and circulating it through the first floor.

A group of laughing soldiers appeared to their right, startling the men. Liam looked beyond the soldiers, through an open door, to see the dormitory wing Ifoudan had described. He kept his head down, pretending that the burden on his back was much heavier, and the soldiers passed him, heading for a shift change. Ifoudan continued to lead them down the hallway, taking a left turn. As they turned the corner, Liam looked down the short hallway into a large gym. The walls were lined with posters of weapons, including exploded views that showed the interior of each gun and rifle.

Tables were lined around the perimeter of the room, and though at a quick glance Liam couldn't be sure, he thought they held weapons and ammunition. In the center of the room, about two dozen men practiced martial arts; as they passed, one man took another down onto a mat.

Just beyond the big room, Ifoudan opened a doorway, which led to a stairway down to the ancient catacombs built by the Romans. They climbed down, past a grinning skeleton set in a niche in the wall.

Liam had been in such spaces before, and he could tell that these had been expanded and remodeled. The halls were wide enough for a group of men to assemble, and fluorescent lights hung from the ceilings. He felt the same movement of air there that he had felt upstairs.

Ifoudan directed them to storage areas off the main tunnels. As each man unloaded his cargo, he was sent back up to get the next load. Ifoudan left Liam in charge of organizing the materials, giving him a few minutes between shifts to explore the lower level.

Each room had a different purpose. Some contained foods, others supplies for the soldiers. The most dangerous contained missiles, rockets, handguns, rifles, and other materials. Each time he ventured out, fearful that he'd be discovered prying around, Liam's heart rate accelerated.

A soldier stepped from around a corner and confronted Liam, pointing his rifle. "You! What are you doing lazing around down here!" he barked in Arabic.

Liam bowed his head and mumbled an apology. His Arabic was good, but not good enough to pass for a native.

For a moment he thought of disabling the guard, knocking him out and hiding his body in one of the storage caves.

But then one of the porters descended the stairs, his back bowed with a heavy load, and Liam walked away from the soldier to inspect the cargo and direct the man where to take it. His body felt like a taut cord as he kept one eye on the soldier. But by the time he was finished with the porter, the soldier had disappeared.

Liam couldn't worry about the possibility that the soldier might come back with reinforcements and more questions. His training kicked in, and he focused on the task at hand as one man after another descended the stairs into the cool, damp catacomb. Liam kept noticing the grinning skeleton in that niche by the stairs, the rictus of his open mouth a warning of what could happen out there in the middle of the desert.

By the time he switched places with Ifoudan an hour later, Liam had memorized the location and contents of each storage cave. He began carrying his share of the goods through the building and downstairs. Everything he saw reinforced his opinion that the Tagant School and Hospital was a front for a military facility. Then, when he was on his way back to the camels for another load, walking through the first-floor hallway past the door to the gym, he brushed an older Arab man in a Hawaiian shirt.

As part of his SEAL training, Liam had taken several antiterrorist courses where he was required to memorize the faces and backgrounds of many suspected terrorists. Abdul Bin-Tahari was one of those.

A high-ranking official in Al Qaeda, Bin-Tahari dropped from sight shortly before Liam left the SEALs. Rumor was that he had been killed in Afghanistan, but there was no physical evidence. Liam knew Bin-Tahari was fifty years old, five-ten, and stocky, with a close-trimmed beard. He had a penchant for Hawaiian shirts, the more garish the better.

The man Liam saw could be another of similar age and build, with a similar taste in shirts. Hell, it could even be someone who was pretending to be Bin-Tahari.

Liam kept his eye on the man as he walked down the hallway and into the gym. All action stopped as Bin-Tahari entered. He said something to the men assembled there that was received with general laughter.

It was Bin-Tahari; Liam was sure of it. That added urgency to the mission; now not only must the Tagant School be shut down, but Bin-Tahari had to be captured. But what could he do? He was alone, his only associates a camel herder and an ESL teacher from Philadelphia.

All he needed was a plan. Oh, and a SEAL team to back him up.

Dropped off the Face of the Earth

When the men and camels disappeared through the gates of the Tagant School, Aidan went back to Ifoudan's tent and practiced Arabic phrases. *Aywa* was yes, and *la* was no. *Shukran* was thank you, and *afwan* was you're welcome.

But how did you say, *Please release my boyfriend from custody* or *Please don't shoot me; I am just an English teacher?*

Aidan considered his situation. They had been out in the desert for a week. A week before that, he'd been in Tunis, settling into his apartment, waiting for his appointment with Madame Abboud and planning his new life.

Things had changed so much since then, it was hard to take it all in. When Aidan stopped to think, he was scared—but when he didn't think about it, he was pleased at his ability to act. He'd talked his way into Charles Carlucci's room at the Hotel Africa, he'd escaped from those guys at the souk, and he'd faced every challenge in the desert, from peeing behind palm trees to riding a camel. When he got back to Philadelphia, if he got back, he'd be a different person, a stronger one. He was sure of that.

He went for a walk, past a small field of black basalt pebbles, and climbed the rise to look out at the Tagant

School again. He was there when the muezzin mounted one of the corner sentry posts with the lonely call to the midday prayer. The men in the courtyard, even the soldiers on patrol, stopped what they were doing, knelt on the ground in the direction of Mecca, and prayed. Aidan added his own prayer that Liam and the rest of the men would return safely.

The fine sand at the top of the rise reminded him of the beach during summer vacations at the Jersey shore. It was rippled like the patterns in watered silk, and whenever a light breeze blew up, a white mist of salt swirled over the surfaces.

He'd thought Liam might return at the heat of the day, but he didn't. Neither did any of the other men, though, and Aidan wasn't sure if that was a good sign or not. If one of the soldiers had discovered Liam's identity, they might have incarcerated all the men of the caravan.

He went back to Ifoudan's tent and tried to sleep, but worry for Liam twisted his stomach until he felt like he'd eaten a whole sheep, which was kicking his insides trying to get out. Though there were others in the camp, and many more in the Tagant School, he felt alone. The guidebook said that the Sahara extended for three and a half million square miles, big as the whole United States, and he was struck by how small each person was compared to that vastness.

And yet, one person could make a difference. By accompanying Liam, he'd helped deliver that bank-account information to Ibrahim's tribe, and that money would change the way they lived forever. Tuareg children would be educated, have access to health care, and become connected to the rest of the world because of something he had done.

There was more to do, though. If Liam did not return, Aidan had to make that satellite phone call and then do his best to get the hell out of Dodge—which he might or might not be able to do, depending on how the soldiers reacted to Liam. What if they swooped down on the caravan's encampment and took everyone prisoner? What if Ifoudan betrayed them?

If the soldiers decided to execute everyone on the caravan, he'd be among them. Probably buried in a mass grave under the shifting sands. No one back home would ever know what had happened to him.

It was an interesting feeling to have dropped off the face of the earth, as it were. Even when he'd worked his way around Europe teaching, before meeting Blake, there had been records: passport stamps, employment paperwork, apartment leases. All his life, in fact, he'd been where he was supposed to be. At school, at work, at home preparing dinner for Blake. Once in a while, he'd sneaked off to an afternoon movie by himself or detoured past a bar on his way home from work (in his pre-Blake days, at least). But those moments out of time had been brief, and he'd always surfaced again.

He left Ifoudan's tent once again, paced around the camp for a while, and then returned to his vantage point at the rise. He heard a commotion at the front gate, and then it opened, and a line of men and camels began to move out.

He wished he had binoculars. Was Liam among the men? With his ability to change his posture and gait, there was no way to tell. Aidan hurried down the rise, kicking up sand, and ran back to the camp.

The women and old men who had remained at the camp while the caravan was unloaded didn't share his nervous anticipation. They carried on with what they were doing—sleeping, building fires, preparing food—as the men returned. Aidan waited at the front of Ifoudan's tent until he saw the camel herder coming, accompanied by a grimy-faced man in a blue robe.

They both moved slowly, as if the day had tired them out, and Aidan longed to rush up to Liam and embrace him but held back. Liam and Ifoudan both collapsed to the mats inside Ifoudan's tent. "I've never worked so hard in one day." Liam groaned. "My back is killing me."

"Roll over," Aidan said. "I'll give you a back rub."

His ability to give massages was another legacy of Blake's desire to educate him as a great caretaker. Aidan had gone through three months of training at night, and he put all those skills to use as he worked the knots out of Liam's back, used his knuckles, pressed his weight into the big man to release the tightened muscles.

He loved the feeling of Liam's skin against his fingers, the way his body yielded to just the right pressure. It gave him a hard-on to be poised over Liam, legs to either side of Liam's body, having the big man totally under his control.

Liam groaned with pleasure. On the other side of the tent, Ifoudan snored softly. "Did you get the information you needed?" Aidan asked in a low voice.

"More than I wanted to know," Liam said, his voice low and husky.

"Yes? What?"

But Liam had drifted off to sleep. Aidan gave up and lay down next to him. Liam smelled of sweat and dirt and sand, but Aidan didn't care. He snuggled up beside him, molding his body to Liam's, and they both slept.

For once, Aidan woke before Liam did. He built a fire and started making dinner, and it was only when the rich, spicy scent of the couscous drifted into the tent that Liam woke. It was after dark by then, and he and Ifoudan ate hungrily, both of them still stretching injured muscles. After Ifoudan finished eating, he left to check on the camels.

"What happened today?" Aidan asked Liam as he cleaned his plate.

"They're not just training Libyan soldiers there. I saw a bunch of men from different places. Some who looked Filipino, some Indonesian. Lots of Arabs. A few were Pakistani; a few were Palestinian."

"What does that mean?"

"I think it's a training camp for terrorists," Liam said. "And we've just delivered their course materials."

"Wow. Are you sure?"

"When I was a SEAL, we had to memorize names and faces and backgrounds of dozens of known terrorists so that if we ran across any of them on an operation, we'd know who we were up against." Liam stirred the fire, and it flared up, sending bright sparks out into the night. "One of the men I memorized was Abdul Bin-Tahari, a Saudi national and close confidant of bin Ladin. He has a background as a petroleum engineer. I saw him today, inside the school."

Liam turned to face Aidan. "I have to stop him. I have to stop him somehow."

"Can't you call in the SEALs and have them drop some bombs on the place?" Aidan asked. "I mean, after we get out of here."

He shook his head. "On the surface, this place looks like it's a school and a hospital. And I did see some kids there, in one wing, and there's a small hospital too. If we blow it up, the Libyans will raise holy hell."

"Can you lure this Bin-Tahari guy outside? We could truss him up, throw him on the back of a camel, and head back into Tunisia."

"I love your enthusiasm," Liam said. "But Bin-Tahari's smart, and he's been on the run for years. It wouldn't be easy to trick him out of the camp on his own."

They sat there in silence for a while. "Are you going to call that colonel?" Aidan asked.

"I need to. But I want to have a plan in mind first."

Aidan cleaned up, and Liam lay down to sleep again. He had another heavy day of unloading the camels the next day, and he needed his rest.

Aidan was restless. He'd spent the day napping and worrying, and neither of those led to undisturbed sleep. Ifoudan returned, and he went to sleep too. So Aidan got up and walked around the encampment for a while.

There were a few fires here and there, but most people had already turned in for the night, knowing they'd be up at first light to continue unloading the camels. Aidan ended up atop the rise once again, looking at the Tagant School. The night was so quiet, he could hear the soft whirring of the air-handling units.

An idea started dancing around at the edge of his brain. He stared at the camp for a while as it gelled, and then he knew what he and Liam could do. He hurried down the rise to wake the bodyguard and see what he thought.

Aidan's Plan

Liam woke quickly and soundlessly when Aidan tapped his shoulder. "I have an idea," Aidan whispered. "Come with me."

Not for the first time, Aidan blessed the fact that Liam was so unlike Blake. Blake wouldn't have followed him without a long explanation, without argument and justification. Just thinking of all the time he'd wasted with Blake made him tired.

He led Liam back up the rise, then said, "Listen. What do you hear?"

Liam listened. "I hear a motor. From the school."

"Yes. It's the air handler, isn't it?"

Liam listened again and nodded. "It brings cool air up from the catacombs and circulates it through the buildings."

"There was a big story in the US a couple of years ago," Aidan said. "Somebody sent anthrax to a newspaper's offices. A couple of people died, and the building had to be closed down for years because the stuff had gotten into the ventilation system. I was teaching my students how to evaluate stories in the paper, and we followed that case for a while."

Even in the dark, starlit night, he could see Liam processing this information. "If we can get some anthrax in there and then let them know it's in the ducts, they'll have to evacuate. If you could get a team in place, you could catch your guy and maybe a few more. And then they wouldn't be able to use this place for years."

"It's a workable plan," Liam said when they had debated the idea and considered the details. "I've got to make that call."

"You should get good reception up here," Aidan said. "I'll wait at the bottom of the rise to make sure nobody surprises you."

Liam leaned over and kissed him. "We make a good team, you and me."

"Yeah," Aidan said as he walked down the hill. "I think so too."

He wondered, as he waited, what this effort might mean to Liam. He'd been kicked out of the SEALs, after all. If he brought them a solid target, like this guy Abdul Bin-Tahari, and a plan to capture him, would that make him feel better about leaving the military?

Liam was definitely the strong, silent type. Blake hadn't been much of a communicator either, but Aidan had always believed that was about control. If Blake didn't tell him anything until the last minute, there was no chance Aidan could complain or propose an alternate plan.

With Liam, the silence was different. He wasn't as chatty as Aidan was, for starters. Aidan felt that after two weeks Liam knew almost everything there was to know about him, and yet he knew almost nothing about the big bodyguard.

Aidan knew where he'd grown up, but not what that had felt like. Had he felt different as a kid? What about as a teenager? From his build and his physical grace, Aidan imagined Liam had been a sports star. What was the locker room like for him?

Aidan had tried to avoid showering in gym class because he was afraid he'd get a hard-on and the other boys would tease him and know that he was turned on by their naked bodies. When the other guys talked about girls and sex, he'd kept quiet. He didn't have any interest in getting to first or second or third base with a girl, and at fifteen or sixteen, he didn't know why. He only knew that his body betrayed him at inopportune times.

He had time for a lot of thinking before Liam came down the rise. "We have to stall for at least two days," he said. "It's going to take that long to get things together."

He yawned. "Man, I have to go back and unload camels again tomorrow."

"Talk to Ifoudan. Get the guys to slow down," Aidan said as they walked back to the tent.

Liam was nearly asleep on his feet. Aidan guided him into the tent, where he collapsed on the mat. He was out within a minute, and lying next to him, listening to his rhythmic breathing, Aidan followed soon after.

The next morning the other men seemed as worn-out as Liam. They plodded from the camp to the gate, and it didn't seem like Liam was going to have to do anything to get them to stall. As a matter of fact, they were back in time for the afternoon prayers.

"Something's up," Liam said when he returned to the tent. "Yesterday they were pushing us hard to get everything unloaded. Today there was no pressure, and the colonel in charge of the facility announced that we won't work tomorrow."

"Tomorrow's Friday—isn't that the Muslim Sabbath?" Aidan asked.

"There isn't really any such thing. Muslims are supposed to pray in the mosque on Fridays, but they're allowed to work after that. I have a bad feeling that something's up."

"Maybe they just saw how worn-out you guys got yesterday."

"They wouldn't care. But at least we won't have to come up with a reason to hang around until the team gets here."

Aidan gave him another back rub, and after that they lay back down on the sleeping mats. As Liam snored, Aidan worried about Hassan el-Masri, wondering why he was still inside the compound. He worried about Leila and wondered where she was. He hoped that Ibrahim and his tribe had made it somewhere safe where they could access their money.

And he worried about how his and Liam's adventure would end. They were in the middle of the desert, miles from civilization, and if things went bad, they could be stranded. What if their plan turned into armed combat? They had no weapons beyond what the SEALs might bring. And it was always possible that their approach could be ambushed, leaving him and Liam on their own and under heavy suspicion.

That night, long after dark, Liam climbed the rise with his satellite phone once again, and again Aidan stood guard at the bottom. This call was a lot shorter, and when Liam came down the hill, he was brimming with enthusiasm. "The team is coming in tomorrow night," he said. "They've got a landing site picked out about twenty miles from here. They'll parachute in and then hump it."

"Camels?"

He laughed. "Not that kind of hump. They'll walk."

"Twenty miles? At night?"

"That's a cakewalk for a SEAL," he said. "A buddy of mine is carrying the anthrax. I'll take it inside and leave it in the ventilation system. Then we'll catch them as they come streaming out."

"You make it sound so easy," Aidan said drily. He couldn't believe Liam was so excited; it was the most animated Aidan had ever seen him.

"This is what I do. This is who I am."

"A soldier."

"A SEAL. There's a difference."

"You miss it, don't you?" Aidan asked as they walked back to the camp.

"I do. I didn't realize how much until now. The stuff I've been doing in Tunis, it's been penny-ante. Bodyguard duty, a couple of courier gigs. It's been paying my rent, but nothing to get my juices flowing."

"If they let you back in, would you go?"

"They won't, so it's not worth thinking about."

Aidan stopped. "Things are changing, Liam. Same-sex couples are getting married in different states. More and more companies have antidiscrimination policies, domestic-partner benefits. Someday 'don't ask, don't tell' will be gone."

"I'm changing too, Aidan." Liam faced him. "When I was in the navy, I didn't care about going away on long missions. Hell, I loved being deployed. Because I didn't have anybody back home to care about me."

"I don't believe that."

"Well, you should, because it's true. My mom's dead, and my dad remarried a born-again Christian woman who puts homosexuality right up there with drug abuse, pedophilia, and devil worship. If they knew I was gay, I wouldn't be welcome in their house again. I never had a boyfriend when I was in the navy. The closest I got was running into the same guy in a bookstore in San Diego a couple of times."

"I'm sorry," Aidan said.

"Don't be sorry. I made my choice, and I lived with it. I thought being a faggot was lousy, and I hated myself, and I hated every guy who sucked my dick or let me suck his."

"Wow." The depth of the bitterness and pain in Liam's speech made Aidan want to hug him, kiss him, tell him that he was wrong. But from his body language Aidan could see Liam didn't want that.

"And then I got kicked out, and I just accepted it, you know? It was my punishment. I tried to go back to Jersey after that, but I'd be out somewhere, in the hardware store, say, and some guy would look at me and start to flirt, and I'd get sick to my stomach. Because I'd want to rip my clothes off right there and have sex, and I knew that was wrong."

Liam turned away, and in the moonlight it looked like there were tears streaking his face.

"And then I met you. And for once I didn't hate myself for wanting to get into another guy's pants. You were feisty and smart and vulnerable at the same time." He turned back to face Aidan. "I didn't need you to pretend to be Charles Carlucci. I could have broken into his room at the Hotel Africa. I could have made it all this way without you. But I wanted to be with you."

"I'm glad," Aidan said. "Whatever happens, I'm so happy I met you."

"I've walked into firefights without a second thought. I've parachuted into war zones. I disabled a ticking bomb underwater. And none of it scared me. I think it was because I didn't care if I lived or died. Now, though, I'm scared as hell, because I've seen what kind of life I can have. But I'm determined to get through this and bring you with me."

Liam grabbed him and squeezed their bodies together as their lips locked. When Liam's mouth turned to Aidan's neck and he felt the wetness of the bodyguard's face against his cheek, he whispered, "I'm scared too, Liam. But knowing you're here makes things easier. I hope you feel the same way about me."

Liam didn't have to say anything. Aidan could feel it in the way the big man held him.

Taking Risks

Friday morning the camp was quiet as the members of the caravan rested from the hard labor of unloading the camels and dragging the goods into the school's catacombs. Aidan and Liam sat on their sleeping mats inside Ifoudan's tent and spoke in low voices as the camel herder slept.

"Can you get away from the rest of the men long enough to place the anthrax in the air handler?" Aidan asked.

Liam explained the way the camels were being unloaded. "Ifoudan and I alternate shifts underground, supervising the unloading. I'll only need a minute between groups. There's an air-intake vent in the main storage room, and I can unscrew the vent cover, place the anthrax, and get the cover back on while I'm on my own."

Even though it was hot under the tent, Aidan couldn't help shivering. He was scared but trying not to give in to the fear. He thought that if he kept talking, kept his mind on the details, he wouldn't have time to focus on the danger, to himself and to Liam. "What if you're searched on the way in?"

"The guards aren't inspecting what we bring in, but just in case, the package will be camouflaged. It'll look like something that's been riding a camel for a week."

"What about precautions? Anthrax is pretty dangerous."

Liam shrugged. "They're bringing doses of Cipro with them. It's the only antibiotic that works against anthrax. If I start taking it immediately after exposure, I should be fine." He looked at Aidan. "And in case you were worrying, they'll have doses for everyone who's been in the school. If we do this right, nobody gets anything worse than a case of the sniffles."

"You're not going to unwrap the stuff until the end of the day, right?" Aidan asked. "So that you can get out right afterward?"

He shook his head. "Too dangerous. Too many ways things can go wrong. As soon as I'm alone, after the first set of deliveries, I'm sticking it in the vent."

"But then you could be breathing it for hours."

"It's going to take some time to travel throughout the ductwork," he said. "Most of the men have scarves wound around their faces, so that should minimize the impact. I'll do my best to be careful."

"You have any idea how we're getting out of here when this is over?"

"There should be a chopper," he said. "The only thing is, they need to get in and get out before the Libyans realize we're in their airspace. If the chopper gets caught here, we could be facing a major international incident."

"As if the stakes weren't high enough." Aidan shivered again, and Liam put his arm around him. Aidan nestled his head against Liam's shoulder.

"It's going to be okay," Liam said softly. "This is what we do. These guys, they're the best. You'll see; it's going to go like clockwork."

"I'm scared. I'm scared you'll get anthrax, or you'll do something heroic and get yourself killed. I don't... I don't want..."

"I took a lot of risks when I was a SEAL. I admit, sometimes they were dumb risks." He kissed Aidan on the lips. "But that's all different now. You've taught me something, Aidan. You've shown me that there's a life out there for me, one that I want. And I'm coming back for it, don't you worry."

They slept through the heat of the day and ate dinner with Ifoudan. He and Liam spoke in Arabic, and Aidan wondered how much Liam was telling him. How did they know that they could trust the camel herder? Sure, he'd helped them get rid of Hassan el-Masri, but Ifoudan's loyalties could lie with his people, with his friend Ibrahim, not with two Americans. And what would happen to him and his people after Liam and Aidan jumped on a chopper full of SEALs and terrorists and winged their way out of the desert?

Aidan couldn't eat much dinner, and what he did eat he threw up, out of sight and sound of the camp. He buried the evidence under the sand, wiped his mouth, and went back to the tent, where Liam handed him the sat phone.

"I rigged it to vibrate," he said. "But just in case, we're going to have to sleep in shifts. I don't expect the guys to get here till nearly dawn, so I'll take the first shift. But if that phone starts to vibrate, wake me up ASAP."

"Will do, commander," Aidan said, saluting him.

"I'll have a few commands for you when we get out of here. Once we've both had a couple of good meals and a shower."

Once again Liam amazed Aidan with his ability to fall asleep. Aidan knew that he'd have been tossing and turning for hours if he had the burdens the ex-SEAL had.

Aidan was scared to leave the tent, because he worried that the phone might go off while he was out somewhere and he wouldn't be able to get it back to Liam in time. So instead he sat there in the tent as Liam and Ifoudan slept, as the rest of the camp slept around them. The next day everything would come apart, and things would change in big ways. Aidan tried to relish the moments of peace but couldn't manage it.

He was sitting there, his mind back in time somewhere, when the sat phone began vibrating. He nudged Liam, who was awake instantly. He grabbed the phone from Aidan and jumped up. He was out of the tent before Aidan could even register that Liam was awake.

He was back a few minutes later. "They've landed, closer than they expected, but it doesn't look like anyone's noticed. There's no activity at the school. If someone's monitoring the radar in Tripoli, they haven't let these guys know what's going on."

"There's always the possibility that because this is a secret facility, anyone monitoring air traffic in Tripoli wouldn't even know it's here."

"That's a good thought. Keep that in mind as this starts going down."

He encouraged Aidan to sleep for a while. "You'll need your rest for tomorrow," he said. "I don't want you falling asleep as we're running for a chopper."

"I doubt that'll happen." Aidan was sure he wouldn't be able to sleep, but maybe knowing that Liam was there with him helped him doze off after just a few minutes. When he woke it was still dark, but Liam was moving around in the tent.

"They're setting up camp just over the next rise," he said. "I want you to come with me. You'll be safer back there."

"Is someone going to babysit me? Or are you leaving me alone out there?"

"Don't be scared, Aidan. I don't have time now."

"I'm not scared, I'm logical. I'm safer here, in the middle of a bunch of people, within sight and sound of the school."

"Fine. Stay here, then. I'll be back."

Aidan couldn't tell if Liam was angry with him or if he was just economical with words because he was in a hurry. Aidan had put up with a lot of nasty comments from Blake about everything from his ear hair to his book collection, and he'd developed a thick skin. But somehow even the mildest reproach from Liam hurt more than a dozen of Blake's sharp observations.

Deployment Plan

Liam knew the SEALs were somewhere in the area. It was a feeling in his bones. He'd left the team abruptly after that conversation with Colonel Hardwick. He'd been transferred stateside for the last few weeks of his commitment and then received his honorable discharge. Nothing in his paperwork said that he was gay or that he was leaving because of that. He supposed he owed Hardwick thanks for that.

But he was tired of apologizing for who he was. His brief time with Aidan had taught him that; he had been a damn good SEAL, and it was the navy's loss that they couldn't accept him as he was. He stopped in the middle of a flat open area, between dunes, and said in a loud voice, "My name is William McCullough. Once a SEAL, always a SEAL."

"Hoo-rah to that, brother." Liam recognized the voice of Joey Sheridan, his best friend on the team, standing up from his camouflage behind a dune. All around him, the rest of his SEAL team, including the colonel, popped up like moles.

Joey was the first to reach him, enveloping him in a big bear hug. "Missed you, brother," Joey said. "You just dropped off the face of the earth."

Liam hugged him back, self-conscious at first. He didn't want his old friend to misinterpret anything. Then he figured, what the hell, and hugged Joey with a strength and fierceness that surprised him.

The other SEALs surrounded them, each of them eager to greet their former teammate. Liam realized, on an almost visceral level, how much he had missed the comradeship of these guys, the sense of purpose in carrying out missions together.

"All right, men, listen up," Colonel Hardwick said. "Let's get a situation briefing from Mr. McCullough, and then we'll make a plan."

Liam ran through the details of the Tagant School and Hospital. Occasionally one of the SEALs would ask a question—"How many of the soldiers are armed?" for example. Within ten minutes the briefing was finished.

"You organized all this yourself?" Hardwick asked.

"I have an associate." Liam was embarrassed to call Aidan his boyfriend, and trying to explain how he'd ended up traveling the desert with an ESL teacher from Philadelphia would take too long. So he just said, "He's back with the caravan."

"Sounds like everything is operational," Hardwick said. He was a bit shorter than Liam, with close-cropped brown hair and wire-rimmed glasses that made him look more like a university professor than a highly regarded SEAL team leader. "Sheridan, you've got the anthrax?"

"Glad to get rid of it, sir," Joey said, handing Liam a package about the size of a hardback book, wrapped in brown paper.

"You have a plan for deployment?" Hardwick asked.

Liam nodded and explained his intentions. "Goodwin's our new medic," Hardwick said, motioning to a SEAL Liam didn't know. "He's got the doses of Cipro you'll need. While the rest of us are sorting through the evacuees from the premises, he'll be handing the meds out to the people in the camp."

"Here's your dose, sir," Goodwin said, handing Liam a bottle of pills. "You'd better start taking them tonight, just to be safe. May I see your hands, please?"

Liam held them out, and Goodwin, a young, red-haired guy who looked barely old enough to drink, held a flashlight and examined them. "Just ensuring that you don't have any open wounds, sir," Goodwin said. "Breathing anthrax is bad enough, but if it infiltrates below the skin, you're in much worse shape."

"Understood," Liam said as Goodwin finished his exam.

"You'd better get back to your encampment," Hardwick said. "We'll be in position tomorrow morning."

"A muezzin calls the prayers every day," Liam said. "I'll have everything in place by the time he calls the *dohr* prayer at midday."

"Sheridan's our best Arabic speaker now that you're gone," Hardwick said. "We'll put him on the bullhorn shortly after that prayer." He clapped Liam on the back. "Good luck, son. We'll back you up."

"You've never disappointed me yet, sir." Liam saluted his former colonel, who returned the salute, and then he began the long walk back to the camp.

He returned to the tent carrying the package of anthrax just as dawn was rising. "Is that it?" Aidan asked.

Liam nodded. "Don't worry. It's well shielded."

"How are you going to open it? It's taped up pretty securely."

"I'll figure it out. Some of those storage containers have sharp edges."

"Hold on." Aidan went over to his pack and dug around. "Take this."

He handed Liam a silver knife with intricate carvings and sharp blades. Liam looked at it, popped the blades open, and nodded. "Where'd you get this?"

"Tunis. While you were picking up your duffel bag, you left me in the cab, remember? While I was waiting, I went into a knife store."

Once again Liam realized that the ESL teacher had surprised him. Way back then, before things had gotten crazy, Aidan had realized he needed to be armed and got himself a decent weapon.

Blake had sure missed out when he let Aidan go, Liam thought. He slid the knife into his pocket, and Aidan asked, "What can I do here while you're inside?"

"Just be ready to run. Listen for the bullhorns right after the midday prayer. The rendezvous point is just behind the rise; get there as fast as you can."

He kissed Aidan and felt a fierce determination to make this operation a success, to return to this man and continue what they had started.

"I *will* be back," he said. And then he left.

The Bullhorn

As the men prepared for what would be their last delivery trip into the Tagant School's catacombs, Liam walked over to the pile of materials that had yet to be carried inside. He hefted a long box of rifles onto his back, feeling his muscles strain.

He stretched and felt the paper-wrapped package under his cloak, pressed against his body. He hoped that the packaging was secure, and that anthrax wasn't somehow leaching from the box through his skin. But there was no way around it. He had to trust in the actions of the men he worked with—or had worked with—and in the plan itself.

He took his place in the line, sweating under the cloak. As he walked, the package worked its way loose and threatened to spill out at his feet unless he got it out fast. With one elbow, he kept it pressed against his stomach. But that gave him an awkward purchase on the box of rifles. If he dropped his cargo, he'd call attention to himself, and he couldn't do that.

As the line of men approached the gate to the Tagant School, an open jeep passed them, kicking up sand in its wake. Liam recognized Wahid Zubran at the wheel. He kept his head down, waiting with the rest of the men while

Zubran argued with the guards and then drove into the courtyard.

As Liam watched Zubran park the jeep next to the arched doorway and stride inside, he felt the package against his hip shift again, angling against his kidney. The military in charge of the Tagant School had listened to Hassan el-Masri and summoned Zubran. Once they pieced together Hassan's story, the guards would begin searching for him and Aidan.

Liam was sixth in line as the men traipsed past the guards, through the lobby, and down the hallway. They passed the entrance to the soldiers' dormitory, which was quiet. Liam assumed that all the men were either on duty, eating, or sleeping. They turned the corner, passing the gym, but the door was closed, and Liam couldn't tell if there were men inside or not.

How much time did he have? There was no way to get word to Aidan that Zubran had arrived. He had to hope he would be able to get the anthrax in place before the guards went on full alert.

When the line of men reached the staircase down to the catacombs, Liam was able to put the box of rifles down and adjust the container of anthrax against his skin, relieving the pressure on his kidney. He picked up the rifles again and descended the staircase, feeling the cool air rise up to him.

Liam followed the man before him to the room where most of the arms had been stored. He stacked his box of rifles on the top of the other men's, then took over belowground supervision. As soon as the last man had returned upstairs for another load, Liam shifted a couple of boxes to create a makeshift stepladder so that he could reach the air-intake vent above him. Using one of the blades of the knife Aidan had given him, he attacked the vent cover.

One of the screws had been stripped, and he wasted an extra minute prying it loose. Despite the cold air around him, sweat began dripping down his forehead, and he used the sleeve of his cloak to wipe it away. His body was on alert for the sound of a guard, or another delivery, approaching.

With a painful twist of Aidan's knife, the last screw came loose, and one side of the vent cover dropped open. Liam removed the package from under his cloak, and using another of the knife's blades, he slit the tape wrapped around it. There were several layers, though, and he kept having to stop and look around to make sure no soldier had stopped by, no bearer had returned with the next load.

He unearthed a glass vial, pulled out the stopper, and poured the contents into the air vent. Some of the white powder blew back onto him, and he sneezed just as he heard the heavy tread of a man on the stone stairs. He gripped the knife, ready to throw it if the steps should belong to a guard.

Instead it was a bearer carrying a rectangular box on his shoulder. The man looked at him, but Liam ignored him. Maintaining his focus, controlling his breathing despite the need to cough, he screwed the vent cover back in, then stepped down and asked to see what the man was carrying.

* * *

After Liam left, Aidan packed his backpack and Liam's duffel, then carried them with him to the rise behind the camp and watched the Tagant School's gate. He knew the

SEALs were behind him somewhere in the desert, and he worried that they might have appeared on a radar screen in Tripoli, that even as he waited and sweated in the sun, an air strike was on its way to destroy them all.

He watched the line of men and camels approach the camp and then stop. A jeep approached, passing the line and throwing up a rooster tail of sand behind it. Who was that? Another terrorist come for training? Wahid Zubran, having tracked his inept assistant? How would this character affect the plan?

Despite his long sleeves and long pants, the safari hat over his head, he began to feel his skin burning. He took small sips of water whenever he felt faint, sitting back against the bags. How did Liam manage this level of concentration? What was he doing—had he loosed the anthrax into the ventilation system? What if a guard had caught him, and he was being interrogated as Aidan sat outside, unable to help him?

The heat rose from the sand in hazy waves. Aidan nodded off, then jerked awake. In the distance he saw a dark cloud rising. Another sandstorm? Or just a mirage?

As he directed the men underground, Liam worried about Wahid Zubran and wondered if the anthrax was doing what it was supposed to, making its way through the ductwork. His eyes watered and he sneezed, sometimes several times in rapid succession, but no one else seemed affected.

He switched duties with Ifoudan and joined the men carrying the last boxes of arms in from the camels.

Shouldering a box, he moved through the arched front doorway, passing a pair of guards with rifles against their shoulders. What if they finished the unloading, but the anthrax failed to circulate? The plan would fail, and there would be no way to infiltrate the complex again.

Carrying in the fourth load, he passed the gymnasium and saw Zubran inside, with Hassan next to him. They were speaking with the man Liam thought was Abdul Bin-Tahari, in his Hawaiian shirt. The boy was speaking, the two older men listening.

But Liam could not linger and eavesdrop; he had to keep moving behind the man in front of him, like an obedient camel. Even if the anthrax was passing through the ducts, would anyone believe the bullhorn warning? What if the guards sealed the garrison before he could get out? What if no one left, and the soldiers inside the school mounted an attack on the SEALs outside? He could be trapped inside, with anthrax in the vents and armed guards searching for him.

As they were returning up the stairs, one of the men sneezed and caused a chain reaction. Within minutes, three other men were sniffling and sneezing. "The air is bad down here," one man said.

Liam sneezed himself. He touched his forehead and felt the heat radiating from it. The anthrax was working. He pulled Ifoudan aside. "We have to get out of here," he said in a low voice. "There is something dangerous in the air."

By the time the line of men had returned to the courtyard, almost all of them were sneezing, their eyes watering. Ifoudan went to the soldier in charge and insisted that there was something wrong and his men had to leave.

Liam stood close enough to Ifoudan to hear the conversation. If they could just get out before Abdul Bin-Tahari ordered a lockdown, the plan had a chance of working. He couldn't tell if the sweat that beaded on his forehead was from the heat, the fever, or nerves. Either way it stung his eyes.

The soldier called an older man, who appeared to be in charge of the garrison. He might not have been convinced had he not begun sneezing himself. "Go," he said. "These filthy camels are making everyone sneeze. Don't come back until tomorrow."

The sandstorm swirled closer; Aidan alternated between watching the gates of the Tagant School and turning forty-five degrees or so to keep an eye on the swirling cloud of sand. He couldn't tell if it was heading toward him, staying in the same place, or aimed in a different direction entirely.

When the sun was at its highest and Aidan was sipping the last few drops of water from the bottle in his pack, the gates opened, and the men and camels straggled out. Several men stumbled, and they clung to each other. Sometimes the camels appeared to be pulling them.

Where was Liam? Aidan cursed Liam's ability to blend in so well. There was no way to tell if Liam was there or not. What if he'd been discovered and captured?

The sandstorm looked like it was coming closer. Would it interfere with the ability of the SEALs to capture the terrorists? Would the chopper be able to land?

Ifoudan led the caravan out through the gates. Liam felt lousy, and it was a struggle to keep putting one foot in front of the other. The line of men and camels was halfway back to the caravan camp when he heard the bullhorn.

It was Joey Sheridan's voice, in perfect Arabic. "Your facility has been infected with deadly poison. If you do not evacuate immediately, you will die."

The men of the caravan stopped to listen, then burst into frantic Arabic. Liam pulled Ifoudan aside. "A navy medic is coming to your camp," he said. "Make sure each one of your men takes the medicine he brings you. Every day, until two cycles of the moon have passed. If they do that, they will all survive. Do you understand?"

Ifoudan himself was sneezing, his eyes watering. "I understand."

Liam forced himself to run, shedding the heavy cloak and scarf as he did. He had been planning to rendezvous with the team and help with the evacuation, but he realized as he struggled ahead that he would be no good. He had to find Aidan.

The ragtag group was halfway to the camp when Aidan heard the sound of harsh words in Arabic blasting through the bullhorn. Even though it was the sound he'd been waiting for, hoping for, it scared him.

The orderly line exiting the school dissolved as men ran toward the camp. One, though, took a different tack and headed toward Aidan. As he shed his cloak, Aidan realized that it was Liam, and that he was in trouble. His customary grace had deserted him; he stumbled and nearly fell twice as he ran.

Forgetting his exhaustion and dehydration, Aidan took off down the slope toward Liam, his pack swaying on his back, Liam's duffel banging against his side.

"Stay back," Liam said as he neared. "I'm getting sick. I must have breathed too much of the stuff."

"I don't care," Aidan said, grabbing him around the waist. "Lean on me. We've got to get out of here."

Suddenly there were armed men running past them wearing camouflage BDUs. The last was a stocky man around Aidan's height. "Hoo-rah, brother," the man said, pausing for a second to high-five Liam. "Good job."

Liam could only nod as the man ran off.

Looking behind him, Aidan saw the gates of the facility open and men begin to stream out. The SEALs were in place by that time, though, and even though there were only a dozen of them, they had weapons trained and began shepherding the fleeing soldiers into groups.

Without his vantage point at the top of the rise, Aidan had no idea if the sandstorm was approaching, and when he heard a loud roar, he worried that they'd be engulfed in minutes, and began looking for a place he and Liam could shelter. Liam was moving slowly, stumbling over his feet. He hadn't even been able to carry the duffel, so Aidan was still burdened with both bags.

The sand began to swirl around them, and Aidan despaired. There was no cover anywhere, just acres of empty sand. He risked a glance up and was astonished to see, instead of a cloud of sand, a dark green helicopter hovering overhead.

As he watched, the big troop transport lowered to the ground. A half dozen SEALs ran forward, forcing with them a group of men wearing civilian clothes, including an older man in a gaudy Hawaiian shirt. As the chopper landed, someone on board opened the side door, and the SEALs began shepherding their crew inside.

Liam and Aidan watched. As the last of the SEALs was preparing to jump on, Aidan recognized him as the stocky guy who'd high-fived Liam, and grabbed his arm. "Take Liam," he said. "He's sick. Get him out of here."

"Joey, I'm not going without him," Liam said, but he was weak and could hardly speak without coughing.

"I'll be on the next one," Aidan said. He pointed to the sky, where a second helicopter was preparing to land.

The SEAL grabbed Liam. "Come on, brother. Get in the bird." Between him and Aidan, they forced Liam inside. Aidan threw Liam's duffel inside with him. Then the SEAL climbed in and slid the door shut.

As soon as the helicopter took off, the second one landed, and the other six SEALs appeared on the horizon, shepherding another group of men. Aidan waited until they were loaded, then tried to jump on.

The last SEAL blocked his way. "I'm with Liam," Aidan shouted. "Liam McCullough."

The SEAL peered at him. "You know Billy?"

The oldest of the SEALs, a man in his forties with wire-rimmed glasses and deep lines across his forehead, stepped forward. Aidan didn't know enough about military insignia to tell his rank, but everything about his body language said he was the troop leader.

"You Billy's boyfriend?" he asked.

The question threw Aidan for a loop. What had Liam said when he called for backup? He knew that Liam had accepted a discharge under "don't ask, don't tell," but would Aidan damage him further by acknowledging their relationship?

What the hell? he thought. Liam was a big boy, and so was he. If they didn't want to let a faggot onto their chopper, then fuck 'em all. "Yes, sir," he said.

"Welcome aboard," the man said. "Now let's get the fuck out of here."

The first SEAL lowered his rifle and motioned Aidan inside. He stepped in and found a place for himself against the wall, taking off his backpack but looping the strap around his arm. The last SEAL kept the door open as they rose, firing a few rounds toward the ground to discourage any of the soldiers who'd followed them from shooting.

Aidan had no idea where they were going. Liam was in the other chopper, so he was on his own. Instead of being frightening, though, the thought was exhilarating. They had done what they set out to do and more. They'd delivered the account number to Ibrahim's tribe. They'd managed to evacuate and shut down the training facility, and deliver a bunch of suspected terrorists to the SEALs.

The helicopter shook and banked as it rose, knocking Aidan against the wall. He slid a foot along the floor, then stopped himself by pressing his foot against a ridge in the metal floor.

He looked around him. The man closest to him reminded him of a Filipino student he'd had in class the year before, skinny and dark-haired, with bad teeth and a scowl. Only one of the other men wore a uniform. The others looked too dark-skinned to be Arabs; they might have been Pakistani or Indonesian.

All the prisoners had been cuffed hand and foot, and two SEALs were guarding them. Aidan took a deep breath. Things had worked out as planned, and he'd be safe on the ground soon with Liam.

Then he heard the pilot say, "We've got Libyan military on our tail."

Evacuation

"Hold on," the SEAL by the door said to Aidan. "This might get rocky."

But hold on to what? Aidan's back was to the wall of the chopper; it wasn't like there was a seat belt he could hook into. He grabbed a piece of the bulkhead as the chopper dipped and swooped, trying to avoid missiles being shot at it.

"There's another one on our tail now," the pilot shouted. "The first one's heading for the other chopper."

That was the helicopter carrying Liam, Aidan realized. Could they have come so far only to be shot down now? Goddamn it, what a stupid way for this to end. At the very least, he wanted to see Liam safe on solid ground again, nurse him back to health. And then, if they had to go their separate ways, if he had to return to Philadelphia, leaving Liam in Tunis, he would. It would hurt like hell, but he could do it, if he had to. At least he'd be leaving Liam alive, and he could hold the memory of their time together and the possibility that they might meet again.

He didn't want to blow up over the Libyan desert, even if they'd accomplished what they set out to do. It was a stupid, stupid waste.

The chopper dived, and Aidan thought he might throw up. A couple of the hostages did. And then there was a huge explosion, and the chopper swerved sharply, knocking Aidan against the bulkhead, where his head connected with the metal. Lights flashed behind his eyelids, and he passed out.

* * *

"Come on, buddy. Wake up." Aidan opened his eyes and looked up, not at Liam but at another of the SEALs. The terrorists had been unloaded from the chopper, and only the smell of sweat and vomit remained.

Aidan looked up. "Where are we?"

"We're safe. That's all you need to know for now." The guy put his hands under Aidan's shoulders and lifted.

Aidan had a hell of a headache, and he was disoriented to boot. Where was he? What had happened? The last thing he remembered was standing on the rise in the desert, watching the facility and waiting for Liam.

"Liam. Where's Liam?"

"You mean Billy? He's in the hospital," the SEAL said. "That's where you're headed too."

It was only then that Aidan felt the congealed blood on his head and saw how it had dripped over his clothes. "Holy shit," he said and then passed out again.

* * *

The next time Aidan woke up, he was in a hospital bed. His head still hurt, but at least it was swathed in bandages, and somebody had cleaned up all the blood. His ribs ached every time he took a breath, and he saw a huge black and blue mark on his left arm. His throat was dry as the desert, and as soon as he struggled up to a sitting position, he spied the plastic cup of water on the bedside table and brought it to his lips.

"About time you woke up."

Aidan looked in the direction of the voice. Wearing a hospital gown that had fallen loose over one shoulder, Liam sat amid rumpled sheets on the edge of the bed next to his. He started coughing, his face turning purple with the effort.

Aidan just stared at him. His memory was coming back; he remembered seeing Liam off on that first chopper, then getting on the second one himself. But that was it. "Where are we?" he asked.

Liam managed to croak out, "Hospital," before another round of coughing took him.

"I didn't think it was the Ritz-Carlton," Aidan said. "You sound like shit."

"Anthrax'll do that to you. The Cipro they give you's almost as bad. I can't keep anything down except clear liquids."

He reached a hand out to Aidan, who struggled against the pain in his side to grab it. "Did we...?" Aidan asked. "Did we...? What were we supposed to do?"

Liam laughed, which set off another coughing fit. Aidan wrapped Liam's hand in his own. Liam didn't have his customary strength, but his hand was still warm, and Aidan felt reassured that he could face anything as long as Liam was there next to him.

A male nurse entered the room. "Mr. McCullough," the nurse said. "What the fuck are you doing up?"

"Sorry," Liam said, releasing Aidan's hand and sinking back to his pillow.

The nurse surveyed the situation. He walked across the room and around to the far side of Aidan's bed. "Hold on," he said. He put both hands on the side of the bed and pushed.

That wasn't close enough. He had to move around to the far side of Liam's bed and push it as well. By the time he was done, Aidan and Liam could reach across the narrow gap between the beds and hold hands again.

And they did.

Return to Tunis

Two days later, Colonel Hardwick arranged seats for Liam and Aidan on a military transport returning to Tunis. That way they could avoid issues of passports and why there was no exit stamp that showed them leaving Tunisia. Liam had turned Charles Carlucci's passport over to the SEALs to be returned to his next of kin, the bank account information carefully excised. He'd even spoken to the woman who held Aidan's and Carlucci's belongings in Tunis and arranged for her to deliver Carlucci's luggage to the US embassy.

The morning of the flight, Aidan woke up in his hospital bed and looked over at Liam, asleep in the bed next to his. Liam was still sick, prone to coughing fits, though his fever was gone. He was weak, and it would be six weeks before he had run through the course of Cipro. Even then he might need additional medication; he'd had a lot of exposure to the anthrax.

He and Aidan hadn't talked much; hospitals weren't great places for private conversations. They held hands now and then, thanks to the nurse who'd moved their beds close enough. Aidan had spent some time sitting on Liam's bed next to him, some time in the chair next to the bed. But they hadn't talked about the future, only the past.

What did that mean? Aidan wondered as he stared at Liam's sleeping form. He resembled one of those warrior angels in Renaissance paintings, strong yet pure. Aidan couldn't look at him without feeling his heart flood with emotion.

They'd both admitted to love—but had they been telling the truth? Was it love between them or just lust? Had the passion of the situation overwhelmed both of them? If he had a reason to stick around Tunis, maybe a real relationship could develop. But he couldn't imagine Liam on a date. His "don't ask, don't tell" experience in the military seemed to have scarred him, made him unable to express himself, and probably unable to commit to someone in the way Aidan wanted.

And he did want that, he recognized. He had been happy with Blake, and not just because Blake's money allowed him a comfortable life. He liked being in a relationship, having someone to come home to, someone to look after. He didn't see a strong, competent soldier of fortune like Liam McCullough ever being able to settle down in that way.

What would happen when they returned to Tunis? Liam had invited Aidan to stay at his little house as long as he wanted. The invitation had been carefully couched, though. It wasn't a "come move in with me"; more like a "you can crash at my place, if you want." Not exactly the commitment that Aidan longed for.

He considered his options. He didn't have a job in Tunis, and his only contact was Madame Habiba Abboud. Had enough time passed that she could apply for a teaching permit for him again? It seemed so long since he had been in her office, like another lifetime.

If he wanted, he could go back to Philadelphia, sleep on his friend Coral's couch for a few days, and find himself an apartment and some adjunct work teaching. Liam had promised him enough money from Charles Carlucci's foundation to get him settled again.

But was that what he wanted? That life seemed awfully boring after a couple of weeks of being pursued through the desert by Libyan intelligence agents, riding camels, hiding inside a burka, and being evacuated by a military helicopter from the middle of nowhere.

Realistically, though, what else could he do? He had friends scattered around the US, and he could always decide to try out San Francisco, Chicago, or Miami. If Carlucci's foundation came up with enough money, he could even go back to school, get a degree in something else. He'd always been good with computers, had built a couple of Web pages, and played around with various kinds of software.

Maybe he could write a book. He'd been thinking about writing an ESL text for a few years, unhappy with the materials that were available. Or maybe a novel about two gay guys chasing through the desert and falling in love.

No, no one would believe that one.

Liam woke and yawned. "Morning," he said, turning to look at Aidan.

"Morning. We've got about two hours before we get to the plane."

Liam was still weak, so Aidan helped him shower, both of them naked, Liam propped against the wall. He soaped Liam's body carefully, paying attention to every muscle, and Liam's dick swelled to Aidan's ministrations. His hand slippery with soap, Aidan grabbed it and began stroking it. "Oh." Liam groaned.

"You're not going to pass out on me, are you?" Aidan asked. "I don't think I could explain that to the nurse."

"I'll try to hold on," Liam said. He was having trouble catching his breath, a combination of the sex and the infection in his lungs, and Aidan sped up his hand, using his other to penetrate Liam's ass with a single soapy finger. The big man's body writhed, and he whimpered as he shot a load in Aidan's hand.

"I want to"—he panted—"take care of you."

Aidan shook his head. "I'm doing the caretaking here. You just need to get your strength back."

Aidan rinsed Liam, once again marveling at how the water cascaded off his tall, muscular body. He remembered that first glimpse he'd gotten of Liam showering behind the Bar Mamounia. He couldn't even imagine how long ago that had been.

He left Liam leaning against the wall of the shower stall as he hurried through his own cleaning. He was hard but tried to ignore the pressure of his dick, swiping the soap past it quickly. "No," Liam said, reaching out to grab his hand. "More."

Aidan's eyes grinned mischievously. "You want a show?"

"I want you to do what I can't."

"You can do this," Aidan said. He raised Liam's right hand and took his index finger into his mouth. He sucked on it, tasting the polished surface of his nail, the roughness of his skin.

He soaped up his own hand and began stroking himself. Liam groaned next to him. "You are so sexy," he said, moving his finger around inside Aidan's mouth. Aidan sucked it, closing his eyes and trying to imagine it was Liam's dick. Nope, that didn't work. Liam's dick was so much thicker, and it pulsed with blood and lust when Aidan had it in his mouth. But the finger was all he was going to get, so he sucked it.

It was the closest they'd come to making love since that night on the desert dune when Liam had fucked Aidan's ass bareback. Aidan felt all that closeness flooding back, his body swelling with passion, his dick pulsing under his hand. He longed to grab Liam, pull him close, rub his dick up and down on Liam's smooth skin, but he knew he couldn't.

He pulled one last time on his dick, whimpered, and then let his body sag. Liam pulled his finger from Aidan's mouth and rubbed his grizzled cheek against Aidan's. Aidan was so tempted then to say, *I love you*, but he held back.

Out of the shower, Aidan dried them both off, then shaved himself and helped Liam. As Aidan combed Liam's light brown hair, grown shaggy during their time in the desert, Liam said, "I could get used to this kind of pampering."

He kicked the bathroom door shut, wrapped his arm around Aidan, and pulled him close. Aidan felt himself melting into the bigger man's arms, pressing his cheek against Liam's. "I want to kiss you so much," Liam said. "But I don't want you to catch this shit." He turned his head aside and coughed.

"Shh," Aidan said, rubbing his back. "Feeling you next to me like this is enough for me." He felt Liam's chest rise and fall against his own, inhaling that scent that was so Liam, like sand and sunshine, even after being cooped up inside for so long.

Liam faltered, and Aidan pulled back. He opened the bathroom door and led Liam to the bed, where Liam sat as Aidan threw the last few items into their bags. A soldier arrived a few minutes later to drive them to the airfield. Aidan could tell that Liam hated being helped to stand or walk in front of someone else.

"Look at us," Liam said as they hobbled together across the tarmac. "Like a pair of old men."

"Speak for yourself," Aidan said, but then he stumbled, and they both laughed. They managed to climb the stairway to the plane, then collapsed into adjacent seats. The rest of the plane filled up quickly with soldiers and a couple of men in plain clothes Aidan supposed were either diplomats or spies. As he buckled his seat belt, he stole a glance at Liam. Savor the moment, he thought. This whole fantasy adventure might be about to end, but he could enjoy every last minute of it. The memories would sustain him through the long winter ahead.

Once the flight back to Tunis had taken off, Liam looked over at Aidan. He'd always thought he couldn't fall in love— because of his military career, because he wasn't attracted to the only men he could tell were gay, because who could love someone who was too afraid to face himself and his desires?

But maybe that was all wrong, and this was why he'd never let himself fall in love before. Because it hurt too much as it was ending. They'd get back to Tunis, and within a day or two Aidan would be on another plane, this one back to Philadelphia. And Liam would still be in Tunis, alone. He'd suffered a terrible depression when he'd left the SEALs, without the camaraderie of men who'd become like his brothers. He'd clawed his way out of that, pretending that he liked being on his own, that everything he'd lost didn't matter. Could he keep on doing that?

He wasn't a wimp. He'd gone through Hell Week at BUD/S, he'd excelled at every SEAL mission, and he'd survived fatigue, dehydration, bullet wounds, and now infection with anthrax. He'd get through this. On his own. He forced himself to look at Aidan and smile. "You got your adventure," he said. "Didn't you?"

"I guess I did. Though it wasn't exactly the one I was thinking of when I left Philadelphia."

"So you'll be going back there now?"

Aidan looked over at him. "Not sure."

"What do you mean? You have some other city in mind?"

Aidan shrugged. "I've got to get on the computer, see what kind of offers I can drum up." He paused. "It might take me a while."

Liam felt something surge in his heart. Maybe Aidan wouldn't have to leave so soon. "Like I told you, you're welcome to stick around Tunis, bunk with me for a while, if you'd like."

"I'm not showering out there in the courtyard, where everybody in the bar can see," Aidan said.

Liam laughed. "Come on, Aidan. You've got a great body. Why not show it off?"

Aidan leaned close to Liam and whispered, "This body is for your eyes only."

A smile twitched at the corners of Liam's mouth. "It's going to take me a few more days to get my strength back. But then..."

"But then, we'll see," Aidan said and squeezed his hand.

An Unexpected Visitor

They took a taxi from the airport to the Bar Mamounia. Liam hobbled into the bar first, where he was assailed by a young Tunisian. "Liam! You come back to me!" the man said.

"Sorry, Abdullah," Liam said, pushing him gently aside. He pointed to Aidan, toting his backpack and Liam's duffel, and said something in Arabic.

"Maybe you like three," Abdullah said. He looked at Aidan and smiled.

Aidan dropped the bags on the tiled floor and put his arm around Liam. "La," he said. "No."

Liam laughed and said something more in Arabic. The Tunisian crossed his arms, pouted, then turned and stalked out of the bar. Aidan helped Liam through the courtyard and in through the back door of the little house. The bartender had repaired the broken front door and assured Liam that nothing had been taken while he was gone.

Liam thanked him, then closed the courtyard door. "How about if we get you to bed?" Aidan said.

"Only if you come with me."

"I thought I wore you out this morning in the shower," Aidan said.

"You don't know me, then."

"We'll see."

Liam tried to walk to the bedroom, but his step faltered, and Aidan had to steady him. "Hold on, tiger," Aidan said. They walked together into the bedroom, and Aidan slowly unbuttoned Liam's shirt, then unbuckled his shorts. "You can't walk, but you've got a hard-on," Aidan said. "Your body sure knows how to channel its energy."

"What can I say? This body was built for action."

"Yeah. Right." Aidan pulled off Liam's sandals, then tugged his jockstrap down. "Lie down, Romeo."

Liam sat hard on the edge of the bed. He struggled to lift his leg, and Aidan had to help him get on his back. "You're coming to join me?" Liam asked.

"I don't know. I thought I might go out and walk around a little. See some more of the city." He smiled.

"Get your clothes off and get that cute ass over here," Liam commanded.

"Yes, sir," Aidan said, saluting. He pulled off his clothes in record time, then crawled into the bed next to Liam, nestling his naked body against Liam's. "This is nice," he murmured. "When was the last time we were actually in a bed together?"

Liam reached his arm around Aidan, and Aidan nestled into his chest. "The Hotel La Gazelle, in Tataouine."

"You've got a good memory," Aidan said.

"I do. I remember that you like this." He leaned over and took Aidan's right nipple between his teeth. Aidan arched his back, inhaled, and said, "Oh yeah."

They moved slowly, turning into each other and rubbing their bodies together. Aidan pushed Liam back onto his back, then mounted him, careful not to exert too much pressure. He rubbed his dick against Liam's, lubricated by their precum, resting his hands on either side of Liam.

"I won't break, you know," Liam said.

"I'm not taking that chance." Aidan leaned down and kissed his cheek. "You're worth too much to me in good shape."

Though his body wanted to move fast, Aidan forced himself to take his time. He arched his back like a cat, began to hump Liam, rubbing his dick against the bigger man's. They were well matched, even though Aidan was circumcised and Liam wasn't. Aidan had always thought Liam's dick was bigger than his own because Liam's body was so much bigger, but seeing them pressed against each other, he realized that his own dick was just a little longer than Liam's.

"What?" Liam asked, noticing Aidan's smile.

"Nothing," Aidan said. Both their dicks were slippery with precum, so they kept slipping apart. Aidan shifted a little so that his dick was rubbing against Liam's crotch, sliding through the dark, curly pubic hairs, and Liam's dick rubbed against Aidan's belly.

He clenched his ass and increased the speed and pressure, keeping his eyes focused on Liam's. He'd never noticed how deep Liam's eyes looked, the black pupil surrounded by green. They were eyes he could spend a lifetime falling into, he thought.

His dick throbbed until it was painful to continue but impossible to stop. His groin began churning, his whole body shaking as the orgasm swept through him. He felt Liam's body constrict beneath him, heard him panting, then grimacing as cum shot out of his dick. That pushed Aidan over the edge, and he threw his head back and howled.

"They're going to hear you in the bar," Liam said, laughing, as Aidan flopped down on the bed next to him.

"They'll know I'm taking care of you. Keep that Abdullah guy at bay, at least."

Aidan snuggled against Liam, regardless of the cum seeping into their pores and dripping down through their pubic hair, and both of them fell into a deep, dreamless sleep. They woke as darkness fell, and Aidan ran out to pick up food for dinner and breakfast. First, though, he wanted to make a small detour.

His former apartment building looked the same. He no longer had a key to the front door, though, so he stood outside staring at the facade. Then he felt the touch he had been hoping for, a wet nose sniffing the back of his knee.

"There you are, girl," he said, leaning down and scratching the dog behind her ears. "Did you miss me?"

The dog sat on her haunches and looked up at him. "I guess we'll have to give you a name," Aidan said. "How about we leave that up to Liam?"

The dog wagged her tail, then followed Aidan all the way back to Liam's house, waiting obediently outside the small grocery as Aidan shopped.

"You just can't resist the urge to domesticate, can you?" Liam asked, sitting at the kitchen table stroking the dog's back as Aidan fixed dinner, a simple pasta primavera he'd made a hundred times in Philadelphia. He boiled water in a battered pot, then steamed some peas, carrots, and squash.

As Aidan cooked, Liam ruffled the dog behind her ears, then scratched her belly as she lay on her back waving her paws in the air. "How about we call you *Hayam*?" he said to her. She looked up at him and panted. "Guess you like that."

"What does that mean?" Aidan asked. "Hayam?"

The pasta on the stove overflowed, and Liam began coughing. By the time Aidan had plated up the pasta with the vegetables, though, Liam had recovered.

When he had gone back to his old apartment building to retrieve the dog, Aidan knew he'd already made up his mind to stay in Tunis for a while, as long as that was okay with Liam. "What was it like, working with the SEALs again?" he asked.

"I can't go back," Liam said. "If that's what you're asking. But I did like it—that feeling of working with a team. It's hard being a lone wolf."

The question hung in the air. Aidan felt foolish suggesting that he and Liam could be a team. In the bedroom, no question. But Aidan wasn't a bodyguard, and he had no training in whatever it was that Liam normally did when he wasn't chasing through the desert.

They had made a few wrong turns, though. The first had been letting Wahid Zubran and his thugs jump them in the souk. The second had been at the pharmacy in El Jem, when they hadn't planned on Zubran getting to the pharmacy before they had. And the third? Probably taking off from Tataouine without preparing for the trip into the desert. That had been the most serious; Liam had been forced to leave Remada for the supplies he needed, and if he hadn't been able to catch up with the caravan at the oasis, the whole operation could have fallen apart.

But they'd done a lot of things right too. They'd both been resourceful, overcoming obstacles and doing what they set out to. Aidan smiled as he looked over at Liam.

"This is really good," Liam said, holding up a forkful of pasta. "You ever think of a career as a chef?"

"I did," Aidan said. "But it's such an all-or-nothing job. I took a ton of little cooking courses, but I couldn't take a restaurant job, because the hours were too long. Had to take care of Blake, you know."

"How much did you give up to stay with that jerk?" Liam asked.

"He wasn't always a jerk. He took care of me for a long time. I could never have had that life on my little salary." He laid his fork down next to his plate. "Blake was attractive and charming when he wanted to be, and he was generous with money when it was something he thought worthwhile. He liked to pick out my clothes and buy them for me. I wore designer labels, slept on high-thread-count sheets, drank good wine."

A former friend had once accused Aidan of being a high-priced rent boy, living off Blake's money, and he'd warned Aidan that he was a disposable asset, easily replaced by someone younger or better-looking. At the time Aidan had dismissed the comment, believing there were much more complex threads tying him and Blake together. Looking back now, he wondered if his friend had come uncomfortably close to the truth.

"I'm just saying," Liam said, holding his hands up. "I think Blake always undervalued you."

Yes, Aidan wanted to say. But Blake wasn't shy about taking what he wanted. Long ago, he had wanted Aidan and made that very plain. Aidan wasn't sure what Liam wanted.

After dinner, they took Hayam out for a short walk and then began writing a report for Carlucci's foundation. It took some time that evening, and then most of the next day, recounting in detail everything that had happened from the time Liam had been asked to serve as Carlucci's bodyguard until their return from Sicily.

"Wow," Aidan said when they finished proofreading the final draft. "This was pretty amazing, wasn't it?"

"Not your typical bodyguard job," Liam admitted. He leaned back in his desk chair, and Aidan looked at him and smiled.

Liam e-mailed the report to the foundation's headquarters in New York, along with his bank information, as requested. Hayam got up from her place by the front door and padded over to them, then sat on the floor next to Aidan and resting her front paws on his knees. "Who's a good girl?" Aidan asked, rubbing behind her ears. "You want to be a bodyguard dog? Can you bare your teeth and growl?" He mimicked the action, which set Liam laughing, though all the dog did was bob her head and stick her tongue out.

Liam's laughter turned to coughing, and Aidan helped him stand up. "Damn this crap," Liam said between fits. "Can't do anything like I used to."

"It'll come back," Aidan said. "Give it time." He reached down and ran his hand lightly over Liam's groin, where his dick was already half-hard. "There's something you can still do." He looked up at Liam's eyes and grinned.

"There's that," Liam said. "Come here, you."

He pulled Aidan close, Aidan resting his head on the bigger man's shoulder. His own dick began to rise as he felt Liam's body so close to his. The doctor had told them that Liam was no longer contagious, so when Liam leaned down to him, he turned his face up for a kiss. Liam responded with surprising ferocity, opening his mouth wide, his tongue reaching out to Aidan's.

Aidan felt like he was being devoured, his body melting under Liam's touch. But then he pulled back. "Easy, tiger," he said. "You're still not up to full strength."

"Strong enough to do this," Liam said. He reached one hand under Aidan's ass and scooped him up. Reflexively, Aidan wrapped his arms around Liam's neck and held on as Liam carried him through the living room to the bedroom, Hayam following behind.

By the time Liam laid Aidan down on the bed, the bigger man was panting for breath, but that only fed his ferocious desire. He unbuttoned Aidan's shirt with fumbling fingers, snatched open the fastener on Aidan's shorts, and tugged them down, then dropped his head to Aidan's stiff dick.

"Slow down, baby, slow down," Aidan said. "You're going to kill yourself."

"What a way to go, though." Liam panted, pulling off Aidan's dick for a quick breath.

Aidan couldn't enjoy the blowjob because he was so worried about Liam. He summoned all his strength to pry Liam off him. "What?" Liam said. "I'm not an invalid. Don't treat me like one. If I want to blow you, I will."

That's what you get, Aidan thought, for loving men who always had to get their way. He lay back against the pillows and let the sensation to his body take over. Liam was right; Aidan had been treating him like a patient, when Liam wanted—needed—to be treated like a man.

Liam raked his teeth up and down Aidan's dick, sending tremors through his body. Liam's mouth was drier than usual, only a little saliva easing the passage of his lips, and Aidan caught his breath a few times at the roughness of Liam's lips.

Liam pulled his head back from Aidan's dick and howled, the sound transforming into a cough. He fell sideways onto the bed, and Aidan took control. "You want a testosterone battle, pal, you've got it," he said. He jerked Liam's shorts down, exposing his stiff dick, and without ceremony or preparation, Aidan sat down on it.

The pain nearly broke him in two, but he didn't care. He began bouncing up and down on Liam, clenching and releasing his ass muscles, and the pain urged him forward, ratcheting through his body so he could hardly breathe, until Liam's dick had lubed itself enough with precum, and Aidan's ass opened.

Liam grabbed Aidan's dick and began jerking it, and Aidan howled himself, just as Liam had done, ending with a little yip of pleasure as Liam's dick pressed against his prostate. Aidan could hardly believe that he was here, with this handsome, sexy, smart, loving man, in this strange place, having survived all they had been through.

He slowed his pace, wanting to savor every minute. He leaned down and kissed Liam on the forehead, and Liam's dick nearly slid out of his ass. But he backed up and down again, and there it was, filling him up once more.

"You're killing me," Liam said, thrusting up into Aidan, building his own rhythm. He laughed, then caught his breath, and Aidan was worried he'd start coughing again, but Liam didn't. He kept rocking his hips up, scratching his pubic hair against Aidan's ass as his dick went deep.

Aidan began to pant, sweat dripping down his forehead. He pressed back against Liam's thrusts, speeding up the pace so that the bed below them was rocking and creaking. "Oh, oh, oh," Liam said, his breath catching; then Aidan felt Liam shoot off in his ass. He closed his eyes and focused on that rough hand on his dick, the thumb riding up over the top and pressing into his piss slit. Liam's hand was warm, and Aidan couldn't hold back any longer, his body shaking with the power of his orgasm.

He looked down at Liam and smiled, then pulled his ass up, letting Liam's dick flop out. Liam released his grip on Aidan's dick, and Aidan turned and slid down next to Liam, resting his head on Liam's chest.

"You really think you can boss me around?" Liam said, smiling a little later as they snuggled in bed together, Hayam on the floor next to them.

"Of course," Aidan said. "And you'll like it too, buster."

Liam laughed out loud, and this time the laugh didn't lead to a cough. "You're a handful, you know that?"

"You haven't seen a handful yet." Aidan yawned. He rested his head on Liam's chest, curved one leg over one of Liam's, and slid off to sleep.

* * *

The next morning, waking up in Liam's bed, Aidan announced that he was going to stay in Tunis for a while. "You need someone to look after you," he said. Liam didn't say anything, just smiled. Later in the morning, Aidan hailed a cab so they could visit Liam's doctor, who pronounced that he was healing as best he could.

He made appointments for Liam each week until the Cipro was due to run out. When they got back to the house, they both napped through the hot afternoon. Liam still tired easily, and the Cipro still upset his stomach, so he could only eat the blandest of food.

"I'm watching you, you know," he said as Aidan prepared rice and steamed vegetables for their dinner. "I remember that trick you played on Blake."

"What trick was that?" Aidan asked, slicing broccoli into tiny florets.

"You said when you were mad at him, you made his food spicy."

Aidan laughed. "You remember that?"

He reached out for Aidan's waist and pulled him close. "I remember everything."

"I'm not sure I'm happy about that," Aidan said. "God knows what I told you when I thought you weren't paying attention."

He had gotten accustomed to life with Liam. He'd begun studying Arabic so that he could tell the shopkeepers what he wanted. He'd already cleaned the little house from top to bottom and supervised the construction of a wooden fence around the shower.

Two days after Liam sent the report to the Counterterrorist Foundation, there was a substantial wire transfer, more than he would have made the entire year. He had Aidan set up an account with a US bank with a branch in Tunis and transferred half the money there. "You can't give me that much," Aidan protested when he looked over Liam's shoulder at the computer screen and saw his new balance. "I was just along for the ride."

Liam shook his head. "Nope. You came up with most of the ideas. I just carried them out. We were a team."

Aidan couldn't help hearing that use of the past tense. As a teacher, after all, he was accustomed to listening for nuances in word use.

"You can always send some money to the desk clerk at the hotel in Tataouine, if you want, and something for his cousin too," Liam said.

"I'll do that."

"I'll take care of Ifoudan," Liam said. "I've got a buddy who says the camel caravan went as far as Ghadames, on the Libya-Tunisia border, and they're on their way back to Remada now."

Hayam began to bark, jumping up from her place on the floor next to Liam and rushing to the front door. A few seconds later, there was a knock on the door. "Expecting someone?" Aidan asked.

Liam shook his head. "Stay there." He pulled his Glock from the desk drawer and crossed to the door.

Aidan worried that Liam hadn't returned to his full strength. Who could it be at the door? They had been unable to find out what happened to Wahid Zubran or Hassan el-Masri after the attack at the Tagant School. Had one of the Tunisians tracked them down? Someone else unhappy with what had happened at the Tagant School?

Liam stood by the door and called out, "Who is it?"

The voice was so familiar to Aidan, and yet so out of place, that he was stunned. "I'm looking for Aidan Greene," the voice said. "My name is Blake Chennault."

Liam looked over at Aidan, who was already rising and walking toward the door, and he stepped back. Aidan crossed the room and opened the door.

Blake looked like he'd been traveling all night. His shirt was wrinkled, and he had a five-o'clock shadow. "Aidan! Thank God you're all right." He stepped in and embraced Aidan.

That was even more startling, to both Aidan and Liam. Blake wasn't a physical man; in the eleven years they'd been together, he'd hardly hugged or kissed Aidan, at least not without prompting. Aidan awkwardly put his arms around Blake's back as his former partner began to cry.

"Come on now; it's okay," Aidan said. This was a Blake he didn't know. Probably the long flight had unnerved him.

"I thought you were dead," Blake said, pulling back from the hug and wiping his eyes. "After you left, I realized what an idiot I was, and I wanted to tell you, I wanted you to come back. I got a buddy to check flight records, and I found you came here, to Tunis."

Aidan led Blake to the table and pulled out a chair for him. He saw Liam slip out the front door, but before he could say anything, the big ex-SEAL was gone.

Aidan sighed as he sat down across from Blake. Here he was again, a place he thought he'd never go back to. Looking after Blake Chennault.

"I checked your activity on the computer," Blake said. "I contacted that Abboud woman, but she couldn't tell me anything other than that you'd walked out of her office. And the place that rented you the apartment said you'd gone. There was just no trace of you."

"I had no idea you were looking," Aidan said.

"You wouldn't believe the strings I had to pull," Blake said. "Finally somebody told me you'd been on a military transport from Sicily to Tunis, that you were with this bodyguard named McCullough. As soon as I could get McCullough's address, I got on a plane."

Aidan reached down to stroke Hayam's head. "Why all this trouble? You're the one who kicked me out."

"I told you, it was a mistake. I didn't realize how much I missed you until you were gone."

Again, Aidan caught the word choice. Missed, not loved. Had Blake missed him or just all the things he did? And where had Liam gone?

"I came here straight from the airport," Blake said. "I wasn't sure if you'd be here or not. I'm just so glad to see you."

"You want something to drink?" Aidan asked. "Some tea?"

"Tea would be great."

Aidan got up and set the water boiling. "It's Tunisian tea," he said as he poured some leaves into the strainer. "Not exactly what you're used to."

"You have no idea what you've put me through," Blake said. "The sooner we get out of here and back to Philadelphia, the better."

Aidan didn't say anything, just waited for the water to just begin to boil, then poured it into the pot and lowered the strainer. There was honey in the cabinet; Blake liked honey with his tea. Aidan brought him the mug. "It's still hot."

Blake looked around. "You've been staying here? Not in a hotel?"

"I've been staying with Liam." Aidan saw the little house through Blake's eyes—the rough walls, the simple furniture. But he didn't miss the luxury of Blake's apartment, the sofas upholstered in floral patterns, the crystal chandelier, or the glass-fronted china cabinet housing Blake's late mother's collection of china birds.

"Do you even get phone service here? We'll need a cab back to the airport."

"Blake, we need to talk," Aidan said.

"I know I haven't been as sensitive as I could be. But you've got to remember, I have a high-stress job. I can't pay attention to every little mood you have."

"Blake, I'm not going back to Philadelphia," Aidan said, the words spilling out before he even knew he was saying them. "I'm staying here with Liam. I appreciate that you tracked me down—I'm flattered. But our relationship was on life support anyway. You just killed it quickly."

"Don't be ridiculous. You can't stay here in this hellhole. And this guy—McCullough. You'd be surprised at all the things I've learned about him. He's some kind of mercenary, a soldier of fortune. He could be dangerous."

"He is dangerous," Aidan said. "I've seen him in action. And you know what? I think that's really sexy. He's smart, and he's gorgeous, and he's dynamite in bed. And when I talk to him, he listens. I'm in love with him."

Blake just stared at him. "But...but..."

Liam opened the front door and said, "I've got a cab waiting out here for Mr. Chennault. Express trip to the airport."

"Guess it's time for you to go," Aidan said, standing up. Hayam sat up too and barked once.

Aidan kissed Blake on the forehead, the way he had so many times back in Philadelphia. "Have a good trip. And keep in touch, all right?"

Blake stood up. "You're making a mistake, Aidan. I won't wait around for you to come to your senses."

"Good. Get back into the dating pool. There are guys in Philly who'll jump at the chance to join your world. It's just not for me anymore."

Blake stalked out, and Liam closed the door behind him. "You sure about that?" Liam asked. "You can still catch him, if you want."

"I know what I want, and it's right here, in Tunis, in this very room." He crossed the room to Liam, and they embraced, their mouths merging in a long, deep kiss. Then Liam's cell phone rang.

Aidan started to laugh. "If I didn't know better, I'd say that your phone is jealous of me."

"It's probably one of Blake's buddies, trying to pry you away from me."

"Not going to happen. But you'd better answer it. Might be a new job."

Liam frowned. "I'm not interested."

Aidan picked up the phone from the desktop and flipped it open. "Liam McCullough's office."

Liam crossed his arms and frowned as Aidan listened to the caller on the other end. "Mr. McCullough's not available at the moment, but if you'll give me the details, I'll make sure he gets the message and gets back to you."

"Aidan," Liam said, but Aidan was busy listening and writing.

"My name is Aidan Greene, and I'm Mr. McCullough's associate," Aidan said into the phone. "Yes. Okay. All right. I've got the information, and I'll have Mr. McCullough get back to you ASAP."

"I can't take on any new jobs right now," Liam said when Aidan had finished the call. "I'm not back to full strength."

"It's a simple, two-man job," Aidan said. "Meet this Spanish businessman at the airport, drive him to his appointment, wait around for him, then drive him back to catch a plane. He's not even staying overnight."

He hesitated but knew he had to plunge in. "We'll work together," he said. "That is, if you want to?"

Liam smiled. "You think you can work with me?"

"I think so. Somebody's got to keep you in line."

Liam grabbed Aidan by the waist and pulled him close, kissing his cheek. Hayam jumped up, trying to get in on the action, and Aidan reached down to pet her. "You never told me what Hayam means in Arabic," Aidan said.

"Deliriously in love," Liam said, smiling. "Just like I am."

Aidan closed his eyes and savored every place where his body and Liam's touched. "You know, I'll need some training," Aidan said. "I've been reading about these bodyguard schools. Five-day programs—defensive driving, CPR, tactical skills. What I want most is to learn to move the way you do."

"Oh, baby," Liam said, nuzzling his cheek against Aidan's. "Let me show you some moves."

ᘐ THE END ᘐ

Neil Plakcy

Neil Plakcy has loved romance novels since he began reading his mother's Harlequins as a teenager. He is the award-winning author of the Mahu series of police procedural novels set in Hawaii, featuring gay homicide detective Kimo Kanapa'aka (*Mahu, Mahu Surfer, Mahu Fire* and *Mahu Vice*). His short erotic fiction, including many stories about Kimo, has appeared in nearly 20 anthologies, and he has also edited two anthologies himself—*Hard Hats* and *Surfer Boys*. His romance novels are *Three Wrong Turns in the Desert, Dancing with the Tide,* and *Guardian Angel of South Beach* (Loose Id*)*, and *GayLife.com* (MLR Press). He is a graduate of the University of Pennsylvania, Columbia University, and Florida International University, where he received his MFA in creative writing. He lives in South Florida with his partner and their golden retriever.

Loose Id® Titles by Neil Plakcy

Guardian Angel of South Beach

The HAVE BODY, WILL GUARD Series
Three Wrong Turns in the Desert
Dancing with the Tide
The above titles are available in e-book format at www.loose-id.com

Three Wrong Turns in the Desert
The above title is available in print at your favorite bookstore